WILD MAGIC

IEUAN LEDGER

Milton, Ontario
http://www.brain-lag.com/

Brain Lag Publishing
Milton, Ontario
http://www.brain-lag.com/

Library and Archives Canada Cataloguing in Publication

1

I hate ghosts.

Nine times out of ten you'll have nothing more than a wee moaning groaner on your hands and all you need to do is give them a shoulder to cry on before you can nudge them off the mortal coil. Job done.

Less commonly, the ones who die in anger or fear might manifest into the much more dangerous poltergeists, known for their tendency to throw folk down the stairs or unhelpfully stacking the furniture. These are more difficult to deal with and can cause serious damage if not treated quickly, but usually a banishment does the trick. There's also the option of helping them move on, but that's dangerous and with all due respect I'm not going to risk my neck for the echo of a person; I'm still alive, and I'd prefer to keep it that way for the time being.

And then rarely, oh so rarely the chance is laughably small, you're going to find your personal ghosts. While not technically ghosts, in that they are formed of memory and emotion rather than being an echo of a scrap of a dead personality, they are the worst. A haunted person soon becomes a phantom themselves.

Fortunately for me, this was not a ghost and instead a loose pipe and some floppy fiberglass insulation. I was on my back in the crawlspace of an attic, swimming goggles over my eyes, nails between my lips and a wrench in my hand as I tightened a nut; I'd learned long ago that what most people assumed was ghosts often turned out to be something as innocuous as a poorly constructed home and I carried tools with me as much as I carried my magical accoutrements.

Needless to say, I wasn't about to tell the owners of the house that their problem had been entirely mundane in nature and as I clambered down the ladder onto the landing, I contemplated the morality of having used less glue than necessary to affix the insulation to the plaster; repeat jobs are the best jobs.

"As far as I can tell, that should be all sorted," I said to the worried woman, not entirely untruthfully. "Though if you have any more issues I can come back and have another look. Discounted, obviously. Here."

From my hoodie I pulled out a half-finished stack of post-its and scribbled my number on it with a leaky biro before handing it over. I needed some business cards. Did people still use business cards?

"Thank you so much!" said the woman whose name I hadn't bothered to remember; it's easier to defraud people if you don't give them a personality. She pushed a wad of notes into my hands which I quickly stuffed into the near bottomless pocket of my hoodie.

"Cheers. Well, I'd best bounce," I said, eager to put as much distance between me and the lie as possible. "Other customers, more ghosts. You know the drill."

"Will you not stay for a cup of tea?" she asked. "I've just put the kettle on."

I glanced over at her husband who was watching me from beneath a furrowed brow; I could tell he wanted me gone as soon as possible and probably had only agreed to hire me to appease his wife and he certainly hadn't been too eager to let a skinny man with a grubby hoodie and a neck tattoo into his house.

"Tempting, but I really have to run. Yours isn't the only house I have to hit up today."

Well, that was a lie. Unsurprisingly, most people didn't put much stock in curses these days which, as Glasgow's only Curse-Breaker, put a damper on my business and even though I had branched out into hauntings as well, commissions were few and far between.

The morning's clear skies had been swaddled in thick grey clouds and a fine drizzle hung in the air so I pulled up my hood over my recently buzzed black hair and tried to ignore the damp that was already creeping in through my ragged Doc Martens. The pay for this gig would absolutely be going towards a new pair.

This house had been in one of my less well-known parts of the city, just off the life-line of Glasgow's Great Western Road, which as a man who liked to brag that he could tell where he was by how the ground felt below his boots was not something I was proud of. I pulled out my phone to double-check my directions and saw a message flashing on the screen.

Meet u at Underbridge. Might have something 4 u.

Even as a teen I hadn't been able to stomach text-speak and it was with a grimace that I changed my direction and began a thankfully short walk out of the labyrinth of modern houses and onto the main road that led almost directly to my destination, leaving me alone with the hot heavy lead of guilt that was now safely settled in my stomach.

I didn't plan this life. Well, I suppose I should say it wasn't my 'Plan A'. Plan A was to study for one degree after another until finally I had enough academic clout to worm my way into a Classics department at some university or other and hide away with dusty books and records until Mr. Grim came about the reaping. But it was those dusty books and records that... side-tracked me, if you like.

It started with a note in the corner of a book. If you're imagining some dusty, leather-bound tome with metal clasps, then I'm sorry; it was your average 1970s paperback containing one specific article I wanted for an essay. The note was nothing special either; a couple of sentences underlined and the title of another book, with page number. So I followed the breadcrumbs, as I thought any student eager to procrastinate would. One book led to another which led to another, almost always with a seemingly random titbit of knowledge highlighted. My procrastination gave way to full-fledged obsession in a matter of months and soon my 'Grecian Urns and History' notebook had become a reference guide to hundreds of texts, each complementing another in a complex esoteric spider web; a paragraph on the history of some obscure ritual in one book, a couple of pages about the secret code of an Elizabethan madman or mystic in another. One book led me to spend another few months deciphering a dialect specific to a region of Slovenia that hasn't existed for centuries. Thus began my foray into the arcane, though at the time I was just putting off doing any actual work.

I pitter-pattered my way down a stone staircase beside an old tenement building, decorated with a mural of flowers and robots, and crossed the River Kelvin. I bet you thought the Underbridge was a mystical waypoint, perhaps where the city trolls like to gather? Try again. Instead picture an unironically hipster bar beneath a bridge across one of Glasgow's major rivers and you'd be more on the mark. The cosy interior, adapted from abandoned train arches, was heaving and I was loath to join a table of strangers, so I settled on a picnic bench mostly sheltered by the bridge above and waited. To pass the time I counted the curses around me; as expected, there were dozens. I'd thought I would make a killing in this line of work, what with the thick fog of curses that surrounded me at any given moment. How wrong I'd been.

There was a ripple through the intangible plane of magic and instinctively I raised my protections, though I knew there was no need; I recognised the energy. I waved Donald over as soon as I caught sight of him. His sandy hair was pulled back into a top knot and, judging by the deep-necked black t-shirt, he had just come off the day shift at the bar. His golden chest hair curled out over the top.

"All right?" he asked, after retrieving a couple of pints of Joker.

"Aye, can't complain. You got something that merits summoning the great and powerful Rudy?" I asked, aiming for powerful and mysterious but landing somewhere closer to conceited and pretentious.

Donald snorted. "I don't think anyone gets to refer to themselves as the great and powerful anything when they're chatting to someone who's washed their boxers."

"Yeah yeah, funny guy. What's the craic?"

Donald doesn't really exist in the peripheries, the realm where your ghosts, ghouls and goblins hold court. Well, not so much the goblins; the fae were reportedly cut off from our world centuries ago, but you get the idea. He dips a pinkie toe in now and again but he never really took to it like me. We'd been flat mates back in uni, and whereas I genuinely developed an interest in the ocult, he'd seen it as a way to cultivate his dark and mysterious backdrop. I'd never let him forget the chipped black nail varnish. But still, he has his ear to the ground in the right circles and his bar is frequented by some of the more... *unseemly* denizens of our great city.

"Before you say yes or no," said Donald with a weird leading tone. "You need to know that you were asked for directly, and this might have a touch of your speciality about it."

"I should hope so," I said. "Otherwise why the hell did you drag me here?"

"There's a lot of money on the line for you," he said, still not giving me a clear answer.

"Oh, aye? Go on then, what's the job?" I asked. "Haunted painting? Goblin in a well that turns out just to be a very large toad? I can handle that."

"Not quite," said Donald. "It's a girl. Seventeen years old. Missing."

"No," I said, instantly. "Absolutely not."

"Rudy—"

"I said no, Donald. I don't do missing persons. I don't do assault, battery, larceny, murder, nothing that's going to get me mixed up with the police."

It's important to have limits. My limit was never having to explain to the authorities that I, a man with no fixed income and Doc Martens held together with duct tape, was only poking my nose in because of magic. Doesn't sound too good, does it?

"Here's the thing though," said Donald, ignoring me. "Police are at a loss. They've got nothing to go on and their investigation is stagnant, apparently."

That piqued my interest.

"How'd you know that?" I asked, frowning. "Police reports? Wee bit above your paygrade, isn't it?"

"I didn't get any of this from the police," explained Donald.

"Then who?" I asked.

"Are you interested?"

"Interested, aye. Committed? No."

Donald sighed. "Look, you've been sought out by name. I know it's not your usual bag but there's a good bit of cash on the line here."

I thought of my leaking boots and relented.

"Go on then. Who's your contact?"

"That would be me," said an unfamiliar voice.

I didn't jump; it doesn't do much for the image to appear easily scared but I certainly pushed some energy into my tattoo. No one was getting in my head today. I calmly took in the young woman watching me from the next table. Mid-to-late twenties, heavy eyeliner, blonde dreadlocks streaked with pink, blue and purple, tied with beads and feathers. She was small, I realised; standing I doubt she'd have reached my chest, though being six-foot-four meant I tended to tower over most people. Glass and plastic jewels adorned her ears, nose and eyebrows to the point that when the light hit her just right I had to squint.

"Older sister?" I asked, sipping my beer and raising an eyebrow.

"Impressive," she said.

"Not really, all things considered."

She joined us at the table. "Laura Baxter. Sorry for the theatre but I wanted to see if you were the real thing," she said.

"Do I pass your test?"

"We'll see. Are you willing to answer a few questions?"

"Do I need a lawyer?"

Not that I could afford one, but I've found it helps to have friends in the right places.

"Funny. First question. Is magic real?"

"Yes," I replied, simply. "Next question."

She frowned, as if I were an exam question that she was struggling with. "Can you find my sister?"

"I don't know," I answered truthfully. "Look, I'm a Curse-

Breaker. Detective work has never been my area of expertise. If your flat is haunted or you think you might have been hexed, then I'm your man. I've never even tried investigation before."

"But you do know magic?"

How could I put this, I wondered. You can't 'know' magic. Saying you know magic is like saying you know the breeze or the stones or the stars. You can study them and know *about* them, but you can't *know* them. I'd been up to my eyeballs in the stuff for years and I could fit everything I knew about the *how* and *why* of magic on the back of a cigarette packet. It didn't matter to me. What mattered was that it *was*.

"I dabble. Look, hiring a private investigator will probably get you further than employing a broke warlock. Or go back to the police-"

"Donald already told you the police aren't doing anything," snapped Laura.

"How do you know that?" I asked.

"I've got a guy on the inside," she said, shrugging. "An hour of passion and I've got him spilling any secrets I like."

"Respect," I said, before I could stop myself.

Laura shrugged. "Meh, he's a good lay and it's smart to keep your pieces sweet. Anyway, after I told him I'd filed a report, he said that he'd not heard anything about it. A couple of days later he calls me and tells me that there's not a single lead to be followed, despite two reports being filed. One from me and one from my parents."

She didn't quite spit the word parents, but it wasn't said with warmth.

"Tell me about your parents," I said, then wished I hadn't; even I could hear the cliché.

"Does this mean you'll help?"

"It means I'm interested. Go on."

"They're textbook narcissists," she scoffed. "Nothing

mattered to them except how good their perfect family appeared on paper. No friends except the ones they pre-approved, no going out past six p.m., we could only wear clothes that they picked out. And then they acted surprised when I retaliated?"

"Why the past tense?" I asked.

"Oh, I've been no contact since I turned eighteen. I couldn't shake the depression the whole time I was under that roof. Go here, wear this, speak to them, ignore the others. I wasn't a kid to them, I was a china doll and it was killing me," she said. "As soon as I was legally an adult I was out of there like a rat out of an aqueduct. Mum howled and wailed and asked how I could do such an awful thing to the people who have only ever loved me."

She blew a raspberry and helped herself to a mouthful of Donald's beer.

"Do you think they do love you?" I asked.

Laura swilled the beer from cheek to cheek, carefully considering her answer.

"I do," she said eventually. "In their own way. It doesn't make up for the years of psychological torture though."

"Of course not," I added quickly. "They did put out a report for her though."

Snorting, Laura shook her head. "If someone stole your car or diamond necklace, you'd report that, wouldn't you?"

"Is your sister like you?" I asked. "Is getting the hell out something she might do?"

"Not at all. She's always been softer than me. I could see her moving away for uni or something, but never running. Look," said Laura. "Are you going to help me?"

"One more question," I said, sitting back. "How did you find me?"

"Oh, that's easy. I drink at his bar," she said, jerking a thumb at Donald. "And this was pinned on the wall."

Laura dug into her pocket and pulled out a crumpled rectangle of card bordered in emerald green; it still bore the name of my predecessor.

Jason MacAffee
Professional Curse-Breaker
Mystic to the Posh and Plebs Alike!

"I suppose I should have seen that coming," I muttered. "Okay, let's say I was on board. Why me? Why do you come to the only consulting warlock working in Glasgow?"

"I told you," said Laura, with a shrug. "I drink at Donald's bar and there's been... whispers."

"Whispers?" I repeated, throwing a glance at Donald. "What whispers?"

"There's something that got a lot of folk on edge," said Laura. "I don't know any more about it than that, but the rumours in his pub are that the night Leigh-Anne went missing, something new to the city had apparently left a few people all of a flutter."

I was certainly interested now. "What was the date?"

Laura told me and I racked my brains to see if anything had stood out to me, but nothing out of the ordinary struck me; it had either been too minor for me to notice, or I'd simply not been paying attention.

"So, that's why I'm sat here and not in some old boy's office," explained Laura. "I don't believe in coincidences and that seemed like a hell of a coincidence to ignore."

Biting my tongue, I resisted the urge to explain how the universe is in fact governed by coincidence and instead gave a resigned nod.

"That night, how do you know that's when she went missing?"

"I couldn't get in contact with her. She said she was going out with some friends and I asked her to let me know she got home safe. Didn't get a text, no response when I called her in the morning," said Laura, her voice suddenly small. "Finally called Mum and Dad and they were frantic."

"And the friends she was with?"

"The police spoke to all her school pals, no one knew anything about her going out that night. That was the last I heard about the investigation."

"And no one knows if she was with anybody?"

"Not to my knowledge," said Laura with a shrug.

So I had no leads from her friends, no indication of who the last person to see her was and a dead police investigation. Great.

"Fine," I said, resigned. "Let's talk rates."

I don't think I'd ever spoken about 'rates' before in my life. That being said, it was easier to be taken seriously discussing rates than if I'd asked her to cross my palm with silver.

"Five hundred quid now, another five hundred when you bring Leigh-Anne back."

God, I hope I didn't look as gob smacked as I felt. A grand! That would cover my rent and amenities for two months!

"That's... acceptable," I managed to squeak.

"And I want to make this absolutely clear," continued Laura. "You bring her to me. Not my parents."

"You're paying," I concurred.

"One thing, before you go," said Laura as I stood up to leave.

"It'll cost you."

She looked briefly taken aback, before she grinned.

"Can you prove to me that this isn't all bullshit? I've just dropped five ton on you. Give me a little something to let me know you're legit."

I didn't say anything. I didn't have to. Instead I clicked out a soft syllable; there was a soft hissing sound and the smell of burned hair, before one of the metal beads on her dreads fell to the table with a soft 'plunk', the singed purple loc smoking where the metal had burned it away.

2

The mushrooms hadn't taken hold yet; I could certainly feel them getting to work, opening up parts of me that otherwise remain closed, and my wallpaper wasn't interesting enough for the amount of attention I was giving it, but I was still compos mentis enough to close the curtains and light some candles. The candles aren't necessary, really. The candles, oils, stones, all of it is just... window dressing. If you want to practice minimalist magic, then more power to you. I, however, think a lilac and patchouli candle to be the peak of the craft. Andy, my flat mate, was out for the night, so I was free to lock myself in my bedroom and have a good chat with myself.

Certain narcotics can help you find the headspace needed to get your engine running; if you can let go of all that baggage that you drag behind you like a Sisyphian boulder and let it fall along the wayside, things tend to slot into place and then everything becomes a whole lot simpler. Obviously, I'm not stoating round the city fleeing every day, but for the occasional ritual it tends to get my engine running. Besides. Watching patterns blossom out of the grain of a door for four hours can be a laugh, if all else fails.

I sat with my legs loosely crossed—nothing worse than getting pins and needles when you're trying to free your mind—and held my hands out in front of me, palms facing up, and closed my eyes. This next part is always tricky; I just start talking shite. Anyone who knows me would think this is right up my street, but chatting shite with no rhyme or reason is a lot harder than you'd think.

Next time you've got nothing to do, I want you to just start talking. I don't care what it's about or if the words that are pouring out of your puss make sense, just talk. Aim for ten minutes. Aim for five. Once you've spouted two or three minutes' worth of garbage, you'll begin to forget every word you've ever heard. Talking this way isn't how we're designed; communication is a part of being a community. To talk to yourself, at length, requires a focus not found in many people. Hence the candles and incense and drugs; create the right headspace and the rest comes easier.

But there's one amazing moment, a moment that you never notice at the time; after a while, the words come unbidden and gush from your tongue like water through a ruined dam. My words began to twist about me, catching in the incense smoke as threads of language, and the innermost workings of my subconscious hung in the air like dew from a cobweb. I could hear only the nonsense I was spewing, forgotten shopping lists and the ingredients to the budget body wash I used four months back. Language deconstructed and words I have used a million times before were alien to my ears.

My palms, previously outstretched and empty, were filled with a pair of warm hands. I opened my eyes and stared back into my own grinning face, complete with acne scars and my too thin, too pale lips. I've lost the little glass gem from my nose stud, I realised as the little piece of jewellery failed to glint in the candlelight.

"Talking to yourself is the first sign of madness," I said.

"It's the only sure way I can get some intelligent conversation around here," I quipped back. We both chuckled.

"So, what's the craic?" I asked.

"Jesus, Rudy," I said, exhaling through my teeth. "I'm being paid a hell of a lot of money to find a missing girl."

"You don't sound too excited."

"Should I? I'm not a PI."

"You could be though. You think you'd be good at it."

"It's just... I'm a low rent warlock. I chase spirits out of houses and break mild curses. This is serious shit."

"Then don't think of yourself as a low rent warlock. I don't think you are. You're a badass caster with an impressive talent!"

"Modest, too." I rolled my eyes before cocking my head to the side, studying me.

"I'm not lying, though. You're clever, everyone growing up always told you that."

That's true. And look at me now. There's little in life more disappointing than being a gifted child who grows up to be a thoroughly mediocre adult.

"This could be life or death though," I muttered. "I don't know if I'm equipped to deal with that sort of responsibility."

Of course, I know what I am talking about, and softly I said, "You couldn't have saved Mum. I've told you that more times than I can count."

"It's not about that."

"Isn't it?"

It's usually so simple to lie to yourself; tell yourself the same thing over and over and you'll begin to believe your own bullshit. But when you're literally sitting face to face with another aspect of your psyche, lying doesn't come quite so easily.

"Okay, so, maybe it is a little," I admitted. "But so what? What if I have to go back to her sister and tell her Leigh-Anne is dead? How the hell am I supposed to take her money with another death on my conscience?"

"Did you kill her?"

"No!" I said, horrified.

"Then why would her death be on your conscience? You didn't kill Mum; it was the cancer that did that. She shouldn't be on your conscience either."

"That's easy for you to say," I snapped.

"I'm you, you numpty. Look," I said, sighing. "You've got a chance to help someone, *actually* help someone. Isn't that what you've been wanting to do?"

"But what if I fail?" I asked, feeling small.

"Then you fail. And afterwards, you'll pick yourself up and get on with it." I was clearly looking unconvinced, because I sighed and squeezed my hands. "Okay. Let's say *I'm* the one taking this gig. Where should I start?"

"I guess... with her online presence?" While I wasn't one for social media myself, I had infuriating memories of Tara posting the minutiae of our lives across Bebo and Myspace, which dated me more than I was comfortable with.

"Good start, thanks. What else should I do?"

"Well, I'd suggest having a poke around her house to see if there's anything interesting there, but that could prove tricky. Unless I can get Laura to get me in. And ask around town. See who's got their nose in the wind."

"Well, would you look at that?" I said in mock surprise. "It seems to me like I've got this all figured out. We're a good man," I added. "We just need to remember that."

I blinked. I was alone again in my dimly lit bedroom, the incense sticks burned down to the stub. Well, I'd made some good points, I reasoned. Standing, I blew out all the candles and climbed into bed, running over the next day's plan in my head, pausing only to pull out the now spoiled stud from my right nostril.

3

It rains a *lot* in Glasgow. Love the city as I do, the weather that blows in from the Irish Sea certainly leaves a lot to be desired and the next morning I woke up to drops like golf balls hammering on my window; hardly the crisp, dry autumn morning I'd been hoping for. After checking my watch and realising it was only just eight, I swung my legs out of bed and stoated to the kitchen, not bothering to put on anything more than my pants since I didn't expect anyone to be in my kitchen this early.

Meeting my surprised eye was a tall man with dark skin and glasses, drinking from my humourous 'Mystic Mug' cup, similarly dressed only in a pair of boxer shorts. His body was muscled, his torso and legs covered in curly black hair. My surprise only lasted a moment as it wasn't unusual to wake up to some guy or girl snooping around the flat after a night with Andy and there'd been no incidents whatsoever after I'd gotten around to putting a lock on my curio cabinet.

"Morning," I said brightly, reaching for a mug. "Pass the coffee, would you?"

"Yeah, sure," said the stranger, apparently a little embarrassed. He handed me the Nescafe Gold and clicked the button on the kettle.

"I don't know why I need to introduce myself to a stranger in my own home, but my name's Rudy. Rudy Renfrew."

"Oh, yeah." He swapped the mug from one hand to the other before holding one out to me. "Mohtisham Bukhari. Call me Moti."

"Nice to meet you, Moti. I'm afraid Andy won't be surfacing any time before noon."

"Ah, no worries. I need to go to work anyway. He told me to make myself at home and let myself out."

"Ever the charmer," I muttered, stirring a tooth-achingly large amount of sugar into my coffee.

"Eh, I'm not too bothered to be honest."

"Where did you end up last night?" I asked.

"Some underground club under the train tracks."

If you know the right people, Glasgow is awash with after-hours raves in hidden places, where the only available drink is Tennent's lager and ecstasy tablets are handed out like breath mints. It's a city with trains running like arteries through the crowded buildings; below the cobbles and tarmac is a sprawling subterranean maze of abandoned shafts and forgotten tunnels, peppered with vast cathedrals of empty space, perfect for the club nights when generators are rolled in and DJs blast house music through echoing halls. Just keep it outside the limits of the subway.

"Look, I hate to run but I need to have a shower before I bounce," said Moti, apologetically. "And I need to dig my clothes out of Andy's floor."

"He didn't tell you about the pig sty, eh?" I asked, grinning.

"No. No he did not."

I reached up to the linen cupboard and pulled out a clean

towel.

"Here, batter in. Just try not to use all the hot water; Andy spends a lot of money on it."

Leaving Moti to it, I took my coffee to my bedroom, sat in my desk chair and dug out my penknife before pulling the long wooden stick that rested against a wall, chest height and slightly thinner than my wrist, onto the desk. Some months back we had suffered a storm that shook the city to its core as gale force winds buffeted buildings and denizens alike while forks of lighting, usually uncommon, crisscrossed the bruised sky in a lattice. It was once the storm had passed that I found the broken tree; initially I thought nothing of it and assumed the winds had torn it apart. But then I saw the charred edges and the jagged wound in the wood; this had been struck by lightning. So, as any warlock worth his sacred salt would do, I dragged the greater part of a tree home. The five feet of ash that I salvaged from the branch had been seasoned, stripped of bark and was now being whittled smooth. I drank my coffee and gently carved away a knot that had been giving me trouble, listening to the shower along the hall, ignoring the flakes of wood that were collecting at my feet.

When I heard the shower stop running and Moti make his way back to Andy's room, I put my project back beside my bed and grabbed my own towel. I didn't take long to shower but after I had finished and exited the bathroom the flat certainly felt emptier, so I could only assume Moti had left. My suspicions were confirmed when I found his name and number on one of the post-its we kept by the Wi-Fi router, which had been stuck to my bedroom door. The brass balls it took to give your number to the flatmate of last night's hookup; it was probably the reason I took it and stashed it in a drawer instead of throwing it away.

I walk most places; lately I avoid using the subway when I

can and I've never been a fan of the city busses, so on days like this when the sky pisses down on me with everything it's got, I tend to lament that I never passed my driving test. The city centre was still flooded with people, despite the downpour, and I had to weave through a sea of umbrellas, getting jabbed by most of them, to get to the shoe store. I picked a new pair of boots and left wearing them, dumping my old ones in the bin outside; paying my rent with dry feet would feel a lot more satisfying than paying it with wet feet, I told myself to stave off buyer's remorse. My detour over, I picked up my original route once more, stopping only to buy donuts as a deal sweetener.

The city centre of Glasgow is a sprawling grid on the side of a hill; a few dozen streets run up the hill perpendicular to the river, cross-hatched by busy roads that result in a labyrinth that no one truly knows the secrets to. You can be sure you are heading one way only to find yourself back where you started; I once found myself going in circles along a straight wynd before the magic shifted and I was spat out onto the road. These little blips of stray magic affect everyone, not only casters, but we're just the ones who tend to notice it. Nearly everyone else pushes it out of mind, wondering why it sometimes takes them ten minutes longer to get to work than usual. Despite all my skills and proficiency, I wandered aimlessly for a wee while before working out which corner I was on. I pushed the buzzer of a door that led into the flats above an Italian restaurant.

"Who is it?" came the tinny, muffled reply.

"It's Rudy."

The door clicked and I pushed it open. By the time I reached the third floor I was out of breath and mentally resolving to try and get into some sort of shape. Annie was waiting for me.

"You're never up this early," she stated, arms folded and eyes narrowed. "What do you want?"

"Can't a man visit his favourite pixie once in a while?"

"Not before ten a.m. if he wants to avoid suspicion."

Regardless, Annie turned on her heel and stalked back into the flat with me close behind. I declined another coffee—my heart was already under enough stress—and pulled out the donuts instead.

"So, to what do I owe the pleasure?" Annie asked eventually, cradling a steaming mug in two hands. "I'm afraid you missed Tara."

"I assumed. Nah, it's you I wanted to talk to," I assured her. "I need your help with a case."

Wow, 'a case'. It still sounded strange.

"Me? Really?" asked Annie, clearly surprised. "I'm about the least magical person you know."

"While that's true, it's not anything magical I need."

As she drank her coffee and nibbled on a donut, I filled Annie in on the events of the past twenty-four hours. To her credit she's a marvellous audience, cocking her head and nodding at all the appropriate moments.

"This is... a little outside of your comfort zone, isn't it?" asked Annie after I had finished. "Wasn't your last gig chasing a ghost out of an attic?"

"For all intents and purposes, aye. But in reality it was some loose pipes and a crack in the insulation," I admitted.

"You're shameless. So why do you need me?" she inquired. "It sounds like you've got a good head on this."

"I need your connections," I explained. "You know what I'm like with technology."

I'm not anti-technology. When I see the latest gadgets and gizmos in the window I can stand there for ages, longing to live in a parallel reality where I understand them all, but tragically that is not the life for me. I can utilise Google Maps, download movies and songs and even mess about with the terminal of my laptop when the occasion calls for it, but Annie is a computer genius. And I'm not just saying that in the manner of a tired old man who thinks anyone who can unlock his phone is a genius. This lass has an undergrad and a postgrad in computer science and is (hopefully) nearing the end of her PhD in the same. As if this wouldn't be enough on its own, Annie also has a plethora of contacts across the globe, equally as tech-savvy as she. These are the people I need her to contact for me.

"I need her emails," I explained. "I need to see who she's been talking to, when, why, eee tee see."

"Her emails?" Annie asked, aghast.

"I know, I know, it's a little intrusive," I admitted. "But I need some leads."

"No, I mean... no seventeen-year-old girl is going to be talking to anyone using a damn 'Gmail' account," she said, as if the concept was nauseating. "Did you check out her social media presence?"

"I don't even know what sites are popular these days. Is everyone still on Facebook?"

Annie sighed and dug out her phone. "In the current social climate, you're going to want to look at Instagram and TikTok... maybe Facebook and Reddit, but I wouldn't bet on it," Annie said as her fingers tapped away on the screen. "Any conversations are going to be through WhatsApp or Messenger. Maybe her DMs."

"DMs?"

"Direct Messages," said Annie, before seeing my lost expression and adding, "Remember MSN?"

"Vaguely."

"Basically, every social media platform has that built in. Is this her?" she asked, handing me her mobile.

Scanning through the tapestry of a life in snapshots, I could immediately see that yes, this was indeed Leigh-Anne. You take away Laura's dreadlocks, feathers and eyeliner and there stands her sister. I nodded.

"Yup, that's her."

Annie moved to take her phone back but I jerked it away and held up a hand, frowning. Something was wrong.

"Does something seem a bit... *off*, with these pictures?" I asked, turning the screen back to Annie.

"Erm... selfies, landscapes, black and white alleyways... Seems pretty standard to me."

"Yeah," I said, nodding vehemently. "That's my point. It's almost *too* standard, isn't it?"

"How do you mean?"

"This looks like the Instagram page of someone who is actively trying to make... look, it all seems a bit bland, no?"

Annie took her phone back and furrowed her brow, scrolling idly down.

"I see what you mean, but maybe she's just a bit of a vanilla person."

"Vanilla gets a bad rap," I said, absently.

"Do you think she has a private account?"

"Is that a thing?"

Annie sighed. "Yes, Rudy. It's a thing. If a kid's got pictures or videos that they don't want their parents to see, then a private account under a different name is a good way to keep them hidden."

That struck something in me.

"Laura said the parents are controlling narcissists. Do you think this page is just for them? Keep them off the scent of her life outside their walls?"

"It's possible," said Annie. "But if it's under another name you'll have a job finding it. What?" she added, seeing my sheepish grin.

"This is why I need you. All those sites you mentioned, will any of your contacts know about hacking them?"

Here's the thing I learned about computer buffs from Annie; they all know each other, like farmers or rich people. From what I have gleaned, under the moniker 'Bonny' Annie has a whole slew of online cohorts of skill equal or greater than her, and right now she is my port in the storm.

"Probably," shrugged Annie. "What's in it for me?"

"My undying gratitude."

"Anything more tangible?"

I sighed. "Let me know how much I owe after the fact and I'll see what I can do."

"Much better," said Annie. "You can leave the donuts too."

"My duty to her ladyship."

We sat a while and shot the shit like friends do, Annie reminding me that we had her and Tara's much belated engagement party in a week's time. As I was leaving, Annie stopped me and handed me Tara's wood burning tool.

"It's pissing down outside and your hoodie is barely dry. Why aren't you wearing a coat?"

"I'll be fine," I insisted, sticking the bundle of metal and cable into the pocket at my belly. "I don't have a coat."

That's not strictly true. There's one coat, barely worn, the phantom in my wardrobe. But I'd never been able to bring myself to make it my own.

"You have to start dressing better," said Annie.

"I could always go back to my trackies," I said, sulkily, stretching out the creases from my jeans.

"Rudy, this isn't largely fraudulent mysticism, you're being to paid to find another person. You have to start looking professional."

"I'm a Curse-Breaker. Unless people already think I'm legit, how professional I look isn't really going to convince anyone."

"Well, you'll still get ill out there."

"I'll risk it," I said, smiling as I left.

While thankfully the rain had eased slightly, my hoodie turned out not to be 'barely dry' but in fact 'not dry at all' and I stepped out of the close into an autumn chill that instantly clung to my skin. I did need a coat, it was true, but the hoodie always felt cramped under another layer. It was an issue with the magic of it that I hadn't been able to work out yet.

We're all cursed. Well, not me because I'm a Curse-Breaker, but almost everyone else. Most curses aren't all that much; maybe you'll always trip on the fifth crack you step on, or perhaps you'll always be the one to feel the first drop of rain. I found one curse where the guy was barked at by every nineteenth dog he came across. Most of them are harmless on their own but they can mount up and eventually they become noticeable to the more paranoid. Others are a shade more potent; they latch onto you, imperceptibly leeching parts of you, until suddenly you realise you're a little less than you were before and a part of you that you weren't aware of has been lost. And that's where I come in. You call me or send me an email, or occasionally bang on my door in the middle of the night, and I come to reverse them. Easy money.

Except, of course, most people these days don't believe in curses. There was a time when you could go pay the woman who lived in a hut on the hills to remove your curses and she'd take a dozen eggs as payment. In this day and age, I am that white witch on the hills and I would take a dozen eggs in a heartbeat. But instead, I remembered, I had the best part of five hundred quid in my wallet and it was there for a reason. I pulled my hood tighter and set off down Buchanan Street, following the gentle decline towards the river. It took me a good hour to find who I was looking for and when I finally did, she ushered me under her umbrella and I followed her under the outcrop of an Edwardian building.

"I've been looking for you," I told her, pulling down my hood and doing my best to wring it dry. "No sign of you at the shelter."

"Aye, they kick us out between nine and five," Naomi said, apologetically. "I understand why but..." She trailed off and glanced upwards at the rain.

"Come on," I told her, squeezing her shoulder. "Let's get a coffee."

Being homeless sucks. I'm not going to sugar-coat it. It takes a certain resolve to live without a fixed address, living only off what others can spare. I wouldn't have lasted much longer than I did. I hadn't really accounted for how quickly my already lacklustre funds would dry up with nothing to replace them. I found myself papped out of the charming garden flat I had lived in as a student, paid for by my bursary and a discretionary fund from the uni. It's all too easy to forget that financial security is often an illusion, an illusion more convincing yet more delicate than any I can cast. For a few months I crashed on couches, in empty beds and eventually in doorways.

But I met Naomi and a few others like her, people who had lost everything yet went out of their way to make each other's lives a little better. Naomi herself had looked after me even after her bawbag boyfriend lost all their possessions to pay for a smack habit. I met her years ago doing the best with what she had and taking care of others at the same time. While I had been fortunate enough to only be homeless for a brief time, she was still here, inching her way towards solvency once more. At least I hoped. Curses have a way of latching on to those around their hosts, and what is misery to do if its host is determined to reach happiness once again? So, I did what I could when I could, funnelling her what I could spare and doing what I thought was best. I never asked where the money went.

We sat down in the nearby Café Nero and I pushed a panini

across the table to her.

"I need a hand," I said, apologetically.

"What's up?"

"Missing girl. Maybe a runaway. Could you ask around and see if anyone has a seen this girl?" I showed her a picture on my phone.

"Never seen her myself, but I can ask around," said Naomi, nodding.

"Thanks."

I peeled off sixty pounds in notes and handed it to her. She just stared at it.

"Rudy, pal, I can't," she said, flicking the crumbs from her fingers. "It's too much."

"Naomi, I haven't earned this money yet so it's not technically mine. Get in there before it is."

Chewing, Naomi seemed to consider this and eventually took the money. "I'll dig up what I can, I promise," she insisted.

"Thanks so much."

As I stood, I grasped her hand and willed her as much fortune and protection as I could; it's not magic, but it should be.

The rain was still trying to soak my already sodden frame so I thought, hell, I'll take the subway. I beeped my way through the turnstile and found the train waiting helpfully for me at the platform. I hopped in, sat down and rested my head back as we pulled away.

I remember the first time I ever saw anything unnatural. It had been about a year since my treasure hunt began and I had made what I like to think was my first big breakthrough. I was sitting with scans of pages from twenty different books, all of which boasted at least a line referencing illusions in almost forgotten cultures and tribes. Armed with an encyclopaedia of notes and a dearth of experience I coughed out a rough sound;

all of the printed letters fell from the page torn from my notebook and jumbled to the desk in front of me. Left on the lined paper were only four letters.

h

A

h

a

It was only an illusion; with a couple of blinks and a squint the original page was back to normal, yet I knew I wasn't. That was when everything changed; the world, my priorities, me. The old me suddenly stopped mattering and there was only Rudy.

I'd like to say I noticed something was wrong as soon as the train stopped, though I would be lying. We'd been sitting in the station for at least a minute before I realized no one had got on or off; not too unusual by itself but the other passengers... They seemed normal enough at first, still breathing, still blinking, but not *reacting* to anything. Almost frozen in a momentary activity.

My heart began to beat violently against my ribs as I thought *NO NO NO NO NO* in time with it. My fears were confirmed when I glanced through the window behind me and saw not the platform on the opposite side of the station but instead a plain brick wall.

"Master Renfrew?" called out a soft but authoritative voice.

I sighed. "I'm coming," I said as I got up and stepped out of the train into a brightly lit subway station, the white walls blinding and pristine, the orange paint fresh and unmarked. A tall man in a tan suit and highly polished shoes waited for me.

"He would like to see you."

"Aye, no shit," I said. "Never would have guessed."

He would like to see me. Him.

The Clockwork Man.

4

Gods exist. I thought I'd rip that plaster off quickly. Gods exist and there are fucking *billions* of them. Think about the last time you stubbed your toe and, while hopping up and down on one foot in agony, you cried out 'OH GOD'; that god exists and that was his summoning ritual. Or perhaps last week when you bought a ticket for the EuroMillions and you said a silent prayer to whatever deity might have been eavesdropping. Well, there *was* a deity eavesdropping and they heard you. Most have less potency than a fart on the breeze but there are a few who can leave an imprint on this world. The Gossamer Lady, god of Glasgow's lost and dead, resides in the necropolis, the vast cemetery that climbs one of the city's hills and guides those who die here to what lies beyond. The Green God and the Blue God live in the stadiums of Glasgow's two football teams, grown from the energy and rivalry of the Old Firm; living in the shadow of the Blue God's temple leaves me often at the mercy of his followers on match days. The Clockwork Man is another and, in my eyes, a truly frightening being.

As the Clockwork Man's most devout led me up the stairs and back into the outside world, we were greeted by what was by now a distressingly familiar forest, the station out of place amidst the tall trees and dense vegetation. We walked in silence along a delicate gravel path that snaked around the thick trunks and eventually out onto a well-manicured lawn that sloped up towards the rear of a bright sandstone tenement block. I couldn't resist glancing behind me at the trees; what had seconds ago been a vast forest whose edges could not even be guessed at was now contained neatly between the walls that separated this garden from the next.

Our destination was the glass conservatory at the head of the garden; there sat an older man, small and wiry, drinking a cup of tea and reading from a tablet. From his waistcoat pocket extended a fine chain that fixed onto one of the buttonholes.

"Sir, Mr. Rudy Renfrew," said my guide.

"Yes, thank you, Campbell," said the Clockwork Man, glancing up from whatever he was reading. "Rudy, what a pleasure. Please, sit down."

By now I knew there was no point arguing, so I sat down while Campbell poured tea for me.

"Milk and sugar?" he asked. I didn't reply, instead staring straight at my host, who sighed.

"Rudy, you should know this by now. You can drink the tea and it's not going to place you under a geas. I'm not a damn fae," he said, taking off his wire-framed glasses and placing them on the wrought-iron table.

"Milk, two sugars please," I said, not taking my eyes off the Clockwork Man.

Gods are neutral, in the grand scheme of things. They are neither benevolent nor malevolent, instead they act as they choose, bestowing their graces on those they deem worthy. I'm sure it sounds fair to the majority but remember that the ocean is neutral. Volcanoes are neutral. A coastal village will exist for centuries, reaping the shoals of fish that has kept its inhabitants well-fed and happy for generations. Until, that is, the wall of water twice the height of a building barrels down on the beach and rolls inland faster than a horse can gallop, and a whole culture is lost. Farmers long benefitted from the fertile soil at the foot of volcanoes, delighting in the spoils of their harvest. Except, that is, on the day the mountain blows itself apart, incinerating the farmers and burying the town alive. Too many people forget that neutral is not *good* and is probably closer to *bad*.

"I know you're more than capable of getting my mobile number from somewhere," I said, sipping my tea.

"I could, but then you would either ignore my call or not come," said my host. He's got me there. "Either way, my method is quicker and guarantees results."

"What do you want from me?" I asked.

The Clockwork man frowned. "You've been poking around town, asking questions," he said. "Might I enquire as to what about?"

"Missing girl," I said, curtly. I didn't want to have to tell this story for the third time today. "Look, I've been at this... Five hours? How can you already know about this? I didn't even ride the subway into town."

"It was the very fact that you were in town without having ridden me—"

"Please don't say that," I groaned.

"—that made me suspicious," finished the Clockwork man, loudly.

"So I can't win. If I take the subway, you abduct me. If I walk, you notice and plan to abduct me next time I *do* take the subway."

"Please stop moaning, it's very tiring. I'm a god, I have privileges. Now, tell me about the missing girl."

I list off the major points; quiet girl, overbearing parents, resentful older sister. "If I had to trust my gut, I'd say she's a runaway," I said as I swallied the last of my tea.

"Are you so sure?"

"No, of course not," I scoffed. "Why does everyone keep acting like I'm Taggart? I'm a Curse-Breaker. I've never done this before in my life. But her sister's gone no contact with her parents; if they're that bad, I wouldn't be surprised if she'd followed suit."

Campbell came and filled our cups again.

"Have you spoken to the girl's parents?"

"No. I don't even know how I would go about it," I admitted. An idea struck me. "Can you get me in?"

"The address?"

I told him but he shook his head.

"It's outside my reach. As well you know, I can only directly affect the city centre and the neighbourhoods within the boundary of my tracks. I have no power in that neighbourhood, only influence. You'll have to find your own way in."

"So much for being omnipotent," I muttered.

"I have never claimed to be entirely omnipotent, nor entirely omniscient for that matter," said the Clockwork man, clipped. "I'm a minor deity with a limited scope. I'm not a cure-all for all of life's problems."

"And there I thought that's what religion was."

For the briefest instant this man was gone and in his place sat another man, soot on his face, unshaven and teeth crooked. Then the Clockwork Man was back, albeit with a slight scowl on his lips.

"You know what I am. Do you need to be reminded?"

"No!" I insisted suddenly, mouth dry. "No, sorry, I mean—"

But the damage had been done, and the god magic had been worked.

I am looking at a man.

Or I am looking at him as best as I can, because it is as dark as shit down here in the tunnels and the only light is the soft yellow glow of the lantern that the man is holding. I catch a glimpse of his weathered face beneath the flat cap, a face coated in soot that stains his skin and darkens the three- or four-days' worth of coarse stubble on his cheeks. Crooked teeth protrude out over his lips. His face is drawn, his jaw aquiver, his eyes panicked.

There is a crash that echoes around me, chattering birds in a murmuration that races down, down, down into the gloom as the lantern bursts at his feet; the oil burns away in one huge flare, and then... shadow.

"Damn," I hear him say, crouching over the shattered pieces of his escape. *Damn, damn, damn, damn...*

This isn't the present day; I'd know that even if I hadn't been here before; someone smarter than me might be able to judge the decade by his clothes, though I doubt it. Clothes caked in smoke and grime are rarely remarkable and always timeless. He wipes his brow, succeeding only in smearing the filth a little more.

"Hello?" the man calls out. "HELLO?"

HELLO, Hello, hello, hello, hello...

A billion strong chorus echoes in harmony. The man is lost, and understandably so; beyond the well-trodden tunnels of Glasgow's infant subway, the unused miles twist and turn, ever shifting as the beast below waits and writhes. Already, the track still freshly laid, a handful of stations have been lost to the annals of time, forgotten even by those who built them and now belonging only to the dark. This tunnel, however, will never be forgotten for none have ever remembered it; it exists only now, in this instant, for the sole purpose of luring this man into a place where he can be truly alone.

Fear begins to grip the man; I hear his frantic breathing and maybe even the rhythmic thump of his laboured heart; what hard-hearted wanker could watch this unfold before them, yet do nothing? Me, it turns out; I realised the first time I was here that I was only a guest in this memory, not a part of it. Echoes that should have faded into nothing instead tremble around the edges of perception, lilted syllables rippling through the labyrinth.

The man walks on in darkness, alone. Save for me, though phantom outlines are rarely comfort to the blind. He falls to his knees, despair writ large across him. The susurrus loudens and I recognise the urge to run, but even if I tried I'd not get anywhere; this is not an event that can be escaped. This man does not know it yet, but his fate was sealed the moment he set foot in the tunnels this morning.

This one, says a whisper from the walls, *this one will do,* and the lonely man looks up in shock. Imagine, if you will, that you had called out into a tunnel, listened to your words echo along impossible miles and then return, altered and threatening. *Thisonethisonethisonethisonethisonethisone* the disembodied whisper repeats, the sound of a thousand creatures crawling along the walls in a frenzied hunt, and even as you listen the voices blend until all that remains is the thrashing howl of the oncoming entity.

A pinprick of light appears in the tunnel and grows before my eyes. No. Not grows. Approaches. In seconds, the light is all-consuming and where before I could not see for the shadow, the light is now more oppressive than the darkness had ever been. The train is upon us, swirling around us like the River Clyde above. If I were to glance at my feet, although you hear the screech of metal on metal as the train runs along its rails, there are no rails for the train to run along. And then I am alone; no train, no lost soul, only me and the terrible echoes. I am swallowed by darkness again; a thick, almost tangible shadow that can only be found in the world below ground. Around me is heard the tongue of engine; inhuman howls, hissing steam and above the sound of tendons tearing and bones breaking, with a bile-inducing scream that is cut off and fades to a gurgle, this man's link to mortality severed forever. And thus… how to build a god.

⊹

Blinking, I found myself back in the conservatory, fingers gripped pale about the edge of the cold table. The Clockwork Man glanced at me over the top of his reapplied spectacles. I hated it when he did that.

"All well?"

What I wanted to say was 'no, not really' but instead what came out of my mouth was a twisting whine of metal. I shut my mouth abruptly and coughed before trying again.

"Just fantastic, thanks," I panted. There was cold sweat in every one of my crevices.

"Sometimes I feel you look at me and you see a stern old gent," said the Clockwork Man. "Which is exactly how I intend it to be, for the most part. But you chose to look behind the curtain and now you must see me for what I am. I am tens of millions of souls, I am countless revolutions. I am the barrier between the centre and all that rests beyond and that which waits below. While to you I may look affable, never forget that I am efficiency and engineering and depth made flesh by the lives that benefit from me. Do not mistake me."

The smell of oil and cold stone was overpowering in my nostrils.

"I'm sorry," I said. "I shouldn't have said that."

"Apology accepted," said the Clockwork man. "Now, to business."

"Wait! This wasn't business?"

"Of course not. I haven't employed your services yet, have I?"

"Oh, you're going to pay me?" I asked, before seeing his expression and adding, "Or, you know. I'll do it pro bono."

"Excellent. This shouldn't be outside of your bailiwick," said my new employer as he picked up his tablet. "I have a couple of matters for you to attend. Nothing too strenuous; a couple of individuals outside my reach whose baggage has become a little too heavy. I can send you the addresses."

"If they're outside the lines, why are you getting involved?"

"They are my devoted," he replied, shrugging. "And they live close to my stations. This cancerous growth spreads and should it take root on holy ground, it will only have a negative effect on the populace at large. I'm sure we can agree this is in both our interests." He quickly looked me up and down. "You might think about changing your getup, too. You're a warlock, for god's sake. Dress for the role."

On the one hand I wanted to bite back but honestly, I'd had a day, so I simply said, "I'll consider it."

"Wonderful. Well, if that will be all."

The Clockwork Man picked up his tablet and I realised I had been dismissed without being dismissed. Campbell escorted me back along the garden, through the forest and down onto a platform where a train was waiting.

"*Sir*," he said, as I boarded.

How can you make *one* word sound so condescending?

5

I'd hoped that my day would end once I crossed the threshold to my flat but fate, it seemed, had other plans. Upon seeing Andy in the hallway I knew something was up because he was dressed. I was used to finding him his underwear, sprawled out over the sofa, yet here he was in jeans, tee shirt and shoes.

"Oh gods, what's wrong?" I asked, pushing our two deadbolts across and hooking the chain. "Is everyone okay?"

Nearly a foot shorter than me, Andy peered up at me through his chin length black hair, pushed it from his eyes and frowned.

"Nothing's wrong. You have a customer."

"In the house? Did you get a name? Any issue with the door?" I turned to the door frame and inspected the scratches I had made when I moved in.

"Linda MacDonald, nothing so much as squeaked and I've drunk so much tea with her these past two hours I've got to piss like a racehorse."

"Two hours? Why didn't you ask her to come back?"

"I did!" Andy stage-whispered. "She wouldn't go. Fairly insistent that she speak to you. Now, if you'll excuse me."

Andy turned on his heel and walked straight into the bathroom. With a sigh I wriggled out of my hoodie and hung it on the peg above the radiator; I'd give it a proper wash later. I straightened my clothes out as best I could, tried to channel some of the professionalism I absolutely was not feeling, and opened the door to my kitchen.

Sitting at the kitchen table was an elderly woman with a shock of white curls, her handbag clasped in her hands. She was wearing a pink parka even though the heating was turned up gut-wrenchingly high; Andy liked a warm house.

"Did my flat mate not offer to take your coat?" I asked.

"Oh no, he did, but I prefer to keep it on, son," she said, hands tightening over her handbag.

"Fair enough," I said. "Rudy. Rudy Renfrew. How can I help you today, Linda?"

"A friend down at the centre said you might be able to read me some cards?"

I tried to not loom too much but when you're a six-foot-plus man in front of a five-foot-three-on-a-good-day wifie it's hard not to. Of course, the community centre down the road. My mum had spent most of her free time there, right up until the end. I think I'd known more people through that building than I had from school.

"Your friend was right."

"You're not what I'd expected," she said.

"I get that a lot."

When you hear about a self-proclaimed warlock and Curse-Breaker who will also do you a tarot spread, you might picture a spindly old gent; pale eyes and pale skin and pale hair, pale everything. When you instead get a tall, young(ish...) man with a nose ring, it tends to put your guests on the back foot. Which can be handy; a surprised person tends to let go a little more easily. After I sat Linda at my designated round table, artfully stained with candle wax and what I like to pretend is blood, I turned to the kettle.

"Two and a coo?"

"Aye, son, that's grand."

As the water boiled, I sat across from my customer and studied what I saw; her face was drawn and the wrinkled skin around her eyes was puffy, weighed down by the heavy bags below; she hadn't been sleeping well. That handbag was still firmly clasped in her fingers so she could make an exit at speed if need be. This was a woman who had been living her recent life in a state of panic, if not outright fear.

"So why are you here today?" I asked her. "I mean your reading. What do you need to know?"

She glanced down at the grain of the table, mouth open, but it seemed that no words were coming.

"I need to know some background details, love," I continued. "It's how all this works. For the time being, we're partners. We talk, we drink tea, maybe have a biscuit if we're feeling daring. You'll tell me about yourself and we'll get to know each other. Blind readings don't give the best results."

Linda nodded, still unsure but hopefully on the same page as me. "Well, where to begin...?"

It wasn't a new tale to me. Hell, it wasn't even a second-hand tale at this point. She'd married young, a child of the age when a daughter's job was to give her own parents grandchildren. Her husband had, of course, been her very own champion, a prince charming promising her castles and carriages. As the decades went by, however, his true colours bubbled to the surface and he revealed that he was in fact not the paragon he had at first seemed to be. They rarely are.

To cut a long, harrowing and sadly familiar story short, after one too many smacks with his signet ring hand, Linda up and left to the safety of her friends from the community centre. See? We've all known a Linda. Most of us have known several.

"So that's that," she concluded. She lifted the mug to her lips and sipped, shoulders looser. "And now I'm living in my pal's spare room and... Look, I'm an old girl with no trade who left school at fifteen. I'm here because I've no clue what the hell I'm supposed to do with myself."

I didn't need cards to tell her what to do with herself. I *couldn't* tell her what to do with herself; I'm not her and I've never been in her position. But I can certainly tell her what she needs to hear.

"Pick a number between one and seven," I said, standing and making my way to the curio cabinet on the kitchen wall.

"Four," she said immediately. They always pick four. I picked out the deck of cards in the centre of the shelf and, after removing the green bandana they were wrapped in, began shuffling them slowly.

"I want you to think hard about the dreams you had as a child. What you wanted from life. Not the things you were told you wanted, or the things expected from you, but the things that you wanted deep in your soul. Don't tell me!" I added quickly as she opened her mouth. "Just mull it over."

After she had cut the deck, I flipped over the top cards.

"One way to look at your situation," I said, gesturing to the first card, the Star reversed, "is the obvious; it's an ending. Of course it is, but after any ending, there always has to be a new beginning. even if it's only the beginning of the life without that person. The stars dim, but they always return."

"But that's what I'm worried about," said Linda, gesturing to the centre card. I nodded and she picked it up, studying the iconography. "That new life. What am I going to do with it?"

"What do you want to do?"

Linda just blinked at me.

"What do you enjoy doing? What are your hobbies?"

As soon as the word fell from my lips, something in my mind fell into place; what were Leigh-Anne's hobbies? I was fairly sure the magic worked the night she vanished was pertinent, but I hadn't entertained the notion that she might have been the one working it; could she have fallen in with a cult of junior mages, teamed up to give me a migraine? A reminder of the money on the line started blaring like a klaxon in my brain and I did my best to give Linda the advice she needed.

Here's the thing about giving readings. Anyone can do them with enough practice, not just the mages and wizards and soothsayers. It's about a relationship between the reader and the readee; when you pick up enough about another person, you can tune into their energies and truly get a feel for them. You don't need cards either. Get them to boil some spaghetti and dump it on the table, or turn out their pockets, lint included, and you're going to get the same result. For some reason most people find the soft allure of ink and paper more palatable than the idea of being read themselves, but I'm not reading the cards; I'm reading her. All I am is the audiobook.

Anyway, once we've discussed at length how now truly was the time to pick up that brush and finally start painting like she had always wanted, Linda seemed about ten pounds lighter and had something close to determination on her face. She stood and tried to push two crumpled tenners into my hand. I peeled one away and handed it back.

"Call it a discount, hen," I told her before taking her mug. "Just be sure to keep the narrative flowing down at the centre."

"I will do, laddie. Thanks so much!"

When I started my business, I hadn't expected to become the local medium, but you took what kept the roof from leaking.

Or what kept saucepans under the leak, if you were a soft touch like me and kept giving discounts. As soon as Linda left, I pulled out my phone and called Laura.

"What's up?" she asked, picking up.

"What does Leigh-Anne do in her spare time?" I asked. "What are her hobbies?"

"Hobbies? I don't think anyone has hobbies anymore, do they?"

"That's really unhelpful," I said, though she had a point.

"Well, she played the piano when she was wee, but I don't know if she still does. She sings, too. Great voice."

"Is that it?"

"Whenever I've spoke to her recently she's just been telling me about hanging out with her friends, just like any seventeen year old," said Laura; I could almost hear the shrug.

My patience was beginning to wear thin. I had had a very busy day and I wanted to take my boots off and sit down.

"What can you tell me about her friends?"

"They're mostly girls from her school," she said. "They've been hanging out since they were fourteen. I saw her with a boy once, but she wouldn't say much about him."

I wanted to stare at her in shock. "That didn't seem like something you wanted to tell me about before?"

"I'd forgotten all about him until you asked. I picked her up from town one day and I saw her talking with him. That was it."

"What did he look like?" I asked, pressing.

"Jesus Rudy, this was months ago. Erm, tall kid, lanky. Blond hair, black clothes. Tatty denim jacket. You know the type."

"And you only saw him the once?"

"Like I said. I get the feeling I haven't helped you much. Sorry."

I thanked her anyway and hung up. I could add skinny emo

kid to my list of leads, I said to myself, with more acid than I deserved, and went to my room, kicked off my boots and fell fully clothed onto my bed. Reaching up onto my windowsill, I pulled down a tiny light bulb, the type used in a secondary school physics class.

I wouldn't say it was the most aesthetically pleasing craft I've ever poured my effort into but if all went well it would come in handy should the need arise. I meditated, drawing energy from the infinite ribbons that trail around me at all times. The energy from every spell you cast, every magical syllable you utter, leaves behind trace amounts of energy that, with a bit of practice, you can harness. While there was certainly enough energy hanging from me, there was nowhere nearly enough within me and after only about fifteen minutes I was crawling out of my clothes and under the covers where I slept the dreamless sleep of the terminally exhausted.

6

I woke to the sound of my phone buzzing by my ears and sleepily slapped at the screen a few times; there were two messages displayed. Neither was from Annie, to my dismay, but there were two messages from a private number. They were both empty, save for an address, postcode and closest subway station. I showered, shaved and did my best to look respectable (no mean feat when you're wearing a six-year-old hoodie). I returned to my room and opened my chest. Which, if I'm honest, isn't really a chest; it's just a wooden box I picked up at a junk store. Inside was where I kept what I liked to call my 'Items of Magical Potential', or 'IMP's for short.

Magic is strange. Big shock, right? Some items can become imbued with energy which, if harnessed correctly, will provide you with a hefty surge of power. Some, like my light bulb, take time and effort and personal strength; your own power pours into the vessel, stores up over time and gives you something to draw on. Having such a reserve can be very handy if you find yourself in a tight spot; ever since the incident with my first poltergeist I've made sure to have a backup like that on the larger jobs.

Some items, however, can take on energy of their own with no help from you. A branch falling from a tree after being struck by lightning will always be magical; how could it not be? But other items have only a potential energy, a deep spark way down deep inside that might go its entire existence without being realised. That energy is, in open defiance of the laws of physics, *new* energy and as a result is utterly chaotic. Useful little trinkets.

But the best thing about it is, as hokey as it sounds, your imagination. *Ooooh*. Let's take, for example, this small cube of shattered windscreen I found in the gutter. For all I know, maybe some poor guy just had his car broken into. Or maybe it was a horrific crash leaving two dead and another seriously injured. Not the most pleasant of images and probably entirely inaccurate, but what matters isn't what was but what *could have been*.

I set out on foot; the closest address was only a couple of stations away and my new boots still needed to get a feel for the city. Thankfully the day was dry, though the memory of rain crept out from the brick and mortar of the terraces that loomed over me from either side. These Edwardian buildings soon gave way to more modern housing, yellow bricks and maroon PVC cladding and even these were quickly replaced by lifeless warehouses, industrial estates and under the great cement monstrosity that was the motorway above. I'd walked the area before, to and from many a bar and house party through the years, but I didn't like to be away from the centre for too long; it left me feeling stretched, as if the heart of Glasgow was pulling me back.

Google Maps led me straight to the front door of a single-story house beside an open yard of rotting pallets and I knocked the knocker four times. I had to wait a couple of minutes, but the door was opened by a young woman, her hair lank and eyes heavy.

Most curses hang from their hosts like thick knotted rope or vast chains. While initially intimidating, these metaphorical knots are easy to grip and pull apart. This woman though… these curses were piano wire, bound in a razor-sharp net from head to toe. This wasn't like anything I'd ever seen before; *how was she still standing?*

"Can I help you?" she asked; her voice was tremulous.

"I'm a friend of… Mary?" She raised an eyebrow and made moves to close the door; I quickly popped a cough sweet into my mouth, crunched down and let the 'honey' coat my tongue and sweeten my words. "Wait! I'm here about… about your bad luck."

That was certainly enough to give her pause and she pressed her face up to the crack between the door and the frame.

"What bad luck?"

"Lots of things have been going wrong lately, haven't they? One disaster after another. If I'm wrong I'll leave, but I don't think I am."

I don't like using magic to get my own way; a little honey on the tongue and people become a little more suggestible. It seems harmless, doesn't it? Except once you find something so innocuous to make allowances for, you'll find something else to pardon and you'll spend a little less time debating it before you do it. And then again, so continue ad infinitum until suddenly you find yourself taking advantage of everyone around you for the mere fact that you have magic, and *they don't*. Most casters who travel that path don't last long, from what I've been told. The Clockwork Man warned me long ago about the Three, and I'm thankful that I have never caused enough ripples to merit their attention.

"I'm Rudy. Rudy Renfrew."

"I'm Hannah."

My new friend opened the door and invited me in. The house, while fairly tidy and bright, was infested with arcane rot where Hannah's curses had seeped into the very makeup of the building and festered.

"Will I put the kettle on?" Hannah asked.

"Aye, that would be grand, cheers. Mind if I sit?"

"Make yourself at home."

I did, as best I could, though from what I could tell Hannah hadn't made herself at home all that much; there were no tell-tale signs of day-to-day life and other than stale cigarette smoke, the kitchen smelled primarily of bleach. I reached out with my mind and probed the feeling of the house but, save for the curses growing in the walls, there was no energy to speak of, no echoes of activity.

"When did it begin?" I asked as she sat down and placed two cups between us. "The 'bad luck'?"

Hannah shrugged. "A while back now, I guess. Mind if I smoke?" She lit a cigarette and exhaled smoke through her nostrils. "I first started noticing it about eight months ago, but I guess it could have been going on longer than that."

"How did you notice?"

"The third time I fell down the subway stairs, just before I hit the ground it all sort of... fell into place? I don't know, it's stupid."

"Hey," I said, in my smoothest tone. "I don't think it's stupid. I wouldn't be here if I did."

"And I just started thinking, the arguments with family, the trouble at work, the..." Hannah didn't finish but I saw her cradle her belly absent-mindedly. "It's too much, you know?"

"I do know. Don't you have anyone to speak to?"

"Not anymore. No one speaks to me anymore."

This is why curses are so foul; not only do they have their

effects, but the side-effects? The depression and resignation and the damage to those around you, this can break a person's spirit long before you waste away from the curse. I pulled out a half-burned candle from a birthday cake and glanced up.

"Do you mind?"

"Be my guest."

I picked up her lighter, melted the bottom of the candle a little before lighting it and set it down on the linoleum tabletop. As the smoke rose, I took the air in front of me and gave it a little nudge, twisting the white trails into a spiral, spinning slowly above the flame.

"Do me a favour and focus on the smoke for a bit."

"What, is this like hypnotism or something?"

"Or something," I admitted.

"Look, I don't buy this shit," Hannah said, sitting back. "You're, what? A magician who goes from door to door doing magic tricks?"

I opened my mouth to protest but found myself unable to disagree too vehemently. "Basically," I said. "But usually people come to me beforehand."

"And what do you get out of it?"

"Typically, people pay me. But this time, I'm doing it... as a favour. For someone watching out for you."

"Who?"

How the hell do you explain that your local deity sent you?

"Somebody who wants you better." I ran my tongue over my teeth but my honey was spent; I'd need to rely on my natural charm. "There are some people that can see things that others don't; I'm one of them. The person who sent me is another. The bad things that have been happening, you're not entirely responsible. There are things clouding your judgment, affecting your life so profoundly that you're doing things you wouldn't normally do, saying things that you'd never say if you were in your right mind. I can help by taking them away, but it will only work if you're on board with it."

For a long moment I thought Hannah was about to kick me to the pavement as she sat and stared right into my eyes, but eventually she nodded.

"Fuck it, what have I got to lose at this point?"

She stubbed out her cigarette and settled her elbows on her knees, gazing intently into the smoky top spinning in the air. I got to work.

Unless you have spent a really long portion of your life pondering and meditating on the forces that you can use to make reality that little bit *different*, then it's difficult to explain the mechanics of how magic, specifically curse-breaking, actually works, but the closest I could manage would be to suggest spending some time untying dozens of knots from a length of string, with skiing gloves on and in the dark. Usually curses aren't tied all that tight and will fall harmlessly away into nothing but this time they were millimetre thick twists in a tight net. I had never seen anything quite so vicious.

I hadn't even managed to loosen a single curse before I noticed something was very wrong. The feel of a curse is usually unpleasant, a parasite taking advantage of a susceptible host, growing and reproducing as humans do the Earth. This felt more like a virus; inane, malicious and cruel. While I'd never seen the like before, a shiver ran down my spine as I realised what I was dealing with.

These weren't curses caught from too many ladders or black cats. This was a deliberate network of curses, which meant that a) there had been a practitioner in my city without me knowing, and b) they were cursing people, like the dark mages of centuries gone by. I wanted to vomit.

"Keep it together, Rudy," I told myself through a clenched jaw.

I took out the piece of river glass I had pulled from the treacherous Clyde and turned it over between my fingers, savouring the smooth matte feel on my skin. What had entered the water as a polished, sharp piece of glass had been worn down over years and right then I could feel every second of it; the drainage of the city above, the grit that buffed the edges down to a delicate pebble. The brief imprints of those souls burned in me with a scalding flash and a relentless adamant prickled across my flesh. I set to work again, continuing to roll the bead between my fingers.

After some not-too-little effort I felt the first curse fall away and now without a host, fade harmlessly into nothing and the malignant sensations faded too, just a fraction and I found that the next curse was easier to undo. Not by much, but it was fortifying to know that my task could only get easier. In fact, when it came to a certain curse that fell away with greater ease than I expected, I wondered if—

"Someone else has been at this," I said to no one in particular. Even as I said it aloud, I knew it was true. Whoever else had tried to loosen some of these bindings either hadn't had much time or much talent. Possibly both. But that did mean there was yet another caster of some kidney in the city. It didn't summon the warmest of feelings.

From the corners of my eyes I watched the light from the window creep across the wall. This was not a quick process; it took a good few hours and a great deal of my strength, so much so that when finally the last curse slipped away into nothing I fell back into my chair, exhausted. The candle had long since snuffed itself out but still the fine twisted smoke turned idly on its axis until I willed it away with a jerk of my chin. Hannah blinked a few times and glanced up at me.

The way people hold themselves is telling; a carefree person will stride along their path, head high and shoulders down, whereas someone carrying baggage will compress under their own mass. When Hannah had opened the door I saw someone so weighed down that she looked almost to be trying to fold herself up until she could hide in her own body. Even now, as she did nothing but stretch out the stiffness that came with being sat in the same place for hours on end, she looked looser, as if the curses had been knotted into her very flesh.

"How do you feel?" I asked as I wiped the sweat from my brow.

"Er… okay, I think." She looked up at me. "What did you do to me?"

"Honestly, it's easier not to think about it." Realising how that sounded, I quickly added, "But nothing bad! You were carrying a lot of… issues with you. All I did was loosen them a little. I can't promise you that everything is going to be peachy from here on in, but you should feel a little better in yourself."

I pushed myself out of the chair, intent on going for the Irish exit but before I could take a step I felt my entire body threaten to betray me and I had to reach out for the table to prevent me from falling.

"Are you all right?" asked Hannah, alarmed.

"Aye, I'll be fine. I just need to get some caffeine and scran in me and I'll be right as rain. Although…" I bent down and swiped a cigarette from Hannah's pack and used her lighter to ignite it. "I know I said this was a favour, but if you don't mind I'll accept this as payment."

I nodded my thanks and stoated out of the door. The sooner she moves on from her encounter with the roaming warlock the better, honestly.

Smoking has never been a habit of mine but I have found it to be particularly grounding after a heavy session of magic and right then, as I started to look for a café or deli, I could feel myself achieving at least an acceptable level of stability, if not normality. The promise of food steeled me as I held open the door to a sandwich bar for a young woman with a head of dark brown curls; she flashed me a grin of thanks at the exact same time my phone buzzed.

> Found something you might like

> coffee? My treat?

Suddenly, the concept of *free* food outweighed my maddening exhaustion and I slouched back out of the shop, aiming this time for the subway station. When I reached the barriers they opened before I even had the chance to tap my card and I scanned the ceiling until I found a camera. I gave a curt nod and accepted the free journey. I'd need to speak to him face to face soon. Bailiwick my balls.

Annie was sat in a coffee shop, steaming mug in front of her. Before I could sit down she handed me a tenner.

"Before I can share this with you, I want a panini. Grab one for yourself, too." When I returned with a tray of goods, she passed me a tablet. "Now sit and tell me how I'm too good to you," she insisted, taking a bite.

"You're too good to me," I muttered.

What I was looking at, I realised, was an Instagram profile and featuring in most of the photos was Leigh-Anne Baxter. I checked the name but it was unfamiliar; *Saorsa*. I'd put my money on it being Gaelic in origin but despite being Scottish born and raised, I'd never picked up a lick of the language, apart from maybe '*failte*'.

"That was rapid," I said, scrolling down through the pictures. "I wasn't expecting anything for a few days."

"I'd have gotten it to you sooner if I hadn't had errands to run; this was ready when I woke up."

The internet is a more powerful magic than I will ever master, a fact I lamented as I scrolled through the photos. This looks much more like what I imagine social media should look like; here was Leigh-Anne smiling with a group of friends, here was a selfie on one of Kelvingrove Park's bridges and another of her with a boy with a septum piercing. Instantly this paints me a more realistic picture of the girl I am searching for. Here are her emotions, bursting with self and laid bare for anyone to see. Good, this gives me somewhere to start. Wait...

"This is her profile! I mean... I'm in her profile," I said.

"Er... Yeah? I thought that was the point?" said Annie.

"I just wanted to see if she had a private profile," I murmured. "This feels wrong."

"Rudy, you've got an inside look at a missing girl's profile, it shouldn't feel right." Annie leaned forwards and fixed me with the sort of look usually reserved for a stern but well-meaning guidance counsellor. "But it should help you. No one said this was going to be easy. You're a good man, Rudy. You're going to have to get used to the idea that you might have do some stuff that makes you uncomfortable."

Sitting there, with Leigh-Anne's personal life in my hands, I felt the truth in Annie's words. I did try to be a good person; exactly how... *not* good could all of this get?

"How similar are Irish Gaelic and Scottish Gaelic, Annie?" I asked.

"It means 'freedom'," she said, nodding at the screen.

"You speak Gaelic?"

"No, I just recognised the name. Like Saoirse Ronan, you know? So, I googled it," she said simply.

"I should have thought of that," I admitted.

"You have the entire internet in your pocket. Are you sure you're up to this?"

I didn't want to have to say *No!* again so I just smiled and pointed to the tablet.

"Do you mind if I borrow this?" I asked.

"I can just send you the details to your phone though."

"This is bigger. Please? I'll bring it back when I'm done with Tara's wood burner."

Annie could frown someone into submission under gunfire, I thought to myself as I did my best to return her gaze. Eventually though, she nodded.

"If that comes back to me with so much as a scratch, I am turning your balls into earrings," she warned.

"Understood."

We finished our food and coffees, and Annie made a half-hearted offer for me to accompany her shopping. I declined, as she knew I would, and she went on her way while I planned my next move. I didn't want to sit in the coffee shop and dig through Leigh-Anne's personal data in public and I had no other pressing business in the city, so I went home. I had no idea where Andy was. I resisted turning on the heating and instead put on an extra pair of socks before settling down to study, turning the light bulb over in my hand and funnelling some juice into it.

What was I looking for? There was nothing recent, for obvious reasons, so I spent some time studying her history in snapshots; nothing really that stood out so with much hesitation and regret I moved into Leigh-Anne's direct messages. I needn't have worried; each chat was her and a friend sending pictures back and forth from other accounts that they follow with very little text. There was one small message that caught my attention, underneath a picture from Leigh-Anne's own account; a black and white photograph of a desk, cluttered with detritus. It read 'you need to put it closer to your bed'. Put *what* closer to the bed? I glanced at the profile picture and followed it to the sender's profile; it was the boy with the nose ring and suddenly I placed him. A skinny emo with blonde hair. The lad Laura had seen her sister with.

Suddenly bursting with adrenaline, I tapped my way back to the post in question; now I had something to look for, even if I didn't know what it was. What needed to be so close to her bed? I zoomed in on the desk as best I could, eyes scanning back and forth like a 3D printer, desperate for something even a little out of place. What was it that, among the books and notepads and folders, didn't fit? Everything looked normal and... wait...

Sitting at the base of a study lamp was a bundle of twigs, each maybe the length of a finger, bound together with an admittedly pixelated cord. Now *that* was something I wanted to investigate, and as a bonus I had a face to put to Laura's maddeningly vague description. That being said, it was with a sigh that I realised what I had to do next; I had to get inside the Baxter house.

7

I was sat on a faded green bench in the shade of a towering horse chestnut tree. The Baxter residence was in a picturesque part of Glasgow's west end, all curving streets and sandstone and magnolias, a far cry from the flat in the crumbling tenement building I'd grown up in that had belonged to my great-gran, then my gran and finally my mum before it had been demolished in my last year at school after having been deemed 'unsuitable' for habitation. Which was nonsense; the rats and I had lived there happily for years, even with the lack of hot water, holey walls and single glazed windows.

It was my third day casing the joint and even though every spy drama I'd ever seen made it known that you had to watch a property for months before sneaking in, I didn't really have the time, the wealth or the culture capital to spend that much time staking out a house that cost easily upwards of a mil. Instead, I let the cool shadow of the foliage wrap around me and mostly obscure me from wayward eyes. The only way anyone could really take notice of me was if they looked right at me.

At ten past eight, the man I presumed to be Mr. Baxter left via the front door and tottered down the stone steps to his car, something big, black and shiny. He looked like the type of man who muttered to himself as he walked. After he drove away, I knew I still had at least an hour until Mrs. Baxter made herself scarce. In this case, it was two hours and my arsecheeks were well and truly asleep by the time she followed her husband's steps and climbed into a waiting car. An Uber? Or maybe she liked to go the whole hog and hire a driver. Whatever, it didn't matter to me as long as she was out of the house.

Hopefully the shadows would stick as I pulled myself from the bench and across the road. Obviously the door was locked and I wasn't entirely sure how I would make it around into their back garden, so instead I pulled out the old key on a rope and held it in front of the keyhole, where it hung stationary in the air once I let go. Picking locks had become one of the first things I had taught myself, though it never seemed to get any easier and I still had to keep wandering eyes from catching a glimpse of me; imagine trying to thread a needle while simultaneously juggling Faberge eggs and you might get a sense of the difficulty I was facing. My anxiety rose exponentially as time passed and when I finally heard the tell-tale 'shik!' of all the tumblers falling into place, I was clinging to my camouflage by a nail. Before anyone could see the large scruffy man slip into the hallway, the key plopped into my palm and I darted inside. With the door closed behind me, I let out a breath that had begun to strain my lungs.

"Well," I said to myself. "Now what?"

I regretted it as soon as I said it because although I thought I was alone in the house I couldn't be one hundred percent sure, and if I wasn't I certainly didn't want them to know I was making this up as I went. The first thing that struck me was the smell. My sinuses were assaulted by the smell of bleach tinged with lime and pine and lavender and as I stepped further into the hall I noticed that everything white shone like the stars. This went beyond keeping a tidy house, I thought as my nostrils burned. This was borderline obsessive and a little disconcerting.

Humans make mess. It's a well-known fact that ever since we started walking upright and had actual possessions, most of us left them wherever they fell in a state of semi-organised chaos. It's a reflection of the natural turmoil in our heads that we all like to pretend is something that only happens to other people, hence our gut instinct to frantically hide our things before guests arrive.

"So, what kind of psychopath lives in this condition?" I asked as I swept a finger along a skirting board; not a single speck of dust stuck to me.

I contemplated having a poke about but decided that the less time I was in here the better and climbed the nearby stairs instead. I was careful to take note of how things looked so that if I touched anything, I could be sure to set it back into its original place. It was the third door I tried that I recognised to be Leigh-Anne's room.

When I was a teenager, I was a bastard for sticking things to my walls and making a mockery of the paint job. Any pictures I liked from magazines and stickers I had acquired went straight up on the walls to the immense frustration of my mother. Not Leigh-Anne; the walls were bare save for a few family photographs, a cross stitch of a kitten and a single corkboard with a few pictures of her friends. That was something I hadn't seen in a while; in this modern age, if you're taking the time to have physical photos printed, they must be important. Most looked like pictures taken at school or around the city, but one, I realised, was a hard copy of the picture of Leigh-Anne and the boy with the nose ring, an individual whose name I had to learn, and soon. I took the picture and ferreted it away and looked down to the desk below. I did not see the twigs.

"Well. Shit."

I was reluctant to handle too much and was seriously regretting not thinking to bring gloves, when I realised that there was nothing much to handle; the desk was tidy, whereas in the picture it had been a bomb site of scattered papers and books. That in itself wasn't too suspicious, but then I realised that the desk, like everything else, was free of dust. I looked around. The bed looked freshly made and I could smell the fabric conditioner from where I stood. The carpet was fluffy and recently vacuumed. While there was no sign that anybody had been living in here recently, there was also no indication that the room had been *empty*. This had clearly been cleaned regularly since Leigh-Anne's disappearance. An idea struck me.

Out on the landing I nudged open a couple more doors until I found the one I was looking for.

"So, this must be Laura's old room," I said to myself.

Honestly, it could have been any other room in the house; faded pastels, needlework framed on the walls… if it hadn't been for the abandoned plush toys on the pillow I might have passed over it completely. But again, save for the lack of evidence of immediate activity, this room too could easily have been occupied. Everything was freshly cleaned and scrubbed while the freshly cut flowers on the windowsill must have been placed there that morning. Someone was living as if both their children were still present entities. Why was something so innocuous unsettling me so much?

By this point I was beginning to feel that I had long overstayed my welcome (or lack thereof) and was beginning to write off my little foray into breaking and entering as a bad idea and decided to leave. Obviously, my luck being what it is, the universe had other plans.

I was padding along the landing when I heard the front door click open and a woman's voice echo through the (to their knowledge) empty house.

"…but that's not good enough! They said they'd have a quote for us by the end of the week."

Fuck. I heard the newcomer trail along the hallway below me to what I assume must be the kitchen and did my best to make a stealthy exit from the landing and down the stairs.

YOOOOWL!

I trod on a cat. Its cream fur had blended in perfectly with the carpet and I, in my haste, hadn't noticed it, so while the wee demon shot out from under me like a bullet, I tumbled headfirst down the stairs, turning arse over tit and no doubt spewing profanities as I span, coming to rest with my leg bent at an unhealthy angle and my face pushed up against the wall. I just have to make it to the door, I told myself, groaning with effort even in my inner monologue. I turned my head slightly to the right, ignoring the shooting pain that lanced into my cranium, and came face to foot with a sensible brown shoe. Said shoe was attached to a leg clad in white jeans and as I glanced up, I took in the periwinkle blue blouse and shoulder length brown hair.

"Hi," I managed.

There was no response. Unless you count the ear-rending scream as a response.

"Sugar?"

"Yes please," I said, holding out my cup with one hand as I scratched behind the cat's ear with the other.

Rachel plopped a couple of sugar cubes into my shallow willow pattern cup and dropped one into her own.

"Again, I am so sorry for screaming like that," Rachel said, wincing. "I'm not usually so skittish, but you can imagine my nerves are a little frayed these days."

"No worries, it's understandable," I said, waving away her concern. "I think if I came home to find a fully grown male stranger launching himself down the stairs I'd have been shrieking too."

Rachel narrowed her eyes and took a delicate sip of her tea. We were in a kitchen that spilled out into a glass conservatory, sitting at the largest kitchen table I had ever seen, and had a view of a neat garden and quaint, ornate fish pond. The cat, who I had come to learn was called Angus, purred contentedly on my lap.

"So, if you don't mind," said Rachel as she set her cup down on the matching saucer. "Could you please explain what you're doing in my house again? You're looking for Leigh-Anne?"

It was the only bit of information I had been able to squeak out as Rachel had pulled out a heavy golf umbrella from the rack beside the front door to beat me with.

"Yeah. Obviously, I'm not looking for her here," I added. "But I wanted to get a feel for her home and see if there's anything that might point me in the right direction."

"And?"

"Nothing."

Rachel looked as if someone had pricked her with a pin and let all the air out. "Well, at least the police are on the case, I suppose."

My gut churned. Did I want to tell her that the police still had nothing to go on?

"What can you tell me about Leigh-Anne?" I asked. "I'm trying to paint a picture of her in my mind and I'm not having much luck. You could really help me out."

"Gosh, where to begin?" said Rachel, exhaling through her

teeth. "She's never been as wild as her sister, for a start. If Laura had been the one to disappear I wouldn't have been surprised; she's got the devil in her, that one."

That's interesting.

"Do you think she left of her own volition?" I asked.

"Absolutely," said Rachel, twisting a napkin in her hands. "She called me on the night she vanished, you know."

That was news to me.

"She called you? On her phone?"

"On what else? Yes, she called me. She said, 'don't look for me, don't try and find me'." Rachel choked and held the napkin to her mouth, forcing the sob back inside. "Obviously the first thing the police did was try to find her phone, but nothing came of it."

"And have the police been forthcoming with their answers?" I asked, though I was fairly certain I knew the answer. Rachel shrugged.

"They were all over the house for the first few days. Apparently the first thirty-six hours are vital if you want to find someone alive. I didn't know. After three days things calmed down on their end though, as if they were resigned to looking for a corpse now, instead of my daughter. They call me, occasionally, keeping me in the loop and letting me know what they're up to. I want to rage and scream at them to get their thumbs out of their arses but they're the only ones looking for my little girl." She glanced up at me and smiled weakly. "And now you too, I suppose."

I do my best to return the smile. So, Leigh-Anne called her mum and forbade her from looking for her? Either Laura kept that from me or she didn't know. Also interesting.

"Rachel, I'm sorry to have to ask this but… Laura mentioned not having the best relationship with you or her father. Now Leigh-Anne has seemingly run away? What reasons could they have for just leaving like that?"

Rachel didn't reply immediately; instead she rose from her chair and opened a drawer from which she withdrew a beaten-up packet of cigarettes.

"Douglas doesn't know about these, neither does he need to. Come on, let's go sit in the garden."

I followed her through the glass door to the patio and accepted a cigarette as she sat down in a wooden deck chair. She blew out the smoke noisily.

"No one tells you how to be a parent. Well, I suppose they do," she added with a frown. "What with the plague of parenting books available, but for the most part, suddenly a child is dropped into your life and you have to work out how to fit that life around them. Do you have any kids?"

It took all my will power not to either shudder or laugh.

"I don't, no. It's never really been a part of my plan."

"In some ways I envy you. Look, I love my girls. I do. But children and a family were always on the cards for me. I finished school and married, I never went to university, I've never had a job. All that was expected of me was to be a wife and a mother; in my family it was seen as progressive that girls could inherit the wealth if they were the first born, not just boys. What you need to understand is that I'm not just me; I am every member of the whole extended family and every choice I make needs to take into account each aunt and uncle desperate for us to be seen as 'proper'. Have I been the perfect mother? Have I hell." She sniffed and stubbed out her cigarette. "But I love them, in my own way. At this point I don't even need her to come home if she's happy. I just want her to be safe."

I didn't know how to feel. Laura had created a villain, a narcissist hell-bent on turning her kids into carbon copies of herself, but as I sat and smoked with this tiny woman, all I could see was a tired mother with bags under her eyes and nowhere to turn.

"What's your mother like?" she asked.

"She was great," I admitted. "It was just me and her for most of my life in a tiny flat in the southside. She didn't let me run wild, but I had enough freedom to go and do my own thing for the most part."

"Was?"

"She died when I was at university," I said. "Cancer."

"Oh Rudy, I'm so sorry."

"Don't be. It still hurts like hell at times, but it was a good few years ago now. You learn to cope."

"I know. My own mother died a couple of years ago. Old age. I never had the best relationship with the old bag, but when they're gone the wound certainly takes its time to close."

"It does." I sighed and stubbed out my own cigarette. "There's one more thing I have to ask. Did Leigh-Anne ever show any interest in the occult?"

"I beg your pardon?"

"The occult. The esoteric. Weird shit."

"No, I understand the question, I just don't know why you would ask."

"I'm not a P.I.," I explained. "At least, not in the traditional sense. Laura hired me because of my background; I deal with things that most people don't notice or believe in. I'm a Curse-Breaker. She came to me because she thinks someone with my talents might stand a better chance of finding Leigh-Anne."

Rachel stared right into my very soul for an exquisitely uncomfortable minute before rolling her eyes back and huffing. "Of course she does. I blame my aunt."

"Your aunt?"

"My mum's oldest sister. She always had her hand in something strange. Not like dead chickens and crosses made from bones and hair but she knew her herbs and loved wandering in the forest. She used to tell me that there were things older than the city that lived in the trees."

"And did you believe her?"

"Back then? No. But you don't spend fifty-seven years in the Catholic church without beginning to believe in at least a little bit of 'weird shit'."

I couldn't fault her there; the concept of transubstantiation was grimmer than most of the stuff I had to deal with.

"But Leigh-Anne never showed any signs of following in your aunt's footsteps?"

"Not to my knowledge," said Rachel. "Besides, she was very young when my aunt passed away. I could imagine Laura having an interest, maybe, but as you've seen I've never been all that present in my daughters' personal lives."

I heard a voice call out from inside the house.

"Damn!" said Rachel, scooping up our cigarette butts and quickly pressing them into the flower bed. "Douglas isn't supposed to be home until this evening!"

She sat back down and called out 'In the garden, darling' at a decibel that made my ears ring, and we were joined by the man I had seen that morning. He wasn't tall and he wasn't short, neither fat nor thin. His hair was thinning and grey while circular spectacles sat on a thin nose. He looked at me with narrowed eyes.

"And who is this?" he asked.

I would like to add at this point that this wasn't a suspicion that said 'why is there a strange man with my wife'; it was a suspicion that screamed 'who let this commoner into my house?' One of the greatest skills I have perfected is hearing the words that people say without speaking, especially when they relate to class.

"This is Rudy Renfrew," explained Rachel. "He's doing some extra work in the search for Leigh-Anne. Laura hired him."

His focus shifted from me as he snapped his head in the direction of his wife.

"That girl can't leave well enough alone."

"Douglas!" Rachel admonished. "Your daughter is missing!"

"She's not missing, she ran away," Douglas scoffed. "She chose to disappear. Now we just have to leave it to the professionals to do their job."

"And how is that job going, Mr. Baxter?" I asked. "Police got lots of new leads, have they?"

I slipped into the more exaggerated Scots that I used among friends or when I wanted to irritate tourists asking for directions and let the language of my city slick from my tongue like slavers.

"I'm sure the police are more than capable," he said, cold.

"And so am I. The more the merrier, eh?" Rocks might have melted between us as we glared at each other, before I broke into my most charming grin. "Well, I'd best be off. Please don't let me take up any more of your time."

"I'll walk you out," said Rachel, hurriedly standing.

I could feel Douglas's eyes in the back of my head as Rachel led me from the garden back through the house.

"I'm so sorry about him," said Rachel, quietly. "He likes to act like this hasn't affected him much but he's a wreck."

"Yeah, well, don't worry about it," I muttered. "I'm used to it."

"I am sorry though."

"Don't be."

We were almost at the front door when the sharp tang of citrus hit my nose again.

"Why is everything so clean?" I asked, suddenly.

"I beg your pardon?"

"The lime, the pine, the ammonia... Everything is bleached to within an inch of its life," I said. "Both girls' rooms look as if they have been kept pristine. Do you have an incredibly thorough housekeeper, or what?"

Rachel looked embarrassed.

"No housekeeper. I told you, I don't have a job. I usually keep the house neat and tidy but when I have nothing to do all day but worry about my missing daughter... It's nice to have control over something, though perhaps I do go a little overboard. But it helps me fill up the days," she said with a grimace as she held up a pair of dry, cracked hands. "If you find anything, anything at all, please call us. Here."

She handed me a card that had the home phone number and Douglas's work number; apparently, he was a bigwig in a law firm in town. Surprised? Not at all.

8

"Eh pal! You Rudy?"

I stopped fumbling for my subway card and searched for the owner of the voice; there was a middle-aged man sitting against the wall of the station, his clothes ragged and his beard wild.

"Aye, that's me. Can I help?"

"Naomi asked some of us to keep an eye out. This is for you," said the man, handing me a crumpled piece of paper. I took it gently and put it in my pocket.

"Thanks, man. What's your name?"

"Brendan."

"Thanks Brendan," I said, handing him a tenner. "If you ever need anything you think I can help with, curses and the like, get in touch."

"Fucking curses?" said Brendan, incredulously. "You taking the piss?"

"Only sometimes. Other times I wish I was."

I tapped my card and made my way through the barriers, pausing to look at the piece of paper. There wasn't much info, which made sense since I imagine Naomi had written out fifteen of these and stationed someone at every... well, station.

The Last Step
27/09
Young girl. Folk from outside the city.

I pulled my notebook from my pocket and cross-referenced the date. It was the same date that Rachel had told me Leigh-Anne had called. Good job, Naomi. I owe you big time.

The Last Step was a rat warren of venue spaces, connected by narrow stairwells and corridors, and while most of the venues were empty during the day, it boasted a decent pub restaurant on the ground floor. A handful of patrons occupied the external tables and although their chips looked stone cold, my stomach gurgled as I walked past and into the bar. I sat myself on a barstool and pulled the faux-leather bound menu towards me. Once I'd made my decision, the barman came over to me.

"Just a bowl of chips and a pint of Best, please."

"Great. Anything else?" he asked as he punched it through.

"Yes please." I set the menu down. "I need to talk to someone about a girl who was here a few weeks back."

To his credit, I saw him register a red flag and he immediately shut me down. "Sorry mate, can't do that."

"I understand. Though, the girl I'm looking for has been missing for two weeks and I've got it on the best authority that this was the last place she was seen, the night she went missing. I want to know who she was with."

"Shit. You're police?"

"Not quite."

I gave him the date and he shook his head. "I wasn't working that night. I'll go get my manager."

He scurried away and I nursed the top of my beer; it wasn't

my favourite but it was the first I'd seen. I contemplated giving myself a foam moustache, before I heard—

"Rudy?"

I glanced up and was impressed by the speed I placed this man.

"Moti. Hello." There was a brief pause before I added, "So this is work?"

"Aye. And this is?" he asked me.

"Also work."

He raised an eyebrow. "Yeah? Best come with me then." Moti motioned me to follow him and led me to a table near the kitchen door. As soon as he sat, his demeanour changed. "Rudy, what the hell? He's saying you're police or something? What's this about a missing girl?"

"Hey, relax. I'm not police. I've been hired by the girl's sister to help turn her up."

"Are you serious? So, you're what? A P.I.?"

"Again, no," I admitted. "Look, she hired me because of my profession." He looked blank, so I tried again. "What I do for a living? Didn't Andy tell you what I do?"

"Honestly, he didn't even tell me he had a flat mate. I had to work that out myself," he said. And I think he blushed.

"Well, erm…" I rattled through my pockets to see what I had and managed to dig out an inch of matchstick, charred to a point. I held it between my thumb and forefinger. "Watch this."

Moti watched; I think I was lucky that his sheer confusion had outweighed being asked to look at a spent match, but he watched without complaint as the matchstick burst into flame beginning at the bottom of the cinder and creeping upwards, leaving fresh wood in its place. In the speed it would take to burn away, the flame blazed higher until it briefly flickered above a now perfectly blue head, then flickered out.

"That's why she asked me."

My audience? Captive. Their mind? Blown. Their jaw? Dropped.

"What the ever-loving FUCK was that, Rudy?" Moti hissed at me, voice low but sharp. "What. The. *FUCK*?"

"That would be magic. Listen, it's already been two weeks and no one has anything on where she is. I know she was here. I want to talk to someone who was working the night she disappeared. Who was she with, how did she seem?" Moti was transfixed on the match. I tricked it into my palm. "Moti!"

He shook his head and snapped back to my eyes.

"So why are you here? Why isn't it the police asking me this?"

"That is a great question. That absence is another reason I'm here." I spread my palms. "Apparently I'm the guy you come to when you have literally no other choice. I should put that on my business cards."

"You have business cards?" he asked.

"It was a figure of speech."

"You know, you never called me."

"That is correct, I didn't. But," I added, "I kept your number. And... I meant to."

Regarding me briefly, he nodded. "Well. We've got CCTV. If you've got the date, we could run through some of the footage in my office?"

"Love to."

I hadn't imagined Moti's office to be anything too grand, but this was nothing more than a broom cupboard with a safe, an overflowing waste-paper bin and an old Dell computer. By which I mean it was a flat screen, but an early 2000s flat screen.

"How do you even fit in here?" I asked, craning my head to the side.

"I've taken up this wonderful exercise in the morning. It's a mixture of yoga and origami. Excuse me," he said, reaching past me and trying to pull the door shut. It bounced off my arse a couple of times but certainly wouldn't close.

"That's not going to work."

"It has to," Moti snapped. "If I'm going to break the law, I'd prefer to do it in private."

"I could just stand in the doorway and kick you if anyone comes. How about that?" I asked.

"Yeah, sounds great. Date?"

"Eh?" I asked, taken aback.

"The date," said Moti, patiently. "Give me the date."

I gave him the night in question and let him type away.

"Okay," he said as the screen was filled with six smaller windows. "Who am I looking for?"

"Jesus, this is hardly Scotland Yard, is it?" I leaned forward and peered over his shoulder. "She's seventeen, blonde hair. Most pictures I've seen she has it in a plait or an over the shoulder thing."

We fast forward through the night, eyes scanning over the sped-up images and occasionally pausing whenever someone with blonde hair entered the scene.

"Wait!" I said, hurriedly tapping Moti on the shoulder and gesturing to the lower middle screen. "I think that's her."

I pointed at a girl in what looked like a denim jacket, with her hair messily tucked over one side. She was young, definitely blonde and with a boy I recognised from her Instagram page.

"So, she was with this wee shitebag," I muttered.

"You know him?"

"Nope. But he keeps popping up like a spot between the eyebrows. Can you zoom in?"

Moti double clicked the window and it filled the screen. The boy pointed over to a corner booth where a group of people were already sat, and the pair made their way over to join them.

"And who are they?" I wondered aloud. "Pause. Can you

pause it?"

"Yes, my system is sophisticated enough to pause," said Moti as he froze the image. "What about these guys? You know them?"

"Not even a little. Can you go forward, see if we can get a good shot of their faces?"

My technician complied and we jumped forward a few frames until the faces all turned to greet the newcomers.

"And that's the money shot," I said. "Can you print this out?"

"Nope. We went green a few months back."

I glanced around at all the paper pinned to the walls. "Seriously?"

"Or the printer packed in and I haven't got around to replacing it yet. I can send you some screenshots."

"I'd like a physical copy."

"All right..." said Moti, exhaling through his teeth. "How about this; I save these pictures for you and then we go get them printed for you. On the condition," he said, turning around to face me, "you have something to eat with me while we're out."

"That seems like extortion. Isn't that illegal?"

"Oh, do you want to talk about illegal? I've just given a stranger access to the bar's CCTV with the intention of giving him printouts. The least you could do is buy me lunch."

"Now I'm paying?" I asked, raising my eyebrows. "Don't you have a business to manage?"

"I'll tell Chris to mark down an extra hour on his time sheet if he can cover me for an hour. I'm nothing if not magnanimous."

I was conflicted; Moti seemed like a good guy but... I didn't date. I had in the past, but not recently and I'd told myself I never would again. And this was a man I had met in my kitchen after he hooked up with my flat mate. I know I'd been out of the scene for a long time but I'm pretty sure there were unwritten rules about situations like this. But... he had gone above and beyond for me, even after I had just unlit a match in front of him.

"I think I can do that," I said eventually.

"Great. Let's eat." He grabbed his jacket from the back of the door, pausing as we were leaving to chat to the barman.

It was raining, again, but at least this was just drizzle and as I pulled up my hood against the chill, Moti turned his head to me.

"So... that weird bollocks with the match?" he asked. "Where did you learn to do that?"

"Books, forums, trial and error. Some other people like me helped me give it a bit of polish."

"Can anyone do it?"

"Nah," I said. "As far as I know, anyway. There needs to be something about you that takes to the magic. It's like being born with an extra set of hands. Even then, most people who have the ability go their entire lives without realising this stuff exists, and those who do sometimes can't handle it. And everyone else? People are good at blocking out stuff they can't explain."

"This is mental," said Moti. I agreed.

The printing shop was down a wynd, where high street stores gave way to corner shops and greasy spoons; Moti was in and out in a flash and handed me a stack of papers. I nodded towards the nearest café.

"Will this do?"

"I don't think so. Doubt anything they serve is halal."

"Oh. Then, you lead the way."

He fired me questions about my usual line of work and I answered them as best I could. I was used to this; when you find out someone is a Curse-Breaker you tend to have a few questions. I only came up short when he asked me about religion.

"I really don't have the answers for that," I admitted. "I've never been religious, and it's never been tied up with what I do."

"I was brought up in a religious household," he told me. "I mean, I follow all the customs but it's never been for me. A lifetime of rituals and rites and I never saw a thing. I've met you twice and now suddenly there's a whole extra slice of the world that I never knew about."

"I wouldn't think about it like that. There's not a huge underground society of magic users. There's just a few other people like you who can do things a bit differently."

"In Glasgow?"

"Not many. At least not many that I know of. A few dabblers maybe, mostly apothecaries and hedge mages," I said, thinking of Donald and his unseemly bar. "But I've not stumbled on many others. I know a powerful priestess, but they live in Edinburgh."

"Is that it?"

"Well, there's the Three," I said, and then off his look, I added, "Three powerful casters; the closest thing there is to a council. They're there to make sure that none of us get too big for our boots."

"And what are they like?"

"No idea," I said, dismissively. "I've never met them and I plan to keep it that way."

"I bet you all have a pretentious name for yourselves too, don't you?"

I bit my tongue before replying with a sullen, "Yes."

"What is it?"

"The peripheries," I said, grimacing.

After Moti had located a suitable café, we placed our orders and found a spot.

"Am I cursed, then?" he asked over his coffee.

"A bit," I admitted. I'd given him a once over the first time we met. It's a habit I need to get out of; I've been told it's intrusive.

"What the fuck are they, Rudy? Why am I cursed?"

"When did you last break a mirror or knock over salt? Or make a really hard decision that you feel guilty about? Some are picked up, some are born. Others can spread around a location like a cancer and latch on. It's a hideous cycle but luckily there I am, a knight in shining boots."

"Can you take them off me?" he asked. "Now that I know they're there I'd really like them gone."

"Wow, asking me to work on a lunch date. Classy."

His eyes widened. "No, it's fine, I mean..."

"I'm pulling your pisser," I assured him as I leaned forwards. "Of course I'll get rid of them for you. One second."

I reached into a pocket and pulled out the light bulb. He raised an eyebrow.

"Ignore it and just look into my eyes. Usually I'd have a focus for you but we're improvising today."

He took off his glasses and focused his eyes on mine. It took him less than ten seconds to start fidgeting.

"Don't get distracted," I said, as I began on the first knot.

"It's just a bit awkward to stare into someone's eyes like this."

"Then don't think about it. How old were you when you came out?"

"What?" he asked in shocked response.

"How old?"

"Erm, to my parents? Never," said Moti. "Never have, never will. I'm out to all my pals but that's something I'm never going to bring up with Mum and Dad. What about you?"

"Brothers and sisters?" I asked, sidestepping his question.

"Two brothers, one sister. They're all pretty cool with it."

"Silver linings," I said.

"You? Any siblings?"

"Nope. Just me."

Conversation faded and I had Moti locked into position, lost in a glazed-over focus. Most of his curses fell away without hassle but there was one, tightly knotted around his neck and shoulders, that certainly had me working; this had his parents all over it. Still, I've worked with worse and before too long it, like the others, fell away, leaving Moti free, for the time being at least. I pocketed the light bulb and gently cuffed his cheek.

"All done. Avoid cats and ladders for a while and you should be okay," I said, taking a swig of coffee.

"I don't feel different, though."

"You won't. Not immediately, anyway," I said. "Give it a few days, then I'll call you to check in."

"You'll call me?"

"To check in," I repeated. I looked down and saw that while we had, to an outside observer, been staring deep into each other's eyes, the server had dropped off our sandwiches. Our little ritual had left us little time to eat and after we inhaled lunch I rose to take our dishes back; it's only common courtesy. Before I could even say 'thank you' to the girl behind the till, something on a shelf caught my eye. Twigs wrapped around a stone, bound with a leather cord and decorated with brightly coloured glass and clay beads.

"Excuse me, what is that?" I asked, pointing.

"No idea," said the server. "Boss said she bought it off some stall near Loch Ness when she needed change."

That didn't track with anything I had learned so far. A piece of tat from a tourist trap?

"What's up?" asked Moti, joining me.

"I've seen one of these before," I told him.

"Me too."

I span so quickly I almost turned into a full pirouette. "What? Where?"

"At Kelvingrove museum," he said, startled. "In the Highlands section. I took all my nieces and nephews a while back and one of these was in a glass case."

My jaw went slack as my brain processed the new information; I could make it to Kelvingrove in no time at all and the staff would probably be more than happy to help. But if I was with someone who all but controlled the staff...

"Moti, can I catch up with you later?" I asked, flinging too much money at him. "I have to go check this out."

"No worries," he said and with a slight wave gave me his blessing to depart. As with most places in the city centre, I wasn't far from a subway station and hopped onto a train that took me to the base of the hill on which Glasgow University was built.

It cuts a striking cityscape, the university, with its five-pointed tower looming above the west end, all darkened sandstone and Gothic arches. Except it isn't Gothic. This building was erected when the university made the move from the city centre to the (then) green space of the west end and built to mimic the original 1460 design. The building constructed from a Romantic's wet dream is nothing more than a set piece, I had realised bitterly when I first picked up this titbit of information and since then, my alma mater has lost much of the power it had over me as a child, when I would see it floating above the lower buildings and I imagined myself a wizard in a castle. Instead I became a petty warlock in a faux-Gothic façade studying in a communist architecture library. Getting half of what you wished for isn't too bad.

Still, unmerited resentment aside, I couldn't help but feel the familiar rush of nostalgia as I passed the steel and chrome monstrosity that had replaced the crumbling student union of my day. Regardless of the lack of antiquity, the area hummed with potential power, as does any site where knowledge and emotion are bound together, and as I pushed open the door that led into the History department I was struck by the old paper smell of learning so suddenly that I almost dropped into a chair and reached for a dusty tome. Bounding up three sets of stairs like a student late for their third tutorial in a row, I eventually stopped in front of a panelled door, the brass plaque of which read:

Prof. Jennifer Rawlings.

I wiped the sweat from my brow, ran my hand over my hair and, suddenly remembering how I had knocked on this door more than a decade ago when I had come to visit for an Applicant's Day interview, rapped it sharply with my knuckles.

9

Over the course of the years, Jennifer had been my course convenor, my lecturer, my tutor and my dissertation supervisor, but since graduation she had settled firmly into the role of friend and now, as friend, I found myself with armfuls of essays.

"Will you wait your turn?" I snapped at a student who didn't look old enough to be out of school. "I'm taking in the submissions from 1A right now, 2B isn't going to be for a little while."

Jennifer stood beside me, ticking names off a list. "Be nice, Rudy, they want to go to the bar. 1B, please line up here!"

I'd forgotten the mania of hand-in day and if I'd known that reading week had just passed, I might have forgone this part of my journey. I dropped the sheaf of essays into a box and started taking submissions from the second tutor group. Had I looked so young when I was in my first year? And to them did I now look haggard and worn? I knew that when I had been their age, thirty had seemed like the end of the line. Now, at thirty, I felt a pang of loathing for my past self. I also felt a more intense pang of loathing for the PhD student that hadn't turned up and had left Jen down one body before I delivered myself into her hands.

"Will this take much longer?" I asked. "I'm on an admittedly loose schedule, but a schedule all the same."

"It will take the time it takes," she replied, looking up from her lists. "And at least they are handing them in on time. I seem to recall a certain student who had a habit of turning in late."

"It was to avoid the lines. Here," I said to an overly eager young man. "You've not filled out your declaration of originality properly. Take it back and do it again."

Mumbling, the student took their essay and retreated to the opposite end of the hall.

"You'd have made a cracking faculty member," said Jen. "What happened?"

"The university's lax rules regarding the defacing of books happened."

The crowd thinned as more and more students handed over their work, until there was only a handful of bored youths watching me file.

"Give them here," I said, exhausted. "I'll sort them out myself."

I sat with a couple of dozen essays on my lap and separated them while Jen pressed me for details on what I was doing with myself now.

"I'm focussing on some investigative projects at the minute," I explained, not wanting to go into too much detail.

"Academic or your other business?"

"Jen, you know I haven't been in any other business for years now."

She sighed and returned to her screen. "You had a wonderful voice in your academic work, I only wish you could have applied yourself a little more."

It's incredible how a thirty-year-old can be reduced to a bashful student in the presence of their favourite teacher.

"Luckily I've found something I can apply myself to," I said. "Here you go. All sorted."

"You have been a godsend today," said Jen. "That would have been a riot without you."

It had seemed rather like a riot anyway.

"You're very welcome. I'm glad I could help. Hey, I was wondering if you could help me. I need someone to come to the museum with me."

Now that got her attention.

"Young sir, are you asking this old lady out on a *date*?" she asked.

"If madam would accompany me, it would be my pleasure," I said, grinning.

"Well, what a delightful surprise!"

Jen grabbed her coat, took my arm and we made our way down the stairs. A couple of girls glanced at her as we reached the ground floor and turned away, snickering to each other. As we exited, there were two shrieks as one of their bags split and spread its contents across the floor, while the iced latte held by the other girl exploded in her face.

"I'm sorry," I told her, sickened. "But they had it coming."

"I agree," she said with a shrug. "It's the minority, I know, but it's a loud minority and they do tend to get under one's skin."

We walked together along the shaded boulevard that ran perpendicular to the university, and as Jennifer linked her arm into my own I couldn't imagine the torment of trying to go about your daily life as a dedicated academic, repeatedly lauded and decorated, only to have your very existence mocked by ignorant children.

"It's different in the peripheries," I explained after Jennifer questioned the environment of my other world. "Beyond all this flesh and sinew, we're all pathetic specks of carbon bouncing around a mostly empty universe governed by absolute chaos. Bigotry over things like gender and sex seems pointless in the long run."

"It sounds like bliss," said Jennifer.

"That's not to say we don't experience it elsewhere," I added. "I might have a foot in the other world but the rest of me is out in the open. I've always been guarded about letting too much of my personal life bleed out into the public."

She squeezed my arm. "I understand. I always counted myself lucky that my colleagues and students were always supportive, and I suppose bigots will always be bigots. Still, it would be nice to be recognised for my achievements rather than things about myself I can't change."

I squeezed back. "You know I've got your back. If you ever need someone to stub their toe every Thursday for the rest of their life I'm pretty sure I could manage that," I assured her as we crossed the carpark to the grandiose stone stairs that led into the museum. "There's something I need to tell you about this visit."

"I'd guessed this wasn't simply a passing fancy," said Jen.

"There's a missing girl I've been hired to find, and my info isn't adding up properly. I have these pockets of data but no way to tie them up," I explained. "And right now the museum has information on a small bundle of twigs that I'm hoping might be more than... well. A bundle of twigs."

"You do lead an exciting life," said Jen as I held the door open for her. "And why do you need me?"

"You know almost everyone who runs this place," I said. "I might need the VIP experience."

"Rudy!"

"What?" I replied, turning back to her and shocked at her

tone. She rapped the Perspex donation box and raised her eyebrows, dropping a note through the slot. I sighed and fished out a crumpled fiver from my pocket.

"That's better."

"Moving on," I said loudly, striding into the grandiose hall that despite its size seemed dwarfed by the pipe organ that loomed large above me. I stopped and glanced quickly over both shoulders; despite my living in the city my entire life and having visited the art gallery more times than I could count, like an elf in iron shackles I still lost my bearings and sense of direction every time I set foot on the marble floor.

"What are you looking for?" asked Jen, noticing my distress.

"The Highlands. History, culture, mythology," I said, still glancing idly about and wishing that the creeping feeling on my neck would give up. "Any of it."

"This way, then," said Jen, pointing past the great white staircase to an archway that led into a cool green darkness.

I've never been able to put my finger on why the museum has such an effect on me, and I've never been able to ask anyone else; I'm not known for my socialising with other casters and as far as I know gods aren't bothered by petty things such as art or culture or… leaving their townhouse. But as soon as my foot touches the tiles I am lost in a maelstrom of scents and echoes from around the globe. Well, mainly Scotland, but decorated by a few multi-cultural vibrations. I understand *that* it happens but what I can't discern is *why*. Though I have my… I hesitate to say theory, so I will leave it at hypothesis.

History is a guideline that we all must follow, even if we don't realise it. One take on history is that it is 'just one fucking thing after another' and I might be inclined to agree, but I would change 'thing' for 'lesson'. The annals of history are volume upon volume of lessons, some pages more worn or dogeared than others, detailing why *this* course of action is superior to *that* course of action, why some decisions are always going to have worse results than others. Yet somehow we as a species, even with an entire eternity to study so that we might not fall into the same pitfalls and dictatorships as before, find ourselves in the 21st century with neon emperors in their chrome towers, growing fat off the toil of the peasants below. An aeon of evidence and we still crave the same unyielding patterns as before.

But this is not the fault of history. Every flipped coin ripples on the film of reality for the rest of time and pleas that we heed the fallout as we stumble forwards, blind and deaf. Here, in a building where history and modernity meet, where stories and fables and facts are bound together in impossible tapestries, the voices of the past scream and bellow and beckon silently in the hopes that someone will take note. Of course, most people don't experience that and are either fascinated or bored while I get dizzy and wander off. Luckily this time I had Jen to keep me straight and she led me through a tunnel into an exhibit where fibreglass trees housed plastic birds native to the north of Scotland.

"I must go to the Highlands again soon," said Jen, tutting at herself. "I've lived in this city for thirty years and I can count the amount of times I've visited on my fingers."

I said nothing; I, too, had lived in Glasgow for thirty years and had gone north maybe three or four times, but the difference between us was that I had no desire to go back. The untamed countryside is too big, too wild, too *quiet*. Give me my tiny metropolis any day.

"So what exactly are we looking for?" Jen asked after we had studied a few of the exhibits.

"A small bundle of stones and sticks," I said, distracted by a preserved moth the size of my hand; I was sure I could find a good use for that. "Tied up with a leather string, maybe."

"And you're sure they have something like that?"

"Nope. I'm here because of an off the cuff comment made by someone I've known for approximately an hour, based on an ornament we saw in a café. I'm not a very good detective."

Jen chuckled and glanced around before heading over to a rather bored looking attendant.

"Excuse me," she said. "I wonder if you could help me; is Andrea working today?"

The attendant blinked before responding with, "Who?"

"Andrea? Doctor Andrea MacArthur?"

"Oh!" The attendant's eyes bulged. "Sorry! Yes she is. Why?"

"Could you radio her?" asked Jen, pointing at the walkie-talkie on their belt. "And tell her Jenny has popped in to say hello."

"Er…"

I felt bad for this kid; gone was their boring afternoon shift and instead they had a woman asking for one of the most senior figures in the museum's administration by their first name. Finally, however, they nodded with a slight frown and turned away to mumble into the microphone on their collar. After a short exchange, the attendant turned back to Jen with a surprised look on their face.

"She'll, er, be down in a minute."

"Thank you. What was your name?"

"Jamie."

"Thank you, Jamie, you've been so helpful."

As Jen walked back over, Jamie shot me a look that clearly read 'is she taking the piss?' I just gave a shrug and focussed my attention on the dried insects once more.

"Jenny, it's so good to see you!" I was ripped from my entomological reverie as a surprisingly young woman in a grey suit arrived and pulled Jen into a hug. "You should have let me know you were coming; I'd have come to meet you."

"Oh, don't worry, this was a last-minute decision," said Jen, indicating me. "Rudy, Andrea, Andrea, Rudy."

"Pleased to meet you," I said, holding out my hand and being slightly intimidated by the grip it found. "I've heard a lot about you."

It was true; Doctor MacArthur was, in Jen's own words, one of her greatest successes. I doubted she spoke about me in such terms.

"Good to meet you, too," Andrea replied. "So, to what do I owe the pleasure?"

"Young Rudy here has a favour to ask you, with regards to a project he's working on."

"Oh?" said Andrea, focussing her attention on me. "And what sort of project would that be?"

"I'm looking for an artifact, probably from the Highlands. Twigs and pebbles, all tied together. A friend said he saw some here a while back."

Andrea looked at me curiously. "What was this for? A university project or…"

"It's for work."

"And your job is, what?"

"He's a—" began Jen.

"An investigator," I said loudly, not wanting to have to spend the next fifteen minutes explaining what a Curse-Breaker was. "Look, there's a missing girl and as strange as it sounds, this might actually give me a little more to work on than what I have so far."

"That does sound pretty strange, if I'm honest."

"Wait until you get to know me," I said. "I wouldn't be asking if this wasn't important. I've got a worried family desperate for information and if I can find out more about this thing then maybe I can tell them something good."

Andrea stared me down for a few seconds and I couldn't help thinking that if 'curator' hadn't panned out for her, she'd have made a damn fine judge; it took all my willpower not to wilt under her gaze. Eventually, she glanced at Jen.

"Can you vouch for him? Because if I take him into the archives and it turns out he's not legit I will have my tits served to me on a platter."

"I give you my word," said Jen, nodding. "He may not have been the most remarkable student…" Ouch. "But he's certainly one of the better people I've met."

Aw. It wouldn't have done to let my composure slip, but I was touched.

"All right," said Andrea as she checked her watch. "I have fifteen minutes before I'm due in a meeting but if it's important, and Jenny seems to think you're on the level… Fuck it, follow me."

Jenny gave me a wink and followed her favourite creation while I tagged along behind, listening to them chat away and being reminded of visiting my mum's friends; never was there a situation more tedious as a child. We were led through an emergency exit and into a stairwell that instilled a chill that only old, exposed stone could, then down into a dimly lit corridor that ended with heavy double doors. A keypad protruded from the wall to the side.

"Welcome to the future," said Andrea as she punched in numbers to the metal and jerked the handle to the side; it took a couple of attempts before it complied. "The future has a tendency to stick."

Oh, what sights befell my eyes. Whereas above there was order and structure, every exhibit neatly marked and labelled, here in the depths there was screaming chaos. A small square room filled to bursting as artifacts lay in rows on desk after desk and filing cabinets and cupboards lined the walls. Some of the larger items were covered with dust sheets and obstructed the thoroughfares while others still threatened to topple from the precarious positions they occupied. I saw two other doors that I assumed led off into similar rooms, suggesting that beneath Kelvingrove Museum there was a subterranean labyrinth laden with treasures. If my senses had been off kilter upstairs, then down here I was a punch-drunk idiot breathing in intoxicating fumes. Knowledge, power and imagination rolled and broke over me like a wave.

"Impressive, isn't it?" asked Andrea. "Something about the randomness down here puts me more at ease. If people visit the museum and leave a little more thoughtful than before then I count that as a win, but anyone who walks into the archives should be forever changed."

I nodded my appreciation.

"You can feel it too, can't you?" I asked. Andrea narrowed her eyes and walked off, but I knew I was right.

"Well, down this way is where we store most of the stuff that we can't fit into the Highlands exhibit right now, so I would assume what you're looking for should be there."

Resisting the urge to touch absolutely everything I could, I left Jen to peruse the artefacts and I followed Andrea through one, two, three doors, making mental notes of every item of interest that I walked past; consider it the magic-user's equivalent of walking through a market and breathing in all the wonderful cooking food. Which, to be fair, is something I enjoy anyway.

"Here we go," said Andrea after pausing to check some labels.

"Great," I said. "So where should we look? Is it just this cabinet?"

Andrea scoffed.

"This cabinet. And then the rest of them in this room. And possibly spilling out into some of the others."

"And I have fifteen minutes?"

"Well," said Andrea, checking her watch. "Now you have closer to five."

"Christ," I muttered. "Okay."

I bit my lip. While I didn't want to start opening drawers at random and emptying their contents out onto the floor, I also wasn't sure exactly how clued in to the other side Andrea was. But, after debating the pros and cons of adding to the disorder down here, I sighed and sat myself down on the floor, legs crossed.

"What are you doing?" asked Andrea.

"Crossing my legs," I explained. "If I sit with them straight out, I look like an Action Man."

"No, Rudy, I mean why are you sitting down at all?"

"Oh. Fair question. I'm looking for the... thing."

"You know what? Fine," said Andrea. "You do you, just remember you now have four minutes."

"Yes, thank you..." I muttered.

I was working under the assumption that whatever I was looking for had to be magical in some way, shape or form. I mean, why would mystery boy have suggested Leigh-Anne move hers closer to her bed? So all I had to do was find whatever had a magical aura, which was as depressingly unhelpful as being asked to listen for a pin drop. If it were completely silent, maybe you could have a fair stab at it, but if that room is filled with howler monkeys, whistling kettles and jet engines you might be harder pressed. Not everything down there was magical (but there were certainly enough to pique my interest further) but as previously mentioned the vibrations of the past bled into my psyche enough to put me off my game. I exhaled through my teeth and reached out into the din.

There were a few pings around me that I managed to discern as time slowed, my breathing halted and I felt the hairs on my face stop growing. Unfortunately it didn't work on the same level as hearing a noise; the further away you are, the quieter the noise. No, when I managed to tune out the cacophony and focus only on the magic, it was as if I was surrounded on all sides, like I could reach out and gather each object into my arms. Now I had to sort through them all. One was a harsh hacking sensation, all screams and blood and terror. God, I hoped that wasn't what I was looking for. Another wrapped me in what felt like cotton wool but smelled of nettles and barbed wire. I couldn't even imagine what that might be. One by one, I studied each item I could sense, putting them in my maybe pile if I sensed potential and pushing them as far away as possible if I didn't like what I was seeing. So to speak.

I had just backed away from something that was evil grins, shadows and fear when I came across something altogether different. Far from the jagged edges of what I assumed to be artifacts of town and city, this was soft and nurturing. I heard gentle waves lapping on a stony shore, washing over pebbles. There was the scent of wood and leaves on the breeze; a bird's wing brushed my cheek. That had to be it. At least I hoped it was.

I opened my eyes; holding onto that sensation, I stood and followed the intangible thread. After moving some boxes around I unearthed a cupboard and retrieved a small carboard box, moth-eaten and tattered. Inside was another bundle (I was going to have to give these another name soon), much less ornate than the one I had seen earlier that day. Whereas the one in the café had glass beads and a few crystals wrapped around the sticks, this one was simply smooth stones, with some almost entirely decayed plants and feathers bound together with a frayed strand of rope. But this one hummed with an unfamiliar energy.

"So that's what you were looking for," said Andrea, reaching into the box and taking out a card. "It says here this is one of a few items found in old houses near Loch Lomond." She flipped the card over.

"Anything else?" I asked.

"No," she said, brow furrowed. "That's annoying."

"Mmm," I said, barely listening. This was *old*, I realised. Except it wasn't. How could it be? Twigs and herbs? If it was as ancient as it felt, then this whole charm should be dust. So maybe it's not the physical item that is giving me old vibes, but instead...

"Oh, damn."

"What?"

"I think I'm going to have to take a trip to the countryside soon, and you have no idea how much I hate doing that."

"How can you hate the Highlands?" asked Andrea, aghast.

"Easily. Give me the hustle and bustle of my city any day." I glanced up from my studying. "My time up?"

"Pretty much I'm afraid," confirmed my host. "I'm already going to be late for a meeting."

"Ah, right." I put the bundle back into the drawer and slid it closed. "Seriously, thank you for this. Even if it did just confirm that a trip up north is on the cards."

Andrea led me back through the honeycomb of storage rooms and, whereas before my attention had been scattered, now it was focussed solely on the bundle in my hoodie's pocket, next to a box of dried insects. Sleight of hand is ninety percent of effective magic.

10

"So, tell me about this girl," said Jen, splashing an unholy amount of vinegar across her fish and chips. I blew out my cheeks and exhaled.

"What's to tell?" I asked myself. "She's been missing for two weeks or so now. Probably closer to three," I said, remembering that I hadn't been progressing as fast as I would have liked.

"Three weeks!" said Jen loudly, before cursing and glancing over her shoulder. "Three weeks? And her parents haven't done *anything*?"

"That's the problem. They think they have. In their minds the police have it all under control."

"But they don't, do they?" asked Jen. Shrewd as ever.

I shook my head. "Not if my info is anything to go by."

"And that's what drew you in."

"You know me well," I said, nodding.

"Of course I do. I don't buy just anyone supper, you know?"

And I was, as always, grateful. The chippy around the corner from uni had always been a favourite of the faculty and students alike and since its expansion, sitting inside was now an option instead of wolfing down increasingly sodden chips in the pissing rain. Which, incidentally, it now was and the pair of us had to speak loudly to be heard over the sound of the drops on the window.

"But this isn't your thing, Rudy," said Jen. "You've told me before; you break little bits of dark magic."

"Curses, but continue."

"Have you ever been paid for finding anything before, let alone a person?"

"Nope," I said.

"Then why now?" asked Jen. "You do realise what shaky ground you're on here, don't you? I mean, if you're done for impersonating a police officer you're going to need a damn good lawyer. And if, as you say, the police aren't investigating, that smacks of something sinister and what exactly do you think will happen to you if anyone gets wind of this?"

I'd put more than a little thought into both of these outcomes, yet simply shrugged.

"I'm doing it because... because I feel like I should," I said, surprising myself with my candour.

I wouldn't say my response shut Jen up because that sounds aggressive, but whatever the benevolent form of shutting up is, that's what she did.

"You are a good man, Rudy," she said after a pause. "You don't need to convince us of that."

"Who said I was trying to convince you?" I said quietly, before cramming far too much battered fish into my maw. There was silence for a few minutes while I chewed furiously, and Jen just stared at me.

"This is about your mum again, isn't it?"

My chewing stopped briefly, as I did my best to avoid the pained expression that I could feel bubbling below my skin. I swallowed.

"I'm not going to say no, because hell, you're not entirely wrong," I conceded. "But it's not about her, per se. It's about me. It's about me and my decisions and their outcomes."

"Rudy, you can't blame yourself."

"I can," I said emphatically. "I can, I have and will continue to do so."

"Cancer is a vile bitch, Rudy. My mother lost both her boobs when she was your age. It nearly broke her and yet she knew she was one of the lucky ones." Jen pushed some mushy peas around her plate before quietly adding, "I'm so grateful she got to know me as Jennifer. I can't imagine how painful losing her so young must have been."

"And so much of that pain is self-inflicted," I said. "You know what I did. It's on me, I have to live with the blame, and nothing is likely to change that. But maybe, if I can do little bits of good here and there, that blame might weigh a little less. And you never know, maybe I can help some others while I'm at it." My beer was warm and a little flat but holding the bottle to my lips allowed me to assess how badly I was shaking; dredging up the past was always painful. "Are you doing good," I asked, "if you are only doing good for others to make yourself feel good?"

"Oh, Rudy, my office is in entirely the wrong building to answer that. Philosophy is the next street over."

Once our meals were finished and Jen had all but beaten me into the ground to stop me paying for it, she walked me to the subway station and gave me a hug.

"I always enjoy your visits," she said as she let me go. "Do come back soon, I promise I'll have the kettle ready if you give me more notice. Or any notice really."

"Yeah, sorry about that. I swear one of these days I'll think about dropping a line before I turn up somewhere."

The escalator, as per-goddamn-usual in this station, was out of service and I stumbled my way down the now stationary, too-wide stairs to the ticket barriers. Which did not open for me. Frowning, I pulled out my card and tapped it on the sensor; still nothing.

"I swear I just put a fiver on this piece of shit," I muttered to myself as I inserted my card into the ticket machine.

Balance: £05.20.

"Then what the hell?" Oh. Of course. I stomped back to the barriers and stared hard into the security camera. "What?" I said bluntly.

The screen that displayed the arrival times for the next train went blank and was replaced with orange letters that slid from right to left.

SECOND TASK NOT COMPLETE

"Oh come on, you know I have other stuff to do. Stuff I'm actively being paid for." I did my best to ignore the stares from the server behind the glass panel that I could feel boring into the back of my head. "Are you going to ban me until I do what you want?"

A GOD'S PREROGATIVE.

"Christ," I breathed. "Fine, how does tomorrow sound? I mean, it's not like there's a missing person I'm trying to find, so how about I drop everything and get this task done for you?"

I stared at the screen waiting for a response but instead wait times returned and the barriers opened for me.

"Spirit of mercy, you are," I grumbled as I made my way to the platform, which I noticed remained free of train for what was most definitely a deliberate amount of time. However, I eventually got myself a seat on a train home and must have dozed off because after what seemed like blinking, my train was waiting at my station with doors open and other passengers grumbling about how long they'd been sat there.

"Oops," I said, hurrying out of the carriage before throwing a curt nod in the way of another security camera.

I was looking forward to my bed. In one day, I had broken into a house, gone on a date and stolen from the archives of a museum; I think I had earned a rest. Still, I had one final task to complete today.

I closed the front door behind me and leant on it. Andy poked his head out of the living room.

"Oh good, you're back."

"Were you waiting for me?"

"I was." The rest of Andy's body joined his head in the hallway, and he pulled a handful of something from his pocket. "Will you *please. Stop. WHITTLING.* In the living room!" he said, flicking a small wood chip at me with each pause. "I have been picking these from between my toes all day!"

"I'm sorry!" I said, remembering that I had forgotten to clean up properly the night before. "I've been uncommonly stressed."

"Stressed? Who the hell whittles when they're stressed?"

"Me, apparently."

I can honestly say that I had never seen that one coming.

"Well take it outside," Andy insisted, pointing to the great rectangle of communal yard that almost every tenement building in this district had. "And if for some reason you do find yourself whittling inside then for God's sake would you hoover?"

"I promise, I promise," I said, pushing past him and falling face first onto the sofa. "I'm exhausted, man."

"How?"

I relayed my day's events to him and by the time I reached the Clockwork Man giving me the metaphysical business on my way home he was sitting wide-eyed, eyes even wider through the thick lenses of his glasses. Considering that Andy is about as *un*-peripheral as it is possible to be, he'd taken the news that much of Glasgow was under the influence of a deified incarnation of the subway surprisingly well. I'd even seen him picking up litter from the stations and trains before nervously glancing at the security cameras.

"How many times did you break the law today?" he asked.

"Good question." I counted down in my head. "Two or three, depending on how you want to look at it."

Andy nodded. "Well, erm... Look, I hate to add insult to injury—"

"Power through," I said, my mouth full of cushion.

"But I need your share of the rent. I covered you this month but I'm getting tight and I really need some cash."

"Balls. Okay." I sat up and pulled the remainder of the five tonne Laura had given me; what with new boots, paying Naomi and her pal and all the other micro-transactions that you hardly even notice, I had already made a hefty dent in it and I still hadn't paid my god damn phone bill. I threw a couple of hundred to Andy and off his even wider eyes I said, "It's safer to have it on me. Have you ever tried to rob a warlock?"

"No," said Andy.

"Well, don't. Not if you like all your pieces where they currently are. I'll have the rest for you when I've found this girl."

"Are you any closer to finding her?"

"Maybe. Possibly. There's a wee shitebag that I think might be able to tie some of these threads together but I can't even think of how I might go about finding him."

"Locator spell?" he offered. I pulled myself up and stared at him, eyebrows raised. "What? It's what they always used in Buffy."

I grinned. "If I had something of his, maybe. Though I'd probably need to have met him first. It's a lot more technical than you'd think."

"Well whatever you do, make sure you can pay me your rent on time next month, please."

Later, in my room, I sat cross-legged and held the bundle in my flattened palms. This wasn't the one I had seen in the picture, but I could only assume that it worked in the same way and I needed to know what that way was. Reaching out I prodded the aura, but I was rebuffed instantly. Magic unlike any I had ever harnessed pushed back, repelling my probing and leaving me feeling less than adequate while water trickled past my ears and the smell of damp leaves tickled my nose. Working the tension from my shoulders, I tried to let my consciousness expand, just a little, and worm its way in.

This time, I was assaulted by centuries that tore at me from all sides and threatened to strip away my meat and bone to leave me floating through the ether. Beneath this attack I was a suckling babe fresh from the womb, defenceless against the claws of this ancient creature. I fell back into my body, dropped the bundle and collapsed backwards onto the floor until the sickening memories faded. I was going to need help, I realised, and pulled out my phone to call Donald.

"Rudy pal, what's up?" he asked upon answering.

"Work," I replied. "Donald, I need your help, man. Are you able to come over?"

"Christ," was the pained response. "I'm just out of working the dreaded clopen and I'm dead on my feet. Can it wait?"

I felt for him; the 'dreaded clopen' is when someone in the service industry closes the bar, usually during the wee hours of the morning, only to return the same day to open it. These are not legally enforceable and you are well within your rights to say no, but you might find yourself on the receiving end of single-digit work hours if you do.

"It's your bar, why not have someone else do it?"

Donald snorted. "It's not 'my bar', it's the bar I manage. Sometimes you have to take a couple of bullets for the team. What do you need me for?"

"It's Leigh-Anne; I might have a lead, but I need someone to keep me steady while I check it out." It may be uncouth to use guilt to get your own way, but it gets results. Donald folded.

"I'll be there in half an hour," he said, resigned.

That meant I had thirty minutes to get set up. I took the bundle to the kitchen and placed it in the centre of the circular table I used for readings. Using the key hidden under the flour pot, I opened my curio cabinet and took out what I would need: a handful of beeswax candles, a couple of half burned joss sticks and a glass bottle of water scooped from between the subway tracks. I dribbled a little into an egg cup before corking the bottle and putting it back. That water was precious. I retrieved the tin in which I kept my narcotic supply, just in case Donald needed a kick to get into the mood.

When the intercom buzzed, Andy let Donald in and led him to where I was sat. The poor guy certainly looked like he was on the wrong end of a long shift; he was pale and purple rings hung below his eyes.

"Well, I'm going to leave you two to your magic," said Andy, pulling a beer from the fridge. "Don't set anything on fire and don't go changing each other into anything."

"You can stay if you like," I said. "You don't need to leave."

"Nah," Andy said, dismissing me. "I'm good. You two have fun."

Andy doesn't like watching me do magic, especially with another person. I think it reminds him too much of Jason; sometimes I forget it wasn't just my loss.

Donald joined me at the table and picked up the bundle. "Is

this what we're working with?"

"It is. What can you feel?"

Turning it over in his hands a few times, Donald shook his head. "Nothing." Disappointed, I reached out to take it but he jerked back. "No, I mean I feel nothing because whatever was there has gone. It feels empty. Doesn't it?"

I copied his movements but all I could sense was ripples against a shore. "Not to me."

"Well, maybe you're just too powerful," he said, jokingly. "You're so in tune that you pick up on whatever is left."

It didn't sound all that implausible, but I didn't want to sound immodest so I let it go. I pulled out the matchstick I had de-ignited earlier that day and lit the candles. "I don't need too much from you," I told Donald. "You just have to keep me grounded for a while."

"Good, because even if I wasn't knackered it's been a long time since I've done this."

"Well, I've got uppers and downers if you need anything."

He shook his head. "Nah. I'm not twenty anymore; I drop any of that and I'll pay for it with interest tomorrow."

Nodding, I hid the tin away and placed the bundle in the centre of the table as we clasped each other's wrists. Sensing magic is one thing, but to truly get a feel for something you need to dig a little deeper and that can get dangerous, in my experience. Thus, I needed someone hold my kite string while I plunged into the memories of a mindless object, someone who could pull me back if I drifted too far. Ideally I'd have liked a more dedicated user, but I haven't known a practicing mage in this city for years so Donald and the memory of his nail varnish was going to have to do.

Exhaling, I gave in to the effects of the magic already pulsing between us and let go; usually I would need to take more time to centre myself but tonight, with Donald holding me down, I was able to leap into a different consciousness without much risk. I picked up on the magic emanating from the bundle, immediately feeling what I had before, but this time I went further. Cold washed over me, the touch of a place where the sun could not reach. A phantom suffocation began to set in and even though my lungs were clear, breath would not come; while this didn't bother me in my semi-ethereal state, I knew my body was going to suffer and I couldn't lose my connection, so speed was of the essence. The cold seeped into my mouth and down my throat while the pressure on my chest grew, and despite Donald lending me some strength I couldn't feel anything I hadn't already felt, apart from the crushing weight of what I assumed was a vast body of water.

I wrenched my arms away from Donald and I drew in a deep lungful of air, sucking down oxygen as if I had truly been submerged in a loch.

"I didn't like that at all," I said, gasping. "You were right."

"I was?" said Donald, massaging his forearms where two red handprints were beginning to form. "About what?"

"It's empty. That's the reason I can't tell what it's been used for; the magic is gone. All I could feel was where the magic had come from."

"So you're saying I came all this way to help you and you haven't learned anything new?"

"No," I said. "Now I know that these can be charged up, like my lightbulbs. They're batteries, or at least something like it. And it basically confirmed that I am going to have to go to the Highlands. I was hoping to avoid that."

"The Highlands are big," said Donald, unhelpfully. "Where would you even start?"

"I can ask the Clockwork Man if he knows of any magic users out there I could send word to, but apart from that I'm fresh out of ideas. Is there anyone at your bar you could ask?"

Donald laughed. "Mate, I don't usually engage with any of them past pouring their pints. Besides, I don't think any of them are going to be on your level and most of them have been doing their best to silence the peripheries with booze for years."

I pulled a couple of beers from the fridge and handed one over. "I want to know more about Laura. What can you tell me about her?"

"You know her about as well as I do," said Donald with a shrug. "I'd seen her in the bar a few times but until she asked me about Jason's card, I'd hardly said two words to her."

"That wasn't the impression I got," I said, honestly; the way Laura had ingratiated herself into my company had made me believe that she and Donald were at least on a first name basis.

"She's forthright, I admit," said Donald after a mouthful of beer. "I told her I could put her in touch with you, but she insisted on her little spying act."

"And that didn't strike you as at all weird?"

"Rudy, she was asking to meet with a warlock; the entire situation was weird, but that's your life, isn't it?" said Donald. "Why do you ask?"

"Because I'm not entirely sure I trust her," I said. "She drinks at your bar, which should have been at least a yellow alert to begin with. Her sister's missing and she's clearly got at least some background knowledge of the peripheries, even if she doesn't walk in them."

"This sounds a little like she's a suspect to you."

"It does, doesn't it," I said, thoughtfully, before shaking my head. "I'm casting aspersions; I've no proof other than suspicion and the only evidence I have is currently pointing me out of the city. Will you stay for tea?"

"Thanks, but no," said Donald, with a weak smile. "I'm going to go home, shower the smell of seventeen hours of bar work from my skin and forget all about the fact I have to go back tomorrow."

I saw him to the door and locked it behind him before joining Andy in the sitting room.

"How did it go?" he asked. "What did you find out?"

"Nothing, which actually explained a lot. When was the last time you went camping?" I asked him.

"Two years ago, I think. Why?"

"As much as I hate the idea, I think I might need to go spend a few days in the great outdoors. Do you still have all your gear?"

"Yeah, I do. Seriously? You?" said Andy, disbelieving. "You haven't left the city in, what, eighteen months?"

"It's closer to two years."

"And you're breaking your rule, because...?

"Because I have a slight notion that Leigh-Anne is somewhere out the Highlands," I explained. "Though I've yet to zoom in on a specific area."

"Well, you're welcome to everything I have but honestly, I don't know if it's going to help you much," said Andy. "You're going to be a fish on land out there."

There was no point replying; I couldn't disagree. Apparently taking pity on my deflated frame, Andy quickly span together a spliff and we shared it in almost silence while music from his laptop decorated the passing time. Once I was sated and my head sufficiently foggy, I bade him good night and made my way to my room.

Where it turns out I did not undress, seeing as I woke up covered in that cold sweat you can only get from having fallen asleep fully clothed. I groaned and stumbled into the kitchen where I found Andy for some reason already awake, showered and dressed in suit trousers and an ironed shirt. He looked at me over the rim of his coffee mug.

"Well, isn't this an interesting turn of events?" he said. "It's a little eerie, isn't it?"

"Why are you all poshed up?" I asked as I poured myself a coffee.

"I have an actual in person, meat-space meeting today," he said with a grimace. "I work entirely on my computer and have no need for unnecessary human interaction. How have we as a species not evolved past this yet?"

"What is necessary human interaction?" I asked.

"Sex," he said simply. "And hanging out and having fun. If we spend too long cooped up with other people during work hours, we're going to want to be alone for our spare time. It should be the other way around or it's not really living. That's just existing."

I shook my head as I sugared my coffee.

"I'm not awake enough to deal with this right now. Personal rule; no magic before nine, no philosophy before eleven. No theology at all if it can be helped."

As I mentioned the time, Andy checked his watch and swore.

"Well, I've got to love you and leave you, walking dead." He drained his coffee, gave me a gentle thump on the shoulder and exited the flat, leaving me feeling rather more pathetic than I'd hoped I'd feel only ten minutes after waking up. Nevertheless, I hauled myself into the shower and freshened myself to an acceptable standard before dressing.

My hoodie was becoming an issue; I hadn't washed it in… more than a while and I'd just slept in it. The thought of putting it on made me feel a little sick, I'm not going to lie. But my alternative was Jason's Curse-Breaker jacket and even if I was going to wear it, it was years from becoming mine. Turning up my nose, I slipped the hoodie on and helped myself to a liberal amount of Andy's aftershave.

I opened my chest and inspected the remaining contents; the house key on its shoelace, a genuine rabbit's foot on a leather strap and the final piece of a Van Gogh jigsaw; any lost, or in this case lifted, piece of a jigsaw is always the final piece. Did I want to take any more? The previous project had left me exhausted and I would have greatly appreciated any buffs I could have given myself, but IMPs are precious and believe it or not, they're pretty difficult to come across. I decided the cube of windshield in my pocket would have to be enough and shut the lid with only a small pang of regret.

For this address I had to take the subway and once again as I reached the barrier, they didn't open.

"I'm doing it," I groaned. "You're actively preventing me from going!"

The barriers slid open, though somehow grudgingly, and allowed me access. Muttering the few curse words I had picked up from long dead tongues, I made my way down the stairs to where thankfully there was a train waiting for me and after only ten minutes I was at my stop; you can ride the whole system in forty-five minutes and be back where you started, giving rise to the ever popular 'subcrawl', in which the aim is to have a drink at the closest bar to each station. I attempted it once and woke up in the Clockwork Man's station with a blinding hangover and Campbell standing over me with a frown.

The station I needed to get off at was a central hub of human activity, which of course meant it was also a hub of curse energy. From the subway you could climb to the overground platform and catch a train to anywhere in the city and beyond. People streamed in and out every hour of the day and now, as I stood and looked up at the tenement building before me, I had to fight to hear my own thoughts over the tangible roar of the populace. I didn't like this building; even if I hadn't been given the exact address I would have known this was the place. Something I couldn't quite place, something wrong, seeped from this building like pus.

Sensing magic is… well, like an extra sense really, if that's at all helpful. I can't smell it exactly, but when my body registers the sensation it triggers the same reaction as if I had caught a scent, only without the actual aroma. Curses are foul, a scent of despair, emptiness and loss, sometimes enough to make me gag. This smelled angry, a fury that felt more potent than any vengeful ghost I'd ever dealt with; I certainly didn't want to go in blind. So instead I sat on a bench at the taxi rank, dug into my hoodie for a permanently half-finished packet of cigarettes; the interior of a cigarette packet is a slightly curved liminal space that exists around the arrow of time rather than inside it and as such is never quantifiable, instead existing in a constant 'some' space until it is suddenly empty. I'd managed to trick this packet into halting its progress ages ago.

With the flame from a lighter that had been nearly empty for four years I lit my cigarette and stared silently at the giant mural on the wall before me that showed a woman playing hockey.

I'd only been staring for a minute before she sighed, rested her stick on the edge of the wall and looked down at me.

"Wha' ia i'?" she asked before sighing and spitting her mouthguard into her hand. "What is it?" she repeated.

"Well hello to you too," I said to the moving, speaking painting. "I've been fine, thanks."

"You still owe me a kebab."

I pointed to one of the takeaways along the road. "I can go get you one now if you'd like."

"Nah, that place is shit," said the woman; she didn't have a name. I'd asked her once and she hadn't seen the point in having one, so I'd privately dubbed her the Woman of Partick, after the train station. "There's a much better place down the road."

"I'm on a job at the minute, but I promise you as soon as it's done I'll get that kebab."

She nodded. "Aye right. For the time being, gies a fag."

I pulled another cigarette from my pocket and held it out; the painting moved forwards, off the wall and in one massive stride was beside me. The Woman reached down and took my offering between her thumb and forefinger, both over three feet long, and waited for me to light it. She breathed a sigh of relief and sat down on top of the bus shelter.

"It's been a while," she said, exhaling. "I'm trying to keep it a rare habit. Too many side effects."

"Do you even have lungs?" I asked.

"Rude. Why would it matter? I'm a fifty-foot woman made of paint, I don't think cancer is going to affect me. But I don't want my whites going yellow."

I considered this and as we smoked she told me about the interesting people she had seen coming and going lately. Not a soul remarked or even showed any indication that they could see the two-dimensional behemoth of a hockey player smoking a tiny cigarette. What has eyes but cannot see?

"I need your help," I said as I dropped both butts into the bin. "Can you have a look through the top windows of that building?"

"You're up to two kebabs now," the mural said. She put her hands on her thighs and stood, crossing the distance in two steps and pressing her face up against the wall, cupping her hands around her eyes. After a second or two, she pulled back and scowled. "Even if I could fit I wouldn't go in there. It's not nice."

"I got that. What does it look like in there? Any goat's heads, dribbly candles or bloody pentagrams?"

"Not that I could see. Décor's still stuck in the sixties though. Lots of brown and orange."

"I don't understand," I said, only half to her.

"Do you understand running? I doubt you'd get very far before collapsing but you could give it a go."

"Rude," I countered. "We can't all be gargantuan athletes. Well, thanks. I'll be back with the kebabs as soon as I can manage. Give my love to the other murals."

"Will do."

After one final stretch, the Woman popped her mouthguard into place and climbed back into the wall, resuming her previous position on the wall. I could easily have stayed chatting to my flat friend for the whole morning but I tried to focus on the task at hand. The door to the close was propped open with a brick and I took a second to appreciate what I had a feeling was going to be the only good thing that would happen today and I wondered if I might be out of my depth; my self-confidence dropped as my sense of foreboding increased.

I knocked at the door. Malice slicked underneath it like bile and almost made me heave. I was sorely tempted to turn on my heel and go straight to the Clockwork Man to tell him exactly where he could insert this job, but a part of me, that damn curiosity paired with my Post Traumatic Decency Disorder, had knocked on the door before I could scarper.

"Once more unto the breach," I sighed.

The door shuddered as someone gave it a mighty tug and then opened it to reveal the man of the house. Colour me stunned.

There was nothing. Everyone was cursed, absolutely everyone, even if it's only a cute little curse tied around your pinkie finger in a silky wee bow. But this guy was clean as a whistle in the way I thought only a mage could be. I didn't sense any of the usual magics around him though, only that dizzying badness that I still couldn't put my finger on.

"Who're you?" asked the man, frowning.

"I'm here to talk to you about… about the… about the subway!" I said, wondering how the hell I could be so awkward when it mattered most. And me without any cough drops.

"Not interested," he said, closing the door.

I couldn't let this get away from me, so I stuck out my foot and wedged it into the gap, thankful for the stiff leather of my Docs.

"All right, all right, I admit that was the worst lie I've ever told, but I really need to talk."

"Get your foot out of the door, young man, or I will call the police."

"Please just listen. I'm here because someone wanted me to help you. I don't really want me to be here any more than you do," I said, honestly. He at least stopped pushing the door against my foot.

"Help me? What d'you mean, help me? I dinnae need your help."

"Well, okay, but you do," I said. "Have you noticed anything weird in your flat? Maybe an extra face in the mirror, or footprints that aren't yours. Any unexplained slime?"

The man narrowed his eyes. "That your business?" he asked. "Ghost stories."

"Stories aren't always fiction. And trust me when I say I've got over a decade of this business under my belt. So I can tell that there is something seriously off in your home. Tell me I'm wrong."

I was convinced I was about to be told to fuck off once again, but I was tentatively surprised as the man opened the door.

"Look, it isnae that bad," he said as he ushered me in. "Occasionally things aren't where I left them, or I feel someone looking over my shoulder."

I stepped in. If it wasn't that serious, then why was there such a malignant presence in the flat? I was so preoccupied with trying to suss out what the issue was that I almost didn't hear the key turning in the lock. While I managed to spin around and face the man, all that did was give me a front row seat to him hurtling towards me; he wasn't small and I'm sure he could lift a moderately heavy item for an extended period of time if he needed to, but he certainly shouldn't have been able to grip me with such force; even through two layers of clothing I could feel his nails tearing into my flesh. He snarled at me, teeth bared in a way that no human should have been able to do.

"So this is his holy knight," the man hissed.

Whereas I'd often liked to imagine I'd hit back with a witty quip in such a situation, in reality it was all I could do to try and bat away his hands; it took attempting to punch him in the face before I realised that both my hands and mouth were free. I barked out a harsh command and made an intricate little design in the air; four of his teeth exploded and he let go, clutching his mouth in agony. So he could feel pain. Good to know.

I scrambled away as he dropped me and moved as far back as I could. His mouth full of blood and shards, the man bared what remained and charged at me. I rolled through an open doorway and found myself in a living room before what felt like a rocket-propelled brick landed right between my shoulder blades and sent me sprawling across the floor, into a bookcase. I had been right; I was *violently* out of my depth.

I tried to take in a breath that would not come and, sensing my distress, the man raced forwards. I clenched my fist and saw him stumble slightly as an invisible hand gripped his ankle. It wouldn't hold for long but I had a few precious seconds to catch my breath; I couldn't remember the last time I had been winded like this, though I was fairly certain it had something to do with a trampoline.

My spell broke with a vicious wrench that ripped my magic and what little breath I had regained away, and suddenly his hands were around my throat. Dots appeared in my vision and every instinct screamed at me to try and pry them away, but I managed to shout those parts of me down and instead pulled the lightbulb and shard of glass from my hoodie, dropped them both to the floor and, after a couple of misses, crushed them below my boot.

Inches from my face the man froze, illuminated by phantom headlights. Then the air around him shattered and for a split second I could see his image fractured into a thousand pieces, before he was hurled away from me with a screech of tires. He slammed into the edge of the open door and fell to the floor, stirring feebly; perhaps now you can understand why I liked to imagine a tragic car crash. I didn't wait for him to get up; as he writhed on the floor I bent over him and bound him in words and wards, pinning him to the floor as best I could. His eyes fluttered open.

"What the hell are you?" I asked, allowing myself a moment of fascination. That had been my first magical battle, even if I had been the only one using magic, and I had no idea what my opponent even was. "Vampire? Fairy-tale?"

There wasn't a response; just a sickening bloody gurgle that I think was a chuckle. I could feel him pushing against my spells and I knew then and there that he couldn't be entirely human because he was resisting my magic, not just trying to wriggle out of restraints. One of my bindings began to fray, like a rope under too much tension. He's going to get free, I realised. He's going to get free and if he gets his hands on you again he is going to rip you to shreds. I closed my eyes and tried to empty my mind, which proved a little more difficult than usual.

What do I know? He's stronger than he should be. Pain doesn't seem to be as much of a factor as it should. There's a clear awareness of magic, even if there's no practice of it.

Wait. Holy knight.

As he was gripping my now tender chest for grim death he had said I was a holy knight, spitting the word 'holy' like a llama spitting at a tourist; he could only have been referring to the Clockwork Man. I mustered up as much energy as I could and placed one hand above his head with the other over his heart.

"In the name of the Clockwork Man, I demand you tell me who you are!"

Again, he did not respond, but there was a flicker of something else that chilled me to my bones. In the perfect shape of a man there was a shadow. No, not a shadow. Darkness. The image lasted only a microsecond but the brief glimpse of that figure, built of the darkness deep inside a cave that had never seen sunlight, I knew would be forever burned into the back of my skull. Malignance cloaked me. Choking back the gorge that rose in my throat, I filled my mind with the sound of wheels on tracks, of the damp smells and the distant echo of running water (and also every exorcism movie I had ever seen) before taking a deep breath. It was worth a try and you never knew; I might even be right.

"By the screeching steel and holy oils," I said with all the authority I could manage. "By the ancient stone and… erm… mouldy walls, I charge you to go!"

Something pulled on me, as if I were hauling an anchor on my own, dragging a weight from the depths. I knew I couldn't let go but good gods was it heavy. The man below me buckled and his mouth opened in a silent scream, which I counted as a blessing; I didn't want to have to try and explain my way out of an exorcism.

"In the name of the Clockwork Man I cast you out," I said with gritted teeth. "By the all-day ticket and the last train on a

Saturday, I cast you out!"

The strain grew heavier and stars burst in front of me, but I couldn't let go. This was magic unlike any I had dabbled in before; religious magic. God magic. In any other situation I might have said it was beyond me but thinking like that was going to get me nowhere.

"By... by darkness beneath the river..." Sweat was dripping into my eyes. "By the veins of the city. By the feeling of seeing the doors of your train close and leave without you, I cast you out."

You're just dragging something. Just dragging something intangible from an unreachable plane. That's all this is, I repeated to myself. You can do it. Hours that were realistically minutes crawled past as I brought up every aspect of the subway I could think of. My vision blacked out more than once and I wanted to fall, to give in to the exhaustion, but I couldn't. This... this *evil* could not be allowed to continue.

As I thought I had reached my limit and my willpower was running on fumes, the weight released so suddenly that I fell back to the floor.

"No, no, no, no," I hissed to myself, thinking that I had lost my grip on the creature and all that effort had been lost.

I stopped and glanced around the room; whatever wicked presence had been hanging over this flat had vanished, leaving only a regular two-bed. It was gone. I'd done it. My celebration was brief but enjoyable as I checked the man's pulse and breathing; weak but regular.

"I am going to kill him," I said to myself. Gripping the sofa, I pulled myself up to my worryingly unsteady feet and half walked, half stumbled to the landline on the corner table. Lucky for me, some people still refuse to adapt to the 21st century. I covered my hand with my sleeve, noticing a huge rip in the forearm as I did so, and dialled 999.

"Unconscious man," I said as the operator answered. "Broken teeth, possibly broken ribs. Stable."

I gave the address and hung up and got the hell out of there, pausing only to hammer a fist on the door opposite in the hope they might see the open entrance and investigate, though I wasn't about to hang around to find out. No, I was already marching into the subway station and resisting the urge to kick the barrier as it slid smugly aside. This time, I found myself on an empty platform. Good.

"MEETING! NOW!" I bellowed, before setting my jaw and waiting for my train. I sat down and, during the journey, began to reflect on how much I hurt. I had been *flung across a room*. As the adrenalin flushed out of my system, white-hot pain lanced through my left hand and up my arm and I noticed that a finger was bent horribly out of shape; I focused on my rage in the hope that might subdue the agony for now.

When I arrived at the unnamed station I stormed out, straight past Campbell who spluttered and begged me to wait, and out into the forest at the foot of the garden. It was only after I had been pounding up the trail for five minutes did I realise that I had been walking for too long and Campbell was nowhere to be seen.

"All right, all right," I said, taking a few deep breaths. "I'm calm. See? Look how calm I am."

I continued walking and thankfully the trees began to thin. I followed as the trail became the familiar gravel path only to find a smug Campbell in the conservatory, stood at his boss's side as the god in question focused his attention on that damn tablet. I glared at Campbell.

"Leave. Now."

"Young master, I don't take orders from—"

"Get out of here," I snarled.

"Campbell, I think it would be easier for all concerned if you listened to Master Renfrew. Why don't you make a start on lunch?"

Campbell bobbed his head at his master, scowled at me and entered the kitchen, closing the door behind him.

"Well?" asked the Clockwork Man, taking off his glasses and looking at me.

I opened my mouth but was surprised when no sound came out. I wanted to say how furious I was that he had sent me into the jaws of he knows what. I wanted to say that I had nearly been killed because of a mission *he* had sent me on. I wanted to say that my hoodie was not only of great sentimental value but one of my most valuable pieces of equipment. However, what I actually said was,

"I am very busy!"

It wasn't my finest rant.

"And yet I find you here, in my home, berating my staff and trampling my foliage," he said with slight interest. "How peculiar."

"Not today. I am not in the mood."

"You know, not many people could stand in such open defiance of a god and not fear being struck down."

"Try me."

The Clockwork Man regarded me, genuinely looked me up and down before saying, "What's on your mind?"

"What's on my mind? Well for a start, this." I held up my hand to reveal the finger bent backwards at a ninety-degree angle. "And more importantly, you can tell me what that creature was. Tell me what that *thing* that nearly killed me was called."

"Come now, Rudy," he admonished. "You're a smart man. What do you think it was?"

"If I had to go out on a limb, I'd say you just pointed me directly at a demon."

"I'm sure you've read about them," said the Clockwork Man with the essence of a shrug, even if he didn't move his shoulders.

"I have *read* about them, and honestly at no point while reading about them did I think 'I really want to meet one'."

"But now you have."

"How can you be so cavalier about this?" I shouted. "I could have died! I nearly did!"

"But you didn't. You lived to fight another day and shout at a deity. Good effort, I'd say." The god sighed and the door opened as Campbell came bearing a tray with two generous measures of spirits. "Whisky? It might help calm the nerves."

"It's not even midday," I said, though I took it anyway and found myself falling into a chair. The Clockwork Man took a sip.

"I would not have asked anything of you that I did not think you were capable of handling," he said. "You fought, you won."

"Why couldn't you have told me what I was going into? I could have prepared better or read up on demons. Apart from the work of William Peter Blatty, I'm a little short on exorcism experience."

"You are unpredictable, Rudy. You operate on a whim and if I had told you what you were facing, you wouldn't have been at your best. It's one of the reasons I took such an interest in you." He took another sip and motioned for me to do the same; I did. The rich flavour of peat and smoke filled my head and almost immediately I felt my heart rate decrease and my breathing ease.

"What did you give me?" I asked, my voice even and steady.

"One of the finest single-malts in my collection, so I hope it's working." It was, I had to admit. "Give me your hand."

I didn't hesitate; if he could hit me with some god-mojo that would help me avoid sitting in A&E for the next four hours then all the better. I extended my hand and let him inspect the damage.

"Broken," he said, tutting.

"Thank you, Doctor. Cash or cheque?"

The Clockwork Man glared at me, then with a wrench that made the sound of splitting wood and a pain that erupted from my hand to nestle sweetly behind my eyes and nose, pushed my finger back into the correct position; it no longer hurt and looked more like a normal finger, but the ripples of pain would circumvent my body for a while.

"Thank you."

"Do not mention it. It's the least I could do."

"Actually, for you that was pretty above and beyond. The least you could do is tell me where it came from," I asked. "Why was it here?"

"Rudy, I feel like I have to say this more times than necessary. I am a god. When you have gods, you have demons," the Clockwork Man said as if talking about oceans and water. "Forgotten gods and lost energies, weary deities who have trod the roads for too long, corrupted by time and negligence, now little more than hatred at all that still lives. For reasons they do not and cannot remember, they are drawn to familiar energy and begin to absorb their hosts so that they may feel what they have lost."

"I've known you for years, you've never once mentioned that demons were a side effect of your being here."

"Yes, well, that does seem to be the problem at hand." He swirled his glass. "I'm not a young god anymore. Well, I am in the grand scheme of gods, I suppose, but as my power grows, so too will the demonic presence. Slowly at first, I imagine. I shouldn't expect any to be as potent for at least a couple of years."

"Oh well, that's a relief," I said, finishing my whisky. "Why is this my responsibility? Why can't you fight your own demons?"

"If they were foolish enough to come within my boundaries then I would have no issue doing just that. Unfortunately, they know this and won't set foot inside the tracks."

He had me there; thinking back to the tenement building and doing a few calculations in my head, the flat the demon had been festering in had to have been about just outside the tracks. Clever.

"It called me a holy knight. I'm not a paladin, I'm a Curse-Breaker," I said, slowly. "Get yourself an exorcist."

"It's up to you, Rudy," he said. "You are my champion."

"Oh, *fuck*," I said, falling back into my chair with a groan. "I'm your what?"

"My champion."

"What do you mean, 'your champion'? Since when?"

"Since I chose you. Were you unaware?" he asked, frowning. "You serve a god, Rudy, and you reap the benefits. Every time you free someone from their curses, you do my work."

"I break those curses because I get paid."

"A happy coincidence."

"I don't want to be your champion," I said, quietly. Despite the restorative effect of the whisky I was still battered and bruised, and my bloody finger was beginning to throb again and all I wanted was to take as strong a drug as I could get my mitts on.

"I know you don't want to be. But you should be." That made me look up. "I didn't pick you for your power. Your spontaneity played a part, yes, but what really shone in you was your need to do good."

"Don't start," I said. "I had this lecture yesterday."

"I know, at the chip shop. And I have an answer to your question. If helping others makes you feel better about yourself then that is what I would call a 'win-win'. What part of a life of miserably serving others sounds appealing to you? When you intend to do good, the good outcome is all that matters. You know I am neutral Rudy, but you are not. If we can be partners in the servitude of others, then we will be greater than the sum of our parts. I want you to do good for me."

I don't say anything immediately, but… he had got a point. If I'm going to be breaking curses and dispelling hauntings anyway, I guess it's nice that the dormant volcano is trying to help me.

"If that turns out to be nothing but a fluffy sermon, I am going to be so angry," I said eventually. "Do I get a shield? Or a jewelled ring?"

"It was not part of my original plan but leave it with me. I do have something else for you, however."

The Clockwork Man reached inside his waistcoat and retrieved a letter; the paper looked expensive and it was sealed with marbled red, blue and white wax.

"For me? Who from?"

"I suggest you open it and find out."

Before I had even cracked it open, my stomach was in knots; I had a suspicion of who might be sending me such fancy correspondence. Written in black ink in a fine cursive script, the letter contained only a few lines.

Dear Master Renfrew,

It is with great pleasure that I extend to you an invitation to a meeting of the Council of Three; your work has impressed us and we would be delighted to welcome you to breakfast. Please present your RSVP to your host, who will pass the message to us.

Sincerely,

Amelia Bracken, the Third of the Three.

Well, my day certainly wasn't getting any better.

"Why did this come to you?" I asked, turning the paper over in my hands; there was no address, only my name.

"For the same reason I find myself having to steal you away when I require you; they knew you would only ignore it."

"You all think so highly of me, don't you?" I asked, while secretly wondering if there was a way I could still ignore this summons.

"What message should I pass on?"

"Tell them I'll get to them when I get to them."

The Clockwork Man frowned. "Rudy, it would not do to keep the Three waiting. They could make life very tiresome for you."

"Between curses, demons and missing teenagers, my life is becoming stressful enough already. Breakfast can wait."

The god looked as if he wanted to push the issue further, but instead shook his head slightly. "Where are you with the girl?"

"Her name is Leigh-Anne. At the minute there's a boy I want to speak to; I'm fairly certain he made her one of these," I said, pulling out the bundle and sliding it across the table. "He was with her the night she disappeared."

"Do you happen to have a picture of him?"

I dug out the picture I had purloined from Leigh-Anne's bedroom and handed it over; the god held it gingerly between thumb and forefinger.

"Hmm, I've never been a fan of all these facial piercings," he said with clear distaste, before closing his eyes for a couple of seconds. After opening them, he added, "I can send you to him."

"Seriously? How?"

"He's within the tracks. I could have you on your way in a jiffy."

"Can't you just do that for Leigh-Anne?" I asked, dumbfounded.

"She is no longer in the city as far as I can tell, otherwise I would try. You know I am only a little omniscient. Now, do you want my help or not?"

"Well of course I do. Do you have a ghost train or something I–"

The world jolted and for a second I felt entirely removed and disassociated from reality until the pictures in front of me made sense; I was no longer in a sunlit garden but a wet wynd that led to Glasgow Central Train Station. In front of me, mouth slack and eyes wide, was the boy from the picture.

11

First impressions are important, and don't let anyone tell you otherwise. That's why I was sorely disappointed that my first impression to this kid was appearing out of thin air, falling onto my hands and knees and emptying the contents of my guts onto the stones below; it was mainly stomach acid and whisky so it burned like paint thinner coming up. Once I was sure that I was finished, I wiped my mouth on the back of my tattered sleeve and rose shakily to my feet, swearing that I was never going to allow myself to be teleported again.

"Y'alright bro?" asked the boy. He looked younger in person, with a couple of spots on otherwise smooth pale skin and an adolescent blonde fringe that poked from underneath his beanie hat. I didn't answer him. Instead I leaned forwards, grabbed his shoulder, and marched him, spluttering and stammering, into the nearest café, which turned out to be a bakery. Pushing him into a chair I ordered myself a latte and pain au chocolat.

"You want anything?"

The boy just shook his head, clearly confused. I sat back down and waited hungrily for my breakfast/lunch to arrive.

"Listen," he said. "I don't know who you are, but I'm fairly certain I'm not the person you're looking for."

"Wrong," I said, simply. "You're going to answer some questions for me. Where the hell is Leigh-Anne Baxter?"

There it was; the spark of recognition. He eyed me curiously, now less uneasy and somewhat defiant.

"You're a mage," he realised.

"What gave it away? Popping out of thin air? Besides, I prefer warlock."

"Why? You know that means-"

"Oath-breaker, yeah, I've heard," I said, dismissing him with a wave of my hand. "You haven't answered my question. Where is she?"

"I don't know," he said with a shrug.

"You were with her the night she up and disappeared." I pulled the printouts Moti had provided for me and jabbed a finger first at the folk at the table, then Leigh-Anne. "Who are these guys and where did they take her?"

"I'm telling you, I don't know," he said with a shrug. "I asked not to know so if this exact situation came up I couldn't grass her up."

That made me stop; if I didn't know any better, I'd say he was protecting her.

"What's your name?" I asked.

"Johnny Harker," he replied almost instantly.

"My arse."

"Oh yeah? What's yours?"

"Rudy," I told him. "Rudy Renfrew."

He scoffed. "*My* arse."

I couldn't help but grin. "Clever. Listen, 'Johnny'. Leigh-Anne is missing, whether you think so or not. Her family is worried sick and her sister has paid me... what I'm now beginning to think was not enough... to find her. And you're everywhere I look. You were at the bar with her. You're in her pictures. You made her the god damn bundle."

He frowned. "The what?"

"The bundle," I repeated, searching through my hoodie before remembering that I hadn't had a chance to pick it up off the table before my lord and saviour had sent me hurtling through space. "Bollocks. Twigs and stones and feathers all tied up together. I had an example but I left it with a god."

"A god?"

"Later. Let's stay on topic. What did it do and why was it supposed to be closer to her bed?"

Johnny glanced at the door.

"Don't even think about it, pal."

"It's just for protection. It's a charm."

"Another lie, don't push it. You made it for her."

"I didn't make it, I don't have nearly that amount of power," said Johnny, shaking his head and then pointing at the black and white picture. "Some people like them made it for me a few months back so I could give it to her. Didn't work though."

"Who are they?" I asked again, punctuating each word by jabbing my finger onto the image. "Where can I find them?"

"Don't make me," he groaned. "I'm not supposed to say."

"Johnny, you get what's going on here, don't you? A seventeen-year-old girl has vanished from the face of the Earth entirely. I have to find her."

"Why?"

"Because..." Christ, how was this a question I didn't have an answer prepared for? "Because it's the right thing to do."

"You sure about that?" asked Johnny. "If she's safe where she is, why do you need to drag her back to this shithole?"

"Okay, first of all, don't talk about my city like that.

Secondly, what? What do you mean she's safe where she is?"

"Why do you think she left? She wasn't taken against her will, you know. Those people are helping her. Protecting her."

"From who? Or what?"

Johnny shrugged and helped himself to my recently arrived pastry. I ripped it out of his hand and took an obscenely large bite.

"There's someone in Glasgow hurting people," he said. "Someone incredibly powerful and protecting her was way past my level. I couldn't even help that lass in the southside."

Well, that's one mystery solved, I thought to myself.

"And someone was hurting her?"

"She never noticed," said Johnny. "But I did. When I met her I thought it was just normal hexes, but then I felt the hooks and the chains. Cold iron and thorns. It was gross, to be honest."

"And you tried to help her?"

"Tried. Listen pal, whoever is hexing these people is strong as balls. Not my paygrade. So, I reached out to the only other mages I know."

"These guys," I said. "Who are they? If they have her, I need to pay them a visit."

"No," said Johnny, defiant. "No way. If you're just going to stoat over there and drag her back then I'm not telling you shit."

"Christ almighty, Johnny," I said, weak. "All right, how about this. I don't go there with the intention of bringing her back. I let her sister know where she is, then I go to confirm that she is indeed safe and not in any immediate danger. I'm looking for her for her own good. I just have to make sure she's okay."

"She *is* okay, though. I keep telling you."

"And I'm not going to take the word of a novice caster I just met. Johnny, where is she. Where can I find her?"

He stared into my eyes, as if trying to get a read of me.

"I prefer witch."

"I'm sure you do. Although honestly I don't think you're anything yet."

I might have gone too far, I thought. The kid fumed from behind his fringe and I found myself having to be remarkably resilient under the teenager's glare. Eventually though, Johnny sighed. "It's Loch Lomond. That's as much as I know. They're the Loch Lomond community. Heavy magic, heavy hippie. They can take care of her and break some of her hexes, make sure she's free before she comes back."

So, a group of practitioners who live off the land and gave their thanks in sweat and breath to make things grow? Seemingly harmless on the surface, I'd imagine, but a group of casters living together in such close proximity is enough to raise the hackles of anyone with an ounce of talent in their bones. We're solitary creatures. Usually. With a weary sigh, I realised I was correct; I was indeed going to have to make a trip to the countryside and quite possibly spend a couple of days trawling the forests around Loch Lomond. Braw. And on top of that, I'd had my theory about a dark caster purposely cursing people confirmed.

"So... can I go now?" asked Johnny, jerking thumb towards the street. "I've got shit to do."

He stood but I waved my hand. "Sit down." His knees buckled and he fell back into his chair. "You can't go yet."

"Why not?"

"Because," I said, my voice honed to a razor-edge. "This is the part where I get angry."

I don't like being angry; when you're angry you make stupid decisions that you regret when you're calm. It's like being drunk but without the comforting blur.

"You're what, seventeen, eighteen?"

"Sixteen."

"Do you have any idea how dangerous the forces you're messing with are? Curses aren't a joke. If you make a single false move, all of that badness can get turned around on you. Knowing a smidge of magic doesn't make you Alastair Crowley."

"Who's Alastair Crowley?" asked Johnny.

I closed my eyes and counted to ten, before I set my face and went in again.

"How long have you been practicing?"

"I don't know, a couple of years I suppose?"

"And you took it upon yourself to try and break some of the strongest curses I have ever seen in my life? Synthetic curses, at that."

"Wait… you broke that lass's hex, didn't you?" Johnny realised, eyes wide. "How long did that take you?"

"Long enough," I admitted. "And you haven't even heard of the Clockwork Man. Do you have a teacher?"

"No, but my great gran left me her books and notes. She died a few years back."

"So you're going in blind. Typical."

"Here, who are you to get so high-and-mighty anyway?" Johnny asked, face once again a picture of adolescent defiance. "I've never even heard of a 'Rudy Renfrew' before."

I slammed my fist down onto the table, causing some of my coffee to leap from its cup in surprise.

"Do you know what I did this morning?" I asked. "I fought a demon. I got punched in the back so hard I sailed across an entire living room. I smashed that demon into the floor, pulled it out of the guy it was living in and sent it screaming to wherever it is these demons go. And I am still standing. Do *not* test me, boy. I have been in this game since before you could sleep through the night without pissing the bed."

"A demon? You get demons in Glasgow?"

"Apparently we do now," I said. "I do what I can to keep this city and her people safe. What I don't need is you ballsing up all the hard work I've been doing."

"Then teach me."

That took me by surprise, though in retrospect I probably should have seen it coming.

"I don't have the time to take on an apprentice," I lied. "Find someone else."

"Do you know anyone else?"

Not in this city, I thought. Save for whoever was cursing my people, I thought, grimly.

"Tell you what. Come with me."

I knocked back the dregs of my coffee and stood up, leaving him to follow as I strode out into the street. Buchanan Street is one of Glasgow's busiest hubs and even now it was crammed with shoppers and businesspeople on lunch breaks and whoever the hell else inhabited the city centre on weekdays. I stopped in the middle of the human current and turned to face Johnny.

"What do you see? What do you feel?" I asked.

"What do I feel? A little pissed off, really."

I shook my head, then reached out and grabbed his arm; I felt him go rigid under my grip as the other world snapped into his view. Where before there had been nothing but people, now there were shades wrapped in all the curses and hexes and malicious bad luck that could be dredged from nightmares. I knew that beneath his feet he felt the beating heart of the city and below that, the beast that threatened to open its jaws and swallow every living being whole.

"Let go," said Johnny, struggling to free himself. "Let the fuck go!"

"This is the peripheries," I said, tightening my fingers. "This city is a thumb on the fabric of reality; people have been drawn to this spot for centuries, shaving years off their life simply by existing here. Magic isn't fun and games and a way to score points with your peers. It pervades every brick, stone and heart and when you open a door into that world, it opens a door into you. Is this what you want? Do you want to be aware of every echo and entity that hides just out of sight, because I can tell you for free that most people don't have what it takes to survive out here. Why do you think there are so few of us?"

"Please," Johnny begged, trying to prise my fingers apart. It was then I noticed the chipped black nail polish that he sported on both hands. I instantly thought of Donald in his black scarves and eyeliner, and my heart softened. I loosened my fingers and he pulled himself away, wiping his eyes.

"Do you want the advice of a weary mystic?" I asked. "Walk away. Put your gran's books and talismans in a locked box and throw away the key. Go and be a normal teenager. Drink too much cheap cider and discover marijuana. You'll have a much better time."

"What about you?" asked Johnny, his voice thick. "You survived to tell me how dangerous it is."

"Surviving means you get the burden of those that didn't," I said, my shoulder twinging slightly.

Pedestrians swirled around us as we fought against the tide that threatened to wash us away.

"No," he said. "Do you think I could just turn my back on all of this now that I know it's here? I helped you. So help me."

"I'd point out that you were pretty reluctant to help."

"But I helped, so as I see it you owe me."

I hate to say it but… I was beginning to like him. He was as stubborn as a brick wall and far too cocky for his age and skill, but I couldn't help thinking of myself at sixteen and what an insufferable prick I had been.

"Okay. You want to walk the peripheries? Fine," I said.

"Lesson one; pick a new name. Johnny Harker? Seriously? You think most people you encounter won't have read Dracula? It's *the* vampire novel, you fudd. Pick something a little less obvious."

"You're going to teach me?"

"No," I said forcefully. "I'm going to occasionally pop my head in and make sure you're not mucking up my operation too much. So, keep an ear to the ground and please, don't go trying to break any more curses. I've enough to deal with already."

I tried to leave but he stopped me.

"Wait. You mentioned a god. How many gods are there?"

"Oh, billions. I've only ever met a handful though."

"Who?"

"Mostly I deal with the Clockwork Man, the god of the subway and city centre."

"Can... can I meet him?" asked Johnny, eyes wide.

"Let's not run before we can walk, hmm?" A thought occurred to me. "Do you want me to pass a message on to Leigh-Anne, when I find her?"

"Yeah, actually." Johnny thought for a few seconds. "Tell her... tell her I miss her, please. I miss her and I can't wait until she's back."

"I'll let her know."

Without another word I swirled away and strode off into the crowd; I had nowhere to go but once you've failed to make a decent first impression, you can at least strive for the dramatic exit. I found myself at the centre of the squiggly bridge that spanned the river; it had been Jason's favourite spot to stand and think and now served as a place for me to come and talk to no one in particular.

"What a day," I said, leaning on the railing. "And it's not even late enough to merit going to bed."

The murky water didn't respond, as I knew it wouldn't; if there was anything in the river that could understand me, by now I believed it either couldn't talk back or chose not to. Good. I didn't need any more gods in my life and I imagined the god Clyde would have been insufferable.

"I... I still don't know what I'm doing," I admitted. "I thought by now I might have discovered that I'm a first-class detective and solved the problem in a couple of days. Instead I'm manhandling teenagers, getting the shit kicked out of me and now I have to go to the sodding countryside. Even if I do find Leigh-Anne I've then got whoever is cursing folks for pleasure to deal with!" I said, voice growing louder. "If I just had someone to talk to who walked in the peripheries and wasn't a deity I might be able to sort all this out in my head. But since you... left, there's been no one I can talk to about this. Or much else for that matter."

I felt my throat threaten to close and my eyes burned, so I shut up and fished through my pocket; I pulled out a hankie, which worried me a little as I couldn't remember ever having used a hankie in my life, but nevertheless I croaked out a couple of syllables and folded the material over and over until the fabric was gone and what I held instead was a white rose, as fresh as if it had just been cut. I twirled it around in my fingers for a few seconds before leaning over the barrier and dropping it into the water.

"I miss you every single fucking day," I said, before crossing the bridge back into the southside and towards my flat.

I didn't think much of the police car sitting outside the front of my flat at first; the area I live in certainly has its sketchier inhabitants, myself included, and police presence is nothing out of the ordinary, certainly not on match days. It was only when I drew closer to my front door and the two officers stepped out of the vehicle did my alarm bells start ringing.

"Can I help you?" I asked.

"Rudy Renfrew?" one of the officers asked, a woman whose blonde hair was pulled back into a ponytail so tight her eyebrows were fixed into an expression of surprise.

"That's me. What's up?"

The second officer moved with more speed than I'd have assumed from his hulking bulk and before I could even process what was happening, both my arms were behind my back and I felt handcuffs being wrapped around my wrists.

"ANDY!" I screamed, praying that he was back from his meeting. "ANDY!"

"Rudy Renfrew, you are under arrest for breaking and entering," said the first officer. "You are not obliged to say anything, but anything you do say will be noted and may be used in evidence."

"ANDY!" I bellowed again.

A window slid open and Andy's head poked out. His eyes nearly shot out on stalks.

"Call Tara!" I yelled, before I allowed myself to go limp and shoved into the back seat of the panda.

Just my luck. My flat was about twenty metres away from where, below the tarmac, the track ran. I was an atheist alone.

12

I'd gone thirty years of life and twelve years of the craft without being arrested; I'd been a P.I. for under a week and here I found myself sitting on a bench in a holding cell that reeked of piss. It was something indeed that nearly getting killed by a demon turned out to be only the second worst thing that happened that day. They'd taken the shoelaces from my boots and the drawstring from my hoodie, my pockets had been emptied (apart from my hoodie pocket which no one but another practitioner could have reached the bottom of) and I'd been told that someone would see me as soon as possible. That had been roughly two hours ago, and I was mentally beginning to decorate my new home.

Douglas Baxter. This had him all over, the sneering wealthy prick. Rachel had seemed more than willing to let me keep my investigation going, but I'll never forget that filthy look he'd drenched me in; he must have called the police first thing this morning. A part of me was beginning to sympathise with the mystery mage cursing people, a part of me I tried to shake free from my head; drift too far down that road and suddenly you're boiling frogs and newts and making vague prophecies about murderous kings.

As the hustle and bustle died down in the hallway outside my cell, I knew that I had no hope of getting out of there that night. This was more than just me being detained and questioned; I was being worn down. So, Douglas had friends in the police? Of course he did. He's a lawyer, I bet he and whoever is in charge of the Glasgow force drink at the same gentleman's club. Did Glasgow have any gentleman's clubs?

I tried to sleep, but all there was in the way of a bed was a hard bench and the cell had no heating as far as I could tell. So instead I did my best to meditate and remove myself from the situation, feeling the sand drain past me until finally there was a shuffling outside and the hatch slid open on my door.

"Rudy?" said a man's voice.

"Who the hell else—" I paused and remembered how the Clockwork Man had punished me for being too angry. "I mean, yeah. What time is it?"

"A little before eight in the morning."

"Can I get out of here yet? Is anyone ready to hear what I have to say?"

"Not yet. Look, I'm not here officially," the voice stage whispered. "I'm here to let you know I've called Laura. She's raging and told me she's going to talk to her parents."

"You're him, right?" I asked. "You're the one who told her the police haven't found dick all."

"Keep your voice *down!*" my visitor hissed. "You might be right but it's still confidential and if anyone finds out what I've done I'm pretty sure the best outcome would be me being fired."

I stood and crossed the short distance to the door.

"I need more information. Laura says you're her man on the inside."

"Oh, does she, aye?" said the voice, derisively. "I've helped her once and even that was mostly me not watching my mouth. Look, I don't know much, it's not my case. All I can tell you is that no one has turned up anything."

"Parker, what are you doing?"

The voice made me jump back from the door while my visitor did the same.

"He wanted a drink," was his reply. "Could I get him some water?"

"Fetch two bottles and put them in interview room two. I'll be through with our guest in a minute."

"I resent being called your guest!" I yelled to the disembodied voice, which chuckled dryly.

There was the sound of clanking metal and my door opened, revealing a tiny woman in a brown suit with a crew cut so severe that if someone ruffled her hair they might lose a finger. In her grasp was a handful of files. The same burly police officer who had cuffed me was standing beside her, brandishing another pair of gleaming manacles.

"You really don't need to cuff me again," I said, wearily. "I know better than to try anything stupid in the lion's den."

"You say that," said the woman who I assumed was higher up than your average officer. "But according to my reports you made quite the scene upon your arrest."

"I would point out that I was being huckled for something that would usually result in just being brought in for questioning. Also, the big man here was less than gentle with my arms," I said, holding them up to reveal the thin, dark bruises that had formed around my wrists.

I almost felt bad for the officer; he seemed embarrassed and looked past me rather than at me, as his superior gave him some heavy side eye. Then I remembered I was in a prison cell and suddenly my empathy levels plummeted. I stuck out my arms.

"Get it over with."

Officer MacMassive complied and attached the restraints with a little more care than last time and led me from the holding cell, down a corridor and into a bland room the colour of a smoker's curtains where he sat me down. Clearly noticing my distaste at the metal bar that protruded from the table in front of me, he shook his head.

"Dinnae fash yourself. That's just for our higher risk prisoners."

Considering I was probably a much higher risk than the majority of folk who passed through here I thought this was a huge oversight on their part. Obviously I didn't say this, but it gave me a sliver of satisfaction to know how far down I was on their list of worries. I took one of the bottles of water off the table and pointed at it.

"Be my guest," he said.

I'd almost finished the bottle before the same woman I had seen arrived, this time carrying only two files.

"So, Mr. Renfrew, is it?" she asked as she sat across from me.

"In the flesh. You realise I'm being set up here, don't you?"

"I'm sure we'll get there. Let me get ready."

She pulled out a couple of pens and laid them next to the files before retrieving a Dictaphone from her pocket and putting it between us.

"Detective Constable MacLean, interviewing Rudy Renfrew on Monday 14th of October. Please confirm your name for the recording."

"I can confirm that I am Rudy Renfrew," I said, hoping my sarcasm translated to the recording.

"Great. Now, where were you yesterday at ten am?"

"You already know."

"I do," agreed DC Maclean. "But that's the point of the

recording, you see. So we can have it in your words."

"Right. Well then, I'm not going to say another word about that until my lawyer arrives."

Dear gods, I hoped my lawyer was going to arrive.

"Oh, your lawyer? Very well. Let's have a look at another incident then, shall we?"

"Another incident?" I asked, racking my brains. "What other incident? I've never had any dealings with your lot in my life."

"Is that right?" DC MacLean slid the second file from underneath the first and opened it. "Says here you were arrested five years ago. What can you tell me about that?"

My guts froze.

"I'm not going to talk about that."

"Well then, let me refresh your memory. You were taken into custody overnight for... assaulting a police officer? That doesn't look good, Rudy."

The bottle crackled loudly as I squeezed it into a pulp. I could feel my jaw and my shoulders tensing; my heart was in my throat. Of course I'd forgotten that, since I'd spent the last few years blocking the night from my memory. Well, what do you know? I have been arrested before. Jailbird, me.

"I still consider myself justified," I said weakly.

"It was justified to punch an on-duty officer in the face for simply trying to do his job?"

"I think so."

"You were trying to access a crime scene."

"Suicide is *not* a crime," I hissed. "There was no crime scene. Does it say why they let me go?"

"It does! It says you apologised to the officer in question and you were released on compassionate grounds."

"Exactly. So, when my lawyer gets here, you can be sure that the first thing I tell her is how you decided to dredge up painful parts of my past to either paint me as a villain or distress me."

"That's entirely within your rights. So how about we wait here for your lawyer to arrive and we continue then?"

DC MacLean took a phone out of her pocket and started typing away; I couldn't help but feel that this was a pointed attempt to highlight just how cut off I was. I watched the minutes crawl by at a slug's pace on the yellowed clock, praying that Tara would get here soon. Didn't the dear constable have other people to harass? And on that matter, why was a detective constable getting involved in a simple breaking and entering matter, where no one had been hurt and nothing stolen?

There was a knock at the door and DC MacLean went to open it. The big officer was back and by his side stood a woman in a well-cut black suit and a bright orange hijab; I recognised it as her Christmas gift from Annie last year. She walked in and held out her hand.

"Tara Sayed, I'll be representing Mr. Renfrew from here on."

I didn't like hearing my best friend call me 'Mr. Renfrew,' but I knew it was time for lawyer Tara, not tequila-shots-at-6am Tara, so I kept my mouth shut. My lawyer, not finding a third chair, stood to my left and loomed over me like a shoulder-angel.

"Pleased to meet you, Ms. Sayed. Perhaps you'll have a better time coaxing some information out of Rudy here," said DC Maclean, clearly a little thrown that a) my lawyer existed and b) she had actually shown up.

"My client doesn't need to say anything," said Tara, calm. I think I liked 'client' even less.

"True, but I'm sure he understands that silence isn't always the best option." She focused on me. "Rudy, I'm going to ask you again; where were you yesterday morning, at ten am?"

It was time for me to twist events a little and talk my way out of trouble, with Tara at my side to kick me if I started saying anything stupid.

"I was at the Baxter home," I said, giving the address.

"And was anyone home?"

"Unfortunately no. I'd hoped to speak to Mr. and Mrs. Baxter."

"Why? Have you ever had any contact with them before?" asked DC MacLean.

"Not them. I know their daughter, Laura. She gave me their address so I could talk to them."

This was clearly something she hadn't anticipated and quickly scanned the file in front of her.

"The oldest of their children, correct?"

"Right."

"And what contact have you had with her?"

"Hold up," said Tara. "Rudy isn't here to discuss his relationships."

"It's a business relationship." I fidgeted my wrist below the cuff and thought about what a risk I was about to take. "Laura hired me to find her sister. Leigh-Anne. Probably quite the entry on her in that file."

DC Maclean reluctantly leafed through a few papers and frowned.

"There's an ongoing investigation to her disappearance," she said, I think partly to herself.

"Ongoing? It's not really going anywhere, is it?"

"Rudy," Tara growled from beside me.

"You realise you've just admitted to interfering in an open case, don't you?" asked DC MacLean. "You've just upgraded your charges. Congratulations."

"Interfering with a case? You know, out of everyone I've spoken to, it was only the parents that have had any contact with the police at all. I'd hate to slander the good name of the filth, but Laura's got the feeling no one's really pulling the finger out." I said, wondering how far I could push this before

Tara physically shut me up. Not long, it turned out.

"I'd like a moment alone with Mr. Renfrew, please," said Tara, her voice steel.

"This started out as such a simple case," groaned the DC. She stood and glanced at the clock on the wall. "Interview paused at twelve-thirty-seven. You two have as long as it takes me to piss and make a coffee."

After she left, Tara turned to me with a hard stare.

"First, I'm sorry it took me so long to get here. They wouldn't let me come last night and I've had things to send off for paying clients all morning. Second, what the hell, Rudy?" she whisper-shouted. "I came here to help you get out of the breaking and entering issue, not witness you insulting the officer interrogating you while incriminating yourself to hell and back."

"I've been at this a week," I said, whispering back. "And I've found out more than they have. I've questioned folk with valuable information that they've not even spoken to. I wanted to find out if they knew anything that I could use but they've got nothing, have they?"

"Rudy, drop it. You're not a licensed PI. You're investigating without any authority to do so."

"And? I haven't broken any crimes."

"You *broke into a house!*"

"I didn't break in," I said.

"Rudy, the report says the house was locked," said Tara.

"I know. But I didn't break in," I repeated. "I didn't *break* in."

Tara blinked at me a couple of times, then realisation dawned.

"Ooh. That's helpful. I can work with that. Could you do me a favour though?"

"Sure."

"Will you shut up about your damn case?" she snapped. "Let

me do my job and stop being a dick."

"Yes miss," I said, meekly. She glared at me and we spent the next few minutes in a terse silence until DC MacLean returned, stained yellow mug in hand.

"Can we continue?" she asked, starting the recording once more. She had barely pressed the button when Tara jumped in.

"Detective Constable, I would like to know if there were any signs of a forced entry at the Baxter residence," said Tara, in a tone of voice I had never heard from her before.

"As I have stated, this is a breaking and entering case."

"You have, thank you. However, could you please tell me if anything suggested breaking and entering? A broken window, perhaps, or a forced lock?"

The DC peered into the page before her, as if hoping that some new incriminating evidence might bubble to the surface of the paper. Nothing forthcoming, she looked back at Tara.

"There were no signs of a forced entry at any of the doors or windows of the Baxter property," confirmed DC MacLean, sullen.

"There are no signs that this actually *was* breaking and entering, correct?"

"He was still in their house uninvited," said the DC and as her argument changed I felt the tiniest kernel of hope. "What were you doing in their house, Rudy?"

"No one was answering so I tried the door. It was open and I poked my head inside to see if anyone was home. Went in to check if everyone was okay; I mean, who doesn't lock their door in the city? I heard Mrs. Baxter return, went to introduce myself and fell down the stairs at her feet." I paused. "I've not been making the best first impressions lately."

"So, you see, there was no breaking and entering, and Rudy was just doing his duty by checking on his community; I think you'd be surprised at his dedication to the people of this city."

"Rachel and I had tea together in the garden. She offered me cake."

"Does that sound like someone whose home had just been broken into?" asked Tara, with an air of finality.

The good DC didn't answer, choosing instead to suck her teeth.

"Well, if that would be all, I would like to leave with my client," said Tara, motioning for me to get out of the chair.

"Wait!" said DC MacLean. "Maybe I can't make the breaking and entering stick, but I'd very much like to know more about how mixed up in this missing persons case you are."

I watched our victory fizzle out in front of me and might have panicked if at that moment there hadn't been a knock at the door.

"Jesus Christ," said DC MacLean as she got out of her chair again. "This is not a public bloody forum, it is a private interview room!"

On the other side of the door was my friend the massive policeman.

"Sorry."

"What is it?" DC MacLean snapped.

"We're to let this one go."

"William, if you're bullshitting me, you are going to find yourself on Sauchiehall Street at closing time every Friday and Saturday for the next year."

"Sorry, ma'am. Orders from the big wummin; charges have been dropped. Just got the call."

Big wummin, eh? That'd teach me to be making assumptions about gentleman's clubs in future. I could only see the DC's back, but I enjoyed imagining the look on her face. She turned to me.

"Orders from on high mean you're free to go," she said, with a stare that could have carved diamonds.

"Thank you so much for your time, Detective Constable," said Tara, pulling me from the chair by my shoulder. "I'm sure we're likely to see each other again soon."

"Oh, I don't doubt it," said DC MacLean. "I'm going to be keeping an eye out for you, Rudy Renfrew."

"If I were you, I'd keep an eye out for any missing persons."

"Rudy," hissed Tara, pushing me out of the open door. Big William led us through the guts of the police station and out into the reception area where, to my surprise, stood Rachel Baxter.

"Oh Rudy!" she cried upon seeing me. "I am *so sorry*, I didn't know. Douglas didn't tell me until just now and I came right away. I am so sorry!"

"Didn't you tell him that I was... eventually... your guest?" I asked as the cuffs were removed from my wrists.

"Of course I did. I told him in passing that I'd found you in the house and he assumed. I laughed about how we met! You know I didn't want this to happen, right?" she asked, her eyes desperate.

"I do," I said, though I wasn't certain I did; more than anything I just wanted this conversation to end. "Thanks for coming down and fixing things."

"Don't thank me, I feel so guilty. Can I give you a lift anywhere?"

"No thanks. Me and my lawyer are going to go have a pint. Isn't that right, Tara?" I asked.

"I'd say you owe me at least a beer," she said, nodding.

We bade Rachel adieu and walked out into the early afternoon and I leant against a tree.

"Is anyone looking?" I asked.

Tara glanced around before shaking her head. "Not that I can see."

"Good."

I burst into tears and put my head on her shoulder; the stress, relief and dredged up pain washed away the dam I had been holding in place and I couldn't have held it back if I had wanted to.

"I can't do this," I sobbed. "I'm not strong enough to go through this again."

"You are, Rudy," said Tara, stroking the back of my head. "You made it through what was clearly a set up."

"Yeah, and when that prick wants to try and put me in my place again? When he decides that putting the fear of god in me wasn't enough?"

"Then I'll be there to get you out of whatever situation you end up in," Tara assured. "Come on, I'm not letting you go home like this. Let's go get you fed."

"I just want to go home," I said. Gods, that made me sound like a petulant child, but right then I didn't care. Let me be a child for a few hours. Tara, however, was having none of it and sat me in the back of a taxi that drove us to the city centre. Annie was working in the university until the evening and the flat was empty, the lingering scent of spices the only welcome.

"Don't you have to get back to work?" I asked Tara.

"I'm sick." She coughed lightly into a hand. "Besides, they can manage without me for an afternoon. If anything is urgent they can email me. Come on, let's have some lunch."

I hadn't eaten since my pastry with Johnny, which seemed like a lifetime ago, and took the plate of reheated leftovers as if I hadn't been fed in weeks. Her father, a great lover of food, still brought her and Annie vast containers of homecooked meals every weekend.

"I don't even know where to start," I said, mouth full. "Thank you so much. I can't pay you back for saving my arse back there."

"You're welcome, Rudy," said Tara. "I don't want us to make

a habit of this if we can help it, but you know I always have your back in an emergency. Only please try not to get in such deep shit again."

"I could reignite the school business, start selling pills again," I said with a grin.

"Honestly, a minor dug charge I could probably handle. Now, would you please tell me about this case? Annie's given me the bare bones, but honestly she made you sound a wee bit mental."

I gave Tara the run-down, starting at the message from Donald and finishing just before she arrived at the interview room.

"You should have told me about the harassment, I wouldn't have let that fly at all," said Tara once I had finished.

"I'd rather leave it. It was just an angry, empty threat."

"And you're leaving for Loch Lomond tomorrow?"

I groaned. "Yes. I have to take two trains and a bus to get there. And I don't even know where to start looking. Have you seen the size of the loch? It could take me days and if I end up having to sleep out there, I am going to be so unhappy."

"Oh dear, a night out in the beautiful Scottish wilderness, how will you cope?" drawled Tara.

"In October. I'm going to freeze my balls off," I said.

"Pack warm then. I'm sure Andy has equipment you can borrow."

"That man has funded my projects for years. I should cut him into my earnings."

"Honestly," said Tara, a little apologetically, "I think he'd be happy if you paid your rent on time. Just be back by the weekend."

"What's happening at the weekend?" Judging by Tara's glare, I had clearly made a mistake of some kind and it took me a few agonising seconds to remember. "Oh, yes! Engagement party. Aye, nae danger, I'll be well back by then."

Dishes washed and put away, we moved to the sitting room with a pot of chrysanthemum tea and I resisted the urge to sink into the sofa and sleep where I was.

"Have you given any thought to what you'll do if you find Leigh-Anne and... you know," asked Tara, dancing around the words 'death', 'dead' or 'dying'.

I nodded. "I've given it ample thought but I've not come to rest on a decision," I replied. "Even I told me that if the worst happens, it's not my fault, but I've not got the best track record with people around me dying tragically. Besides, she's still just a kid."

"She's seventeen, Rudy."

"And when I look back at the things I was doing at that age, I realise I was nothing but a stupid kid who needed to be looked after more than I knew. Both of us," I added. "How many of our mistakes might have been avoided if we'd admitted that we needed help?"

"Good point," said Tara slowly, as if she wanted to say something and was tasting the words. "But I think you need to have a plan in place in case the worst happens."

"According to Johnny, she's there for the good of her health."

"And you believe him?"

"I'm going to have to start believing some of the people I speak to," I said. "Doesn't mean I trust any of them, but otherwise I'm not going to get anywhere."

"And if she isn't even there?"

"Then I start again," I said with a shrug. "Once I've abandoned Johnny in the tunnels and left him to the darkness."

I sipped my tea; if I was going to drink tea, I wanted it with milk and enough sugar for a layer of tea-syrup to form on the bottom. Chrysanthemum was not a flower I had ever desired to steep in hot water and when I asked for sugar I thought Tara was going to ask me to leave.

"I feel like you've got this," said Tara, after a pause. "You're stronger than you give yourself credit for."

"Yeah? Has your shoulder dried off yet?"

"Come off it. You'd spent the night in a cell and been abused by a tiny tyrant. They wanted to break you. You understand that, right?"

That made sense, though it didn't make my breakdown any more palatable. I refused to let myself cry in front of others and if it had been anyone but Tara I probably would have choked to death on my own sobs.

"Can they do that?" I asked. "Can they treat prisoners—"

"Detainees."

"Detainees," I corrected. "Like that?"

"Hmm," said Tara, picking a petal from between her teeth. "It depends on which modal verb you want to use. They *can*, but they *shouldn't*. It's to leave you weak and vulnerable so they can get what they want from you. It's barbaric and I would have taken great delight in dismantling that cow limb from limb if you'd told me. But you kept it together."

"Apart from me being wide?"

"Apart from that," agreed Tara. "Next time you find yourself in that situation, please don't antagonise the police. I can't promise I'm always going to be able to fudge the facts in your favour. And you certainly can't rely on a wealthy white lady coming to your rescue."

"What do you know about corruption in the police force, anyway?"

Tara snorted and erupted into a fit of coughing laughter. "Jesus Christ, where to begin. For a start, if you're wealthy enough then you'll never be convicted of a crime. You'll get a talking to and your record scrubbed after you donate to a suspicious charity. If you've got a pal inside on the take, then you've got your own militia."

"Gods almighty," I breathed.

"This isn't limited to Glasgow, Rudes. Scratch the surface of any establishment and you'll find the rot that's been left to set in."

"So you think Douglas has got his finger in the bridies?"

"Almost definitely," said Tara, with a sigh. "I fight with and against the law on a daily basis, you learn quickly that this isn't a level playing field. Certainly not for people like you and me."

"And how do you cope with that? In court, I mean."

"I destroy them when I can and let them wallow when I can't. Pick your battles, Rudy. Fight until you bleed, but never expect to win them all."

This sort of thing didn't happen in my city, I told myself. It was the sort of thing that happened in London and New York and Chicago. Glasgow was too small and humble to have such infection. It couldn't be allowed to continue. *I* couldn't allow it to continue.

"No, Rudy," said Tara, vehemently.

I blinked a couple of times. "Did I say that out loud?"

"No, but I know that look. It's the same look you had when your mum said no more sweets, or when a teacher did something unfair to a kid. This isn't your fight. Leave it to those of us trained to deal with this."

"A little help couldn't—"

"I said no!" I didn't like it when Tara shouted. "Your world and mine can't mix. The law won't fix problems caused by magic and magic certainly can't cure the corruption in the real world."

"The real world?"

"Or whatever fancy name you have for it," said Tara. "Look, if I come across anything I think is your gig, you know I'll come straight to you. But until then, let me do my job, you do yours and we might be able to make a crumb of difference.

Deal?"

"Deal," I said, though the word left a bitter taste.

"Do you want to take a nap?" asked Tara, more softly. "If we wait for Annie, I'm sure I can convince her that Chinese is the only viable option for dinner."

I shook my head, drowning out the cry of the orange chicken that was calling my name. "I need to pack for tomorrow, and maybe stitch this."

I pulled open the slash in my sleeve and noticed quite how much blood there was on my clothes. "I spent the night in a police station, covered in gore," I said. "Good job, Rudy."

"I think it's time to retire the hoodie," said Tara, wrinkling her nose.

"I thank you for your concern, and I will take your suggestion into consideration."

"When was the last time you washed it?" I didn't answer but I think my silence spoke volumes. "How've you been sleeping?"

"Great, actually. It's getting out of bed that's the hard part," I said.

She just stared at me.

"What."

"Have you thought about finding someone to talk to?"

I snorted. "There's not a huge market for periphery-aware psychologists, Tara. But hey, it's an idea. Maybe I could take advantage of the gap."

"I'm being serious, Rudy. I think this might be opening up old wounds."

"I'll be fine, I promise. I'll be careful and do some breathing exercises or something."

"Basically anything except actual therapy?"

"How is that helpful?" I snapped, feeling my temper flare. "Do you know of any psychologists that would listen to anything I have to say without having me committed?"

"Rudy, I—"

"Maybe I would love to have someone to talk to but the only other person I know who truly lived in this world is dead, because of this world." My eyes burned and I realised I was starting to shout at the person who probably cared more about me than anyone else, so I reined it in and bit down on the inside of my cheek, hard. "Jesus, I didn't mean to yell. I know I need help, but sometimes there are reasons people don't, or can't, ask for it. I'm sorry."

"Me too," said Tara, gently. "I was out of line. But please, try to take better care of yourself, for your own good. Take today for instance; who are the police more likely to treat better? A man in a ripped hoodie stained with his own blood, or a respectable looking gentleman in a nice shirt with a fine coat?"

"This hoodie has everything I need," I whined. "I don't have the time to spend making another. And it was his," I added, quietly.

"Then at least, please will you sew it up and wash it; it smells like student accommodation."

I ordered an Uber and lifted one of Annie's cigarettes while I waited.

"Listen, I want to say thanks again," I said. "Not just to you but Annie too. If it wasn't for you two, I'd either still be at square one or in prison. Possibly both."

"Thank you. We help you because we love you, Rudy. We're always going to be there to give you what you need, if we can. Just promise me you'll be safe."

"Yesterday a demon popped out of the woodwork and took me by surprise, so I can't promise I'll be safe," I said, apologetically. "But I promise that I will try to be safe."

"That'll do," said Tara, kissing me on the cheek.

13

I looked the part of a happy camper, at least; my thickest jeans were tucked into my old hiking boots, which had been staple getup before my I bought my first Doc Martens. I'd borrowed a rucksack from Andy and had stuffed it with spare socks and underwear, a towel and as many cereal bars as I could feasibly get my hands on, as well as a single person tent; canvas and tarpaulin morbidly stretched into the shape of a coffin. Even now I could hear the larger part of my brain screaming at me to just go back to bed but instead I did the phone-wallet-keys shakedown once more and swung the rucksack over my shoulder. To my immense surprise, I found Andy in the kitchen drinking coffee again, except this time he was wearing only a pair of lime-green briefs.

"So, you're actually going through with this," he asked, eyes bleary. "I thought you were going to bail."

"So did I, for a bit," I said, gloomily. "You can always come with me, if you want."

"I'd rather shit in my hands and clap," said Andy. "Besides, I couldn't even if I wanted to; my entire morning is filled with meetings."

"Hence the early start?"

"Exactly. I'm not leading anything so luckily I don't have to turn my camera on."

"Hence the underpants?"

"On the money, once again." Andy stretched his arms high above his head to iron out the kinks and gave me a once-over. "You all set?"

"I think so," I confirmed.

"Well then. Good luck. I hope you find the girl."

"I'd better. I'm not going to the Highlands for the good of my health."

After Andy had returned to his room with his mug, I helped myself to his thermos, filled it with the rest of the coffee and slipped out of the flat before I could find a reason to stay.

It's amazing how little we have to walk if we really don't want to. In ninety seconds I can reach the subway and be taken straight to the train station; in forty seconds I can be at the next platform; by then I have walked for just over two minutes and I'm on the train that leads me out of the city and into the untouched wilderness of Scotland. My easy life of weak ankles and doughy calves was about to be my undoing.

I don't hate the country because it isn't beautiful. On the contrary, I cannot help but have my breath stolen as every mountain, river and forest comes into view. When it comes to stunning vistas and inspiring panoramas then you could do worse than the great land of Alba. No, it's not the views; as I have said, it's too *big* out here. Mountains that should invoke awe do nothing but make me realise how tiny and powerless I am against the passage of time and entropy, when Bens Nevis and Lomond and Macdui have punctuated horizons since before the human infestation. My city magic is still screaming in its cradle when compared to the wild magic I daren't touch.

It scares me; I don't know it, I can't channel it, but by gods do I feel it.

There are gods out here too, beings that make the Clockwork Man look like a blip on the scale of history; ancient kings and clan-chiefs and beasts, once deified and now forgotten by all but the land, little more than memories of offerings on the air. I didn't plan on bothering them, and hopefully they'd leave me alone.

The bus that awaited me as I alighted from my train at Balloch wasn't one of the recently upgraded services I'm used to, with thick upholstery and central heating. Instead, this was a shed on wheels that rattled down to its bolts on every hairpin bend. It was with clenched teeth and white fingernails that I was shaken along the road that ran parallel to the eastern shore and by the time I was finally dropped off at the surprisingly busy campsite at the end of the route, my hands had cramped into claws.

The view was certainly idyllic, I'd give it that, though the sun was a little low for my liking as I stared into the forest at the foot of Ben Lomond; I'd used up the best part of my day and I hadn't even started my search. I contemplated seeing if I could pay for a night in the campsite but one look at the marshy ground snuffed out that idea, so instead I strolled down a path to the water's edge and had a cereal bar while I pondered my next move; the loch had a surface area of seventy kilometres, making it the largest lake in the British Isles by surface, and dozens of islands, some of which were, again, the largest in the British Isles, I read from a sign in front of the stony beach. So, it didn't really matter where I began, I told myself, chewing my disappointing Coco Pops; I tried to do the maths in my head and work out how large an area I might end up having to scour but soon gave up, leaving it at 'sickeningly large'. And I was feeling even... *less* than I thought I would. I wasn't sure I'd have enough juice to get out of any trouble I might get into.

I dropped my wrapper into a nearby bin and noticed that the site rented out canoes too; that could come in handy if I had to take myself to the islands. But the public shore was going to be of no use to me, so I hopped a short fence and trod off into Loch Lomond and the Trossachs National Park. I was cut off from sound almost immediately as I stepped into the trees and heavy undergrowth; where before I had heard children laughing and chattered voices, now there was nothing.

"Ominous," I said to myself.

From my pocket I pulled an iron nail tied to a cord and let it dangle through my fingers. Hopefully it would give me a nudge in the right direction.

I walked. I walked without any direction, keeping the loch to my left and periodically stumbling over shrubs and exposed roots, once or twice putting my foot right into one of the myriad burns that wove like snakes down the slope of the mountain and into the water. An abundance of interesting flora bloomed around my ankles, and I felt a twang of disappointment that herbs and flowers had never been a part of my usual accoutrements, as I would have been in heaven. Still, I allowed myself the occasional inspection of a plant or tree that caught my eye.

Now and again, as I walked I forgot what I was doing and found myself simply enjoying the scenery; with my powers weakened, I could almost feel any other person on a day out, experiencing nature and breathing the free air. Then, of course, reality would set back in and I would remember that I was there for a reason and the safety of a young woman could be at stake. Grounded once more, I would trudge on.

Something struck me as I continued my path less trodden; I had seen no other walkers in the hours I had been exploring. On the loch there had been the odd boat motoring across the still water, rapier voices from the passengers piercing the quiet. But no one on foot. Every now and again I saw quaint little B&Bs nestled among the trees or another campsite, yet it might as well have been me against the great outdoors, the sole survivor of some final cataclysm. The feeling of being a single pixel in a vast television screen set in and the trees closed in over me.

"Nope," I said, squeezing my eyes shut and gritting my teeth. "The trees are just buildings and the forest is just another city."

I didn't believe what I was saying but nevertheless the gloomy pines pulled back a little and let in a scrap of watery grey light; I could feel the rain coming in. It's a talent I've had for a long time; something in the way the air changes around you, a sudden hush of anticipation of what was to come. Also living in Scotland for thirty years helps. I pulled up my hood and waited.

Sure enough, as the evening light began to fade and a damp chill crept in from the loch, I felt the first drop of rain tap on my hood and the world held its breath as it waited for the deluge to begin. And begin it did. Luckily the tent popped up on its own and I scurried inside as the downpour began in earnest. I lay my sleeping bag down and unlaced my mud-caked boots, kicking them off as I traced out a sign with my finger. The air around me warmed. It wasn't like I was sitting next to an open fire, but it meant I would be able to go the night without shivering myself awake. I wasn't exactly sleepy; it wasn't even seven p.m., I realised as I plugged my phone into the battery pack I had borrowed from, you guessed it, Andy. I had a bar of signal (the most I had had all day), so I sent out a couple of messages to let my friends know that I was still alive and lay back, using the rucksack as a pillow.

There is a kind of magic to being inside, all warm and cosy, while the rain pours around you. Usually I enjoy it from a car or from my flat, listening to the drops beat on my windows, but out here in the middle of nowhere with only a few millimetres of canvas between me and the elements, it was a different beast. I could hear the cascade sliding from leaf to leaf, coating a dozen trees before what was left reached my tiny bastion of comfort. I lost myself in the symphony, a music played for millennia, lulling me to a gentle slumber.

When I woke with the sunrise, I felt remarkably well-rested; the combination of the past few days followed by the most walking I have done in over a decade, with the added bonus of the sounds of the forest at night, had resulted in one of the best night's sleep I have had in a long time. I was surprised considering it had been mostly lumpy and uncomfortable since I had forgotten to pack a roll mat. The light that illuminated the tent looked promising, so I leaned forwards, unzipped the door and poked my head outside.

"Jesus Christ!" I exclaimed, causing a nearby fowl of some description to launch itself out of a bush.

I ducked back inside and retrieved the hat, gloves and scarf I had packed; I hadn't had much success with having the heat spell follow me around and while the temperature was still probably above zero at this time of year, the cold of dawn felt like needles on my face and tasted like tin in my throat. I wrapped up as best I could and made a second attempt; this time, my amount of exposed flesh reduced, I was able to climb out into the morning. And I was glad I did.

A weak sunlight seeped through the leaves that swayed gently in an almost non-existent breeze, illuminating everything below in a dull green glow. Drops balanced perfectly on petals, each a ruby or emerald or sapphire, leeching the hues of the flowers below. And where the sun warmed the ground, weak as it may have been, a silky mist hung above the ground, more delicate than woodsmoke and tying intangible knots around the flora.

I followed the gentle decline that led to the water's edge and whistled in a long, low exhale. The mist floated above the surface, as still as the water below in a perfect blanket; with a sound like a gunshot, a fish surfaced a short distance from where I stood and a series of perfect circles rippled out, the small waves reaching the shore and lapping at my boots. Still, the mist above remained immovable and seemed so solid that I almost felt I would be able to walk on it to the other side of the loch.

With a sigh I turned back to my camp and did my best to put everything back into my bag. I only swore a couple of times as I wrestled the tent back into its furled position. Grabbing another cereal bar (Frosties this time) I zipped up, swung my bag onto my shoulder and set off once more. Wet plants whipped at my shins and within ten minutes my jeans were soaked through to the skin. The beautiful morning lost its charm pretty quickly. Still the iron nail hung from my fist, bouncing loosely off my thigh with every step. I hadn't felt as much as a twitch from it and while disappointed, I wasn't surprised; I still had a lot of ground to cover.

Most of the day passed without anything of merit; my stomach gurgled to let me know it had to be at least one p.m. and I half-satisfied it with yet another cereal bar; by now I was regretting not bringing more of a selection. Midday rolled into afternoon and I was able to stand on the shore and stare out over the satin loch and, almost blinded by the light of the sun on the water, look over to the village of Luss, a simple smudge in the distance. Behind me was nothing but miles and miles of gnarled trees that bore shadows much deeper than those on the opposite shore. It dawned on me that although I had counted on the community being within easy distance of the loch, it could just as easily be hidden deep in the forest that spread out onto the sides of the mountain above me and I was nowhere near prepared to climb. So, I hedged my bets and continued along the shore, within an easy distance of the West Highland Way but cloaked in the gloom of the woods.

Something to my right caught my eye and I snapped my head to the side so quickly my neck pinged. There was a figure moving deep in the shadows that, although mostly obscured by trunks and darkness, broke into view here and there. I stopped and stared; I was fairly certain it was an animal, but not trusting this land and her history, I stayed on my guard.

"It's coming closer," I whispered to myself, sing-song. I gathered what energy I could and held it close, just in case. It was probably a deer. Deer aren't usually a dappled grey though, I thought to myself as I caught a better glimpse, before realising that it was a horse. I didn't know if you got wild horses out here, but I could believe it. Except... I squinted into the gloom. How far away is it, I asked myself? I'm fairly certain I'd never seen a horse that looked about ten or twelve feet from hoof to mane.

And, I added, glancing over my shoulder and looking for a place I could hide, I'd definitely never seen one with three feet of horn sticking out the centre of its head.

"Hey."

I spun around to the source of the voice and instead of a person, came face to face with the business end of a staff.

14

At the other end of the staff was a tall man in hiking boots, shorts, and a woolly jumper so thick I reckoned it could turn a blade. His hair was pale blonde and his long curls were tucked away into a headband. I summoned the energy I had managed to store, but if my body could have puttered and stuttered like a car failing to start, it would have done.

"Easy, city boy," said my acquaintance. "We don't need you hurting yourself out here."

"Did you see it?" I asked, dismissing the stick and turning back to peer between the trees.

"See what?"

"The unicorn!"

"What?"

"Unicorn! Ten foot tall, long mane, *enormous horn*?"

"You saw Her? You?" he asked, clearly surprised.

"Me," I confirmed, a little insulted. "Why shouldn't I have seen it? Her?"

"You reek of city magic," the man told me. "She doesn't

usually show herself to just anyone and you certainly can't be trusted."

"Eh, watch it," I said taking a step forwards.

The stick was suddenly in my face again.

"I don't react well to having staffs in my face," I said, hoping it came off as a threat but doubting if I'd be able to follow through with it.

"Oh, this? It could be a staff I suppose. Mostly it's just a stick." He gave me a gentle nudge between the eyes and withdrew it. "You're out of your depth here, man. If you go wandering off in these woods, I promise you, you won't come out. Not you."

"There's someone I have to find," I said, patience thin. "Let me go. She's out here somewhere."

"Doubt it. I don't think you understand how big this forest is."

"Thanks, I'm actually beginning understand all too well. I'm looking for a commune," I carried on. "I think they can tell me something about a girl who's gone missing from Glasgow."

The man's face hardened. "Who sent you?" he asked.

"No one sent me. Her sister asked me to find her, but I came here on my own."

"So no one knows you're here?" he demanded.

"Only a couple of friends, in case anything happened to me out here," I said pointedly. He slid the stick into a holder on his back.

"Sorry, it's just… yeah, I think you'd probably better come with me."

"Really?" I asked. "I'm supposed to follow the man who just booped me with a walking stick?"

"Well, She seems to trust you," he said, apparently missing my sarcasm. "If it were up to me, I'd have sent you back the way you came, but if you've seen Her… I'm Ben."

He held out a hand.

"Rudy," I replied. "Rudy Renfrew."

Ben raised an eyebrow but didn't say anything, instead pointing in a direction and making his way through the undergrowth. He moved with more grace than I did, slipping between the tree trunks and around bushes with ease, while I huffed and puffed and at one point fell heavily, ripping my sleeve even more and covering the cuffs in mud.

"You know, I could hear you long before I could even see you," said Ben as he pulled me to my feet. "Had you pegged as a city boy without even having to get a sniff of your magic. How are you feeling out here, by the way?"

"Drained. But that could just be due to the number of miles I've walked."

Ben scoffed. "Please, you've been for a pleasant stroll around the loch. Others can climb entire mountains in a day."

"Well, like you said, I'm a 'city boy'," I said, snarkily.

"And what," he asked, stopping and pointing to my hand, "is that?"

I still had the nail hanging between my fingers; in all the confusion I'd forgotten it was there. "It's supposed to act like a compass and point me in the direction of any heavy magic, but I think I fucked it up."

"For future reference, iron isn't going to do you much good out here," said Ben. "Couldn't tell you why but the magic seems to rust far quicker than the metal."

I stuffed the useless nail into my hoodie. Terrific; my magic was currently the arcane equivalent of a fart in a hallway and I'd brought trinkets that were useless. At this rate I was going to find out that unicorn had been an omen of my imminent death.

"How much further?" I asked.

"Less than an hour."

It was almost an hour more than I would have liked but by

this point I was fairly tired and dazed by the turn my day had taken so I followed along in surly silence, save for my tripping and cursing. After what I assumed to be about forty minutes, there was a cough and a middle-aged woman stepped from a tree, as if pulling herself out of the bark.

"Who's this?" she asked, looking at me shrewdly. "You know the rules about outsiders. There's been far too much of that already."

"Clara, She vouched for him," said Ben. There was a knowing silence between them; for me, not knowing what Ben meant, it was more of an awkward silence.

"Are you sure?"

"He described Her pretty well. And he seemed about as shaken up as a city boy—"

I really wish he'd stop calling me that.

"—would be if he'd seen a unicorn."

Clara looked at me before sighing and giving a single nod. "Fine, on you go, the pair of you. But if he starts any funny business, it's on your head."

I guessed we couldn't be far from our destination and I was proven right when we broke out into a clearing; there was an open space about the size of a tennis court, dotted with large flat rocks and simple chairs made of sawn logs around three or four fire pits. Around the outside of the space were various structures of tarpaulin and rope under which mats and mattresses and bedding lay strewn in great nests. There had to be at least thirty people, mainly adults but with a few children, all engaged in various tasks, and each of them turned to stare at me as I stepped into their space. There's nothing like an entire community staring you down to make you feel unwelcome.

"Guys, relax," said Ben. "He's with me. This is Rudy, he's going to be visiting us for a while."

"Hi," I said with a small smile. "Love what you've done with the place."

While the atmosphere didn't exactly change, everyone at least diverted their attention from me and allowed me access. Ben offered to take my bag and he hung it from a branch.

"Come on," he said. "Let's find her."

Leigh-Anne wasn't hard to find, to be fair. The commune proper was quite clearly marked out and I assumed that there had to be some sort of magic preventing wandering hikers from stumbling in. We only had to pull back a couple of tarpaulins before, in a woefully anti-climactic moment, we found her sitting on one of the makeshift beds, crookedly stitching two pieces of fabric together.

This felt like a fist slamming into my gut; I'd spent almost a week hunting down leads, interviewing innocent bystanders and even getting arrested, and now here sat the very person I had been hired to find, large as life and twice as happy. Don't get me wrong, I was delighted to find her alive and well but the morbid, possibly reasonable part of me hadn't held out too much hope.

She looked up and broke into a wide smile.

"Ben," she said, standing. "I thought you said you'd be gone all day?"

"I thought I would, but then I found a stray. Leigh-Anne, I'd like you to meet Rudy."

"Nice to meet you, Rudy," she said, holding out her hand. I shook it.

"You too."

"So, are you moving in?" asked Leigh-Anne, brightly.

"No, gods no," I said hurriedly. "No, I'm here looking for you, actually."

"Oh." Her demeanour suddenly changed, and she glanced at Ben, clearly worried.

"Don't worry," said Ben. "I have it on good authority that we can trust him."

"I'm not here to hurt you," I confirmed. "I've been looking for you for a while now."

"Why are you looking for me in the first place?" asked Leigh-Anne, clearly not convinced.

"Your sister asked me to find you," I explained. "She's worried about you. Worried to the tune of a grand. Your mum's a mess. I'm here to make sure you're safe and get you back to them."

"Well, I am safe. And I'm not going back."

"Leigh-Anne, I understand that you're in trouble but I can help you too."

"No," said Leigh-Anne, more forcefully this time.

"I don't have time for this," I muttered. I stood and held out a hand. "We're leaving."

The hush that surrounded me in that moment was an almost physical presence; birds stopped rustling above me and insects I didn't even realise I could hear stopped their activity. I turned slowly, and the entire community was watching me, eyes hard and mouths thin. From the crowd, a young woman with dark skin, a shaved head and eyes like a storm walked forwards, the figurehead on the prow of a ship. I smelled more power on her than I had in a long time. Perhaps I had misjudged my standing? Ben's hand was on his staff.

"You told me that was just a stick."

"I said *mostly* just a stick. Rudy, we don't like to fight. It's not what we're about. But we can if we need to and if you try to take Leigh-Anne away from here then we will consider that an attack on us, and we will react as such. Step back."

I will admit that for a stupidly long moment, I considered just grabbing her and making a break for it, but I knew that even on my own I wouldn't make it more than twenty feet through the forest before they took me down. Against Ben alone I might have had a chance, but I didn't need to be a genius to know it wasn't just him I'd be facing. I glanced at Leigh-Anne, whose eyes were darting between the two of us, worried.

"Can you promise me she's safe here?" I asked eventually, doing my best to ignore the eyes I felt boring into my flesh.

"She's safer here than anywhere you could take her," said Ben. "And while you're here, so are you. Unless you choose to make us your enemies. Are we going to be enemies?"

Well, that was a stupid question; even if I was going to stand across the battlefield from them, I wasn't going to come right out and say it. However, I shook my head. Ben removed his hand from his staff and gave a slight nod; the birds went about their business, insects carried on eating the plants and the community picked up their chores.

"Good choice," said Ben, with a light smile. I sat back down across from Leigh-Anne.

"I'm sorry. I've been through a lot to find you and seeing you right in front of me... I didn't think about what was best for you. I'm not going to try and make you go back to the city. No one apart from me knows where you are, apart from Johnny, and the police aren't doing anything to find you."

Ben plopped neatly down onto the ground beside me, legs perfectly crossed, and began twisting fallen leaves between his fingers.

"Johnny? Who's Johnny?" Leigh-Anne asked, frowning.

"Oh yeah, that's not his real name. Skinny lad, blonde hair, piercings?"

"You mean—" She bit her lip and stopped speaking.

"Wise. I'd keep that to yourself if I were you."

"Are you like him?" she asked.

"He's like me. Let me show you," I said. I wasn't sure what I had in my pockets, but I saw a withered flower head by my foot; I had enough energy for a little trickery, at least. As I rested it in my palm, it rose slightly and began to revolve in the air; dry petals revivified and expanded, colour returning to the wan membranes. As it regained the splendour it had boasted in life I closed my fist around it, opening it to reveal the same decaying flower I had picked from the dirt.

"Very nice," said Ben, applauding lightly. "My turn."

He closed his eyes and cupped his hands in a small dome above the soil. Then, nothing. There were no words, no gestures, he simply sat in perfect stillness. I didn't want to say anything that might break the spell, as it were, but after probably twenty minutes I felt my arse-cheeks go to sleep and had to shuffle awkwardly on my box. Leigh-Anne, though, did not seem phased by this at all; she sat in wonder, watching Ben with a gaze so intense that I thought I might be missing something. Eventually Ben returned to us, opened his eyes with a sigh and a smile and opened his hands. There, between the three of us, was a perfectly formed thistle, its flower a rich, familiar purple.

"How did you do that?" I asked, astounded.

"Easily, to be honest," he said, thickly, as if the magic had had some intoxicating effect on him.

While botanical sorcery wasn't something I had ever dipped my toe into, I knew that growing something at that speed would require energy at a rate that could kill the average mage if channelled poorly.

"Well, you should see me on my home turf," I said, a little sulkily, before turning my attention back to Leigh-Anne. "Maybe you ought to think about getting a message to your sister, just to let her know you're okay."

"No one can know I'm here," she said, pained.

"And no one has to. I can call her for you."

"Good luck getting a signal out here," said Ben. "If you're lucky you might get something down by the shore, but I wouldn't hold your breath."

I rolled my eyes; This place was going to drive me insane.

"Leigh-Anne, Johnny filled me in on why you're here, but I want to hear your side of the story," I said, putting a pin in the phone call for now. "For my own peace of mind."

"What did he tell you?"

"Only that you're here to get help. And that someone was hurting you."

Leigh-Anne nodded.

"I noticed it last year, I think. Ever since Laura moved out I'd get upset easily. Mum took me to the doctors and I started having meeting with a therapist every Monday. I went every week for years. Anxiety, abandonment issues manifesting into depressive tendencies," she recited, sounding every bit like a medical file. "This emptiness and sadness; as soon as I left my house, I'd feel exhausted and want to go home. Mum tried special diets to give me energy, family day trips, gifts… nothing. So I tried to ush through it, go to school, hang out but everything felt so… heavy all the time."

"Then back around Easter I met 'Johnny'. He was a friend of a friend and we clicked right away. I used to stay with him in his flat—"

"Wait, what? His flat? He told me he was sixteen."

"He's from Skye," Leigh-Anne explained. "His parents moved back to the island and he didn't want to, so they set him up in a cushy flat in the city centre. His dad checks in on him every couple of weeks when he's in town but for the most part he's on his own."

This story was almost enough to make me feel sorry for him. Almost.

"I used to stay the night at his," Leigh-Anne continued, "and he'd tell me all about magic and what his gran could do. I tried a couple of the things he showed me, but I never got anywhere.

Anyway, after a while he started to tell me that something was wrong with me. I thought he was being a dick at first, but then he started explaining to me about hexes and what they did, how they worked and I started to believe him. I asked him to take it off, but he said he couldn't. He'd tried to break some curses on someone else and hadn't managed it."

I was inclined to agree that this was far beyond Johnny; even now, after weeks of what I assumed was curse-breaking by the whole community, curses hung from her like chains from Marley's ghost. It was good to see he hadn't tried to help and made the damage worse; he was the luckiest chancer alive to not have caused serious damage to Hannah. Or himself, for that matter.

"So he put you in contact with these guys?" I asked.

"Not immediately," said Ben. "He contacted a group he knew back in Skye who passed the message on to us. That was when we organised the meeting in the city."

"At the Last Step," I said.

Ben nodded. "Aye. So that's where you found us?"

"More or less. And then you brought her back with you to try and break the curses?"

"We had to," said Ben. "It was a unanimous decision, almost immediately. Someone did this on purpose, Rudy. It's sick."

"I know. You're not the only one either," I said to Leigh-Anne. "I helped a woman not much older than you a few days ago. It was the same deal; cursed up to the eyeballs. These curses are different though."

Something about the way these curses were twisted and threaded was noticeably different than I'd seen in Hannah, as if whoever had made them was trying their hands at different styles. That was a worrying thought; why were they treating people like lab animals? What was the endgame? I was going to have my work cut out for me.

"I'll work it out," I said out loud. Then, off the two puzzled looks, I added, "Sorry. I mean, I'll work out who's doing this. I don't want to think about how many others like you there are out there."

The smell of cooking vegetables reached my nostrils and my stomach growled in response, reminding me that I had eaten nothing but those cereal bars for the past two days.

"You'll enjoy dinner," said Leigh-Anne, stretching as she stood. "Everything we eat is grown here, and anything not used or eaten goes back into the ground to begin the growing process again."

"Sounds idyllic," I said, wishing I could have ordered in a takeaway. However, I joined the huddled bodies as they sat on the strategically placed rocks and logs around the scattered fires.

Though, these rocks hadn't been moved here, I realised; the community was built around the natural land and its residents respected that everything had been there long before them. At the head of the camp was a massive fallen tree, the centre of which was smoothed down into a long, well-worn seat from years of backsides. Both ends, however, as they stretched far either side of the camp, were covered in fungi and lichen so thick I couldn't see the wood beneath. Paths led around shrubs and plants rather than over and through them, and I assumed that the wood that fuelled the fires had fallen naturally; I couldn't see any of these people chopping down a tree.

Ben brought over two wooden bowls and some bamboo cutlery for myself and Leigh-Anne before returning with his own meal.

"There's no meat here," he said, unapologetically.

"I am not surprised," I responded, blowing on a spoonful of vegetarian Scotch Broth. A single mouthful and I already knew I was going to go back for seconds if I could. I didn't know that something made from only vegetables could be so delicious and realised I couldn't remember the last meal I'd had that hadn't had some form of animal in it. This, however... the vegetables were sweet, the flavours seeping into the lentils and barley. It was the best broth I had ever eaten, and I said as much.

"Chef will be pleased," said Ben, mouth full. "Tomorrow I can show you the garden where we grow everything we use."

"Wait, tomorrow?" I said, choking on a large chunk of carrot. "No. I have to get back to the city."

"Tonight?" Ben laughed. "Good luck. Even we don't like to leave the boundaries during the night and the sun is going to set in half an hour or so. You can either get lost in the woods or you can stay with us tonight."

I'd spent one night out here already and I'd no plans of staying for another, but Ben did have a point; I didn't fancy striding off into the woods at night, alone, where I knew for a fact there was a dirty great unicorn roaming around that could skewer at least three of me at once.

"Okay. Well, point me to where I can set up my tent then, please. I'd prefer to do it before it gets dark."

"Oh, no need," said Ben, dismissively. "Everyone shares beds; keeps our space down and helps keep each other warm."

I immediately felt uncomfortable as I tried to picture myself sharing a bed.

"I would honestly prefer my tent," I said. "I have a bit of an issue about sleeping with other people."

Ben just shrugged. "Okay, no worries. Here, I'll help you find a good spot."

It didn't take long; there was a perfect Rudy-shaped space opposite one of the fires and as I popped open my tent for another night, I felt all the eyes on me once again. What, was I too *good* to share with them?

"Do you use magic to stay warm at night?" I asked,

launching my rucksack through the tent's open door.

"No," said Ben. "We use extra clothing and blankets."

"Really?" I was surprised; each of the sleeping areas was fully open on one side and the other walls were only tarpaulin, fixed in place with either heavy stones or wooden stakes.

"We tend to use magic sparingly out here," Ben explained. "If it's something we can do without it, then we do."

"I know a thistle that would beg to differ."

Ben grinned, sheepishly. "I said 'tend to'. Besides, it was to make a point."

"What 'point'?"

"To let you know exactly what you can find out here, city boy."

"Okay, look," I said, wanting to nip this in the bud now. "I will admit that I am off my game, and I'll also admit that this land puts the shits up me. But I doubt you're any less off your game in the city."

Ben didn't respond, but from his stoic features I knew I was right.

"Have you ever harnessed the power of a car accident?" I asked. "Or channelled the energy of a drunken fistfight at three a.m.? Don't play the high and mighty card, Ben. As dangerous as it might be out here, you'd be in just as much danger if you could truly see what was around you and beneath you. City magic might be new magic but it's fast, it's sharp and it will leave nothing behind but your boots if it gets its claws in you. So don't try to make me feel like a child just because we're on your patch."

He said nothing immediately and I thought it might have been the end of our friendship, but eventually he gave a hard smile.

"I see your point. I've never trusted the city, honestly," he said with a nod. "It's too small and not green enough. And it feels like I'm walking on top of an animal that could swallow me at any minute. Like it's alive."

"It is alive," I said. "You must know about swarms? The swarm is alive, made up of hundreds, thousands of bees. If the swarm senses an intruder, it swallows it, surrounds it, and cooks it to death. Nd that's Glasgow."

He frowned. "That's a disturbing comparison."

"Next time you're in town, find me. I'll show you a side of the city you never knew existed."

"I'll hold you to that," said Ben. "Come on, I want to show you something I think you'll appreciate."

He led me through the camp and out past the boundary, down to the shore of the loch, where he delicately dropped into a cross-legged position once more.

"Sit," he instructed; I obeyed and lowered myself with a few more difficult cracks. I couldn't imagine disobeying even if I'd wanted to.

"Are you in charge here?" I asked.

Ben laughed so loudly that it took me by surprise. "Me? God no. I'm just the voice. Most of us don't speak all that much and I'm the chosen mouth."

"So who is in charge?"

"No one, really," said Ben with a shrug. "We don't have a leader. There are those of us who are tasked with keeping the others safe and so our opinions might carry a little more weight, but everyone has a voice, as it were. Nae king, nae quin, nae laird."

I tried not to think of the feeling of the entire community ready to pounce on me if I had made a further wrong move. "I felt power. Lots of it."

"Yeah, you did. Some of these people are much older than me, much wiser and far more dangerous. Are you scared?"

"A little," I admitted.

"Good. Fear is good. It keeps you alive out here. But I don't want you to conflate the outdoors with being scared. That's why I brought you down here, so stop talking and listen."

I did; I wasn't sure what I was listening for, but I listened all the same. The loch was already turning an inky black and I knew that when the moon rose it would cast its blue-white light across the entire length of the water.

"I'd close your eyes if I were you," said Ben.

"Am I meditating?" I asked.

"If you like. Just be quiet and listen."

My eyes now firmly shut, I did my best to tune out the sound of the water on the stones, or the leaves in the trees and search for whatever it was Ben wanted me to hear. But there was only silence, a great pall hanging over the loch and the mountains. There was nothing to hear.

And that, I realised, was the point. The silence of the city was just the absence of unignorable sound; soon the low hum of engines and the patter of foot fall bleeds into the silent symphony, a great cacophony of tiny noises playing forever in the background of city life, each sound almost inaudible but noticeable in its absence. This was not the case here; the gentle lapping of water on stone and the wind on the branches did not pollute the silence, rather they complemented it, as a pair of festive socks might make your tailored suit seem more striking. A beetle could have fallen from a flower on the opposite shore and I think I would have heard it.

"Go further," encouraged Ben.

I wasn't entirely sure what he meant, but I suppose I could listen... *harder*? What else was there to hear? It's difficult to focus on something while trying to meditate; I didn't want to concentrate myself out of this state, so I tried to let my consciousness hover above my body and simply experience the sounds.

Something skittered by in the nearby vegetation, bigger than a shrew but smaller than the unicorn. I think a fish surfaced nearby, feeding on the insects that skate across the water at dawn and dusk. I heard the creaking of the branches as they swayed above... wait. That sound wasn't coming from above, it was coming from behind me. And beneath me.

The sound of the tree roots stretching and bending under the ground grew louder until I could hear dozens of trees spreading out and reaching deep into the earth. Echoes of creatures that never moved from the depths of the lake came in waves to my ears and painted me a picture of the world below. I rode the roots and animals down, down to the bottom of the lake where silt and stone lay undisturbed and then further into the ground itself, deep through layers of rock and clay and soil and heard the rumbling of tectonic plates as they surfed a sea of magma, and heard the roaring molten heart of the planet, hotter than the surface of the sun. Yet even with all these sounds reverberating through my skull, not once did I lose my grasp on that silence that tied me to my place on the shore. I rode a thousand trails yet there I stayed, a fixed point in space while I enjoyed a tour of a history of sounds. I felt a hand on my shoulder.

The day had well and truly ended now and I realised, as the stars above me burned with a light that never broke through the purple-orange haze of the city, it must have been close to midnight, if not already morning.

"How long I was I out?" I asked.

"A good few hours, I'd say. I don't wear a watch, it's pointless. Did you hear it?"

"I heard it," I said. "I heard everything."

Ben's little trick with the thistle made a little more sense to me now; if you can hear the sounds of eternity, where mountains have grown and trees have sprouted, reached to the heavens and fallen back into the earth to feed all that came after, who can it really harm to borrow a few of those years?

"I know it can be a bit much out here," said Ben as he pulled me to my feet. "But I wanted to show you that although your fear is justified, there's more out here than just untrustworthy darkness and threatening scenery."

"I'm beginning to see that," I said. Then, when we were almost back at camp, I said, "Wait, the unicorn. Can we please discuss the unicorn?"

"In the morning," said Ben. "It's late."

I couldn't fault him there; the fires were all but embers now, light forgotten and heat seeping away. Only a few of the community remained awake. Ben pulled a few blankets from a trunk and offered one to me; I hesitated, thinking of my spell, but took it nonetheless.

"Good night Rudy," said Ben.

"Good night."

Ben gently clambered into a bed where two other men were already fast asleep and I climbed into my tent to lay on the thick sleeping bag, which did a passable job of softening the ground below, before I wrapped myself up in the thick woollen blanket like Jason used to do when I was feeling down. I decided against my spell; when in Rome, right?

15

I could smell wood burning when I woke up; panicked, I stumbled forwards, still fully dressed in my now two-day old clothes, out of the tent and onto my feet. A few people glanced at me, then went back to stirring their honest to gods cauldrons, the type I might fantasise about during my campest daydreams. What looked like porridge bubbled away slowly. Ben was drinking tea from a metal mug.

"Morning," he said.

"What time is it?" I asked, looking around to see if there was any chance of coffee.

"Well, it's the morning. I told you, I don't wear a watch. And you haven't missed breakfast," he added, brightly.

"I'm not known for my breakfast habits. I'd love a coffee, though."

"Sorry. Ran out a few months back. Tea?"

I gratefully accepted a cup of unsweetened builder's tea and settled in next to Ben and Leigh-Anne.

"How long did it take them to accept you?" I asked her, watching a mother and child give me a wide berth.

"Oh, not long," said Leigh-Anne; she seemed more subdued than when we had spoken yesterday. "They took to me pretty quickly. Special case, I guess."

"Do you think we could call your sister later?" I asked. "If you could just speak to her and tell her you're okay, I know it would make both her and me feel better."

Leigh-Anne glanced at Ben, who shrugged.

"Just don't tell her where you are. And you're certain it's not her who could have done this?"

"Certain."

I could confirm this. I'd sat with Laura and not got a whiff of the craft from her and while I didn't exactly trust her, I didn't see her being the one to curse her sister like this.

"Then I don't see why not. But not till this afternoon, I think."

"Really?" I said, grieved. "I was hoping we could do it sooner."

"You're the one who said 'later'. Besides, we have Leigh-Anne's daily ritual after lunch." Off my look, he added, "She's here to get better, Rudy. This isn't a getaway."

"It's just… I was really looking to get back to Glasgow by this evening, and I've got a long way to walk around the loch."

"Then stay another night," said Ben. "We're happy to have you."

"Is that right," I said, glancing over at the community that had barely approached me since my arrival.

"There's the rest of the operation I want you to see as well, anyway," Ben added. He passed me a full bowl of porridge and honey despite my protests. "You need your energy. We have a big day ahead."

"I don't want a big day," I protested. "I want to go home."

"Well, that's not going to happen right away," said Ben, with an air of finality.

"I'd really like some clean clothes."

"We can wash them for you. But you'd have to do something for the community. That's how it works."

I gave up fighting my losing battle and made a start on the mammoth bowl of porridge in my lap. Despite not having eaten breakfast in longer than I cared to remember, I found myself powering through my meal as if it was ambrosia. Leigh-Anne took our bowls and left me with Ben. I scooched closer.

"What are we talking about with these rituals?" I asked. "You've been at this for three weeks, and despite your rituals she's still holding onto a good number of them."

"You think you could do better?"

"Yeah, actually. I don't think it would be easy, but I could get it done in a day."

"You're too... you're too quick," Ben muttered, resting his face in his hands, and staring at the ground. "You remove the curse, fine. But then what about all that damage the curse has caused? The trauma, the guilt. The curse might be gone but its effects are still there, Rudy. You take the bullet out and then what? You don't stitch up the wound?"

I didn't know what to say; most curses I'd dealt with had only been small things, no tighter or more durable than a daisy chain. There were others of course, a handful a year that were wound in a little deeper. But in the end, they all fell away without having had too much of an effect. But these newer, synthetic curses... they were bound into the flesh and soul of their hosts; what damage could be done under those conditions? Damage that inevitably would have fallout long lasting even after the curses were broken; my stomach twisted uncomfortably at the thought of Hannah and what I'd left her to deal with alone. The road to hell, right?

"So rather than just treat the affliction, we have a go at treating the symptoms too," said Ben, looking up from the ground.

I couldn't answer immediately; when I eventually unstuck my tongue, I said, "I get it. I may need to re-evaluate my practices."

"Come on," he said, slapping his legs and standing. "I want to show you the farm."

'The farm', it turned out, was two plots of lands, each split into four sections. One plot was filled with plants while the other was unused, the soil tilled and marked out with wood. Through the first there seemed to be a diverted stream that ran through the quarters. A couple of goats idled nearby.

"Some of the community drink milk, and it's good for the kids," Ben explained. "So we keep Esme and Gytha looked after and well fed. The children love brushing them; keeps them occupied for hours."

The vegetables and herbs growing in the soil brandished thick bright green leaves and as I bent down to inspect some of them, I found a carrot bigger than any I had ever seen.

"I've seen hipster farmer's markets with less impressive produce than this." I dipped my fingers into the irrigation channels through which the bitingly cold mountain water trickled. "More thistle magic?"

"The soil is thin here," said Ben with a grin. "We bring in soil from other places to keep it viable and top it up with compost, but we do need to use a bit of a nudge to help us get the most we can. Otherwise we wouldn't get half of what we do now."

"What's with the other plot," I asked, gesturing with my chin. "Out of order?"

"We're expanding. I'm hoping to get this plot up and running for the summer."

Something tickled my senses as he said that; why had a word so innocuous as 'summer' got my warlock senses tingling? I couldn't muse for long, however, as Ben had already made a bee-line towards the shore. I followed, half paying attention and half wondering if the community might have a boat that I could use to save stoating around the whole loch again. No such luck, I realised as we reached the water's edge.

"What now?" I asked. "More listening?"

"Not yet," said Ben. He pulled off his jumper and under-layers in one movement and began to work on his belt. Despite his head of thick curls, I was surprised to see that he was almost entirely hairless, only a few strands of hair leading from his navel into his waistband. He was, however, corded in hard muscle that didn't bulge but gave his torso a ropey solidity.

"Wait, are you going swimming?" I asked, incredulous.

"We both are."

I laughed. "Absolutely not," I said. "It's autumn, that water must be freezing."

It was only now I noticed how cold it was down on the beach; the glade was surprisingly temperate, even when the fires were spent. Last night had been chilly, certainly, but only chilly enough to merit a slight shiver.

"It's nippy, aye," said Ben, nodding and gazing out over the loch, unphased. "But it's not cold enough to kill you off the bat."

"Oh, well, that's a relief. I'm still not going in though," I said.

"You've got to. It's part of the experience."

"Ben, I didn't come here for the experience. I came here to find Leigh-Anne and make sure she was safe; all I want from this experience is for it to be finished."

"You can go soon."

"After the ritual?"

Ben didn't respond, and suddenly I was very aware that no one knew where I actually was.

"Ben, why is it beginning to feel like I'm being kept here against my will?" I asked, the chill from the loch reaching out to me. My heat spell smouldered in my fingertips; if all else failed I could at least try to give him a nasty burn.

"You're not being kept against your will, Rudy."

"Really, because now your whole 'stay another night, you can go home soon' approach has taken on an entirely more sinister tone," I turned to stomp back up to the camp and collect my things but the branches of several trees whipped out in front of me. "Are you serious?"

"You can't leave right now," said Ben, almost pleading. "Not yet."

"Why," I demanded. "Why are you keeping me here?"

"Because you're so *loud*, Rudy," said Ben, exasperated. "Because I wasn't lying when I said I could hear you a mile away."

"I get it, I trample a lot of the nature," I said.

"No, you dunce, I mean all of this." He gestured in my general direction. "You're wrapped in such a din I'm surprised you can hear anything at all."

"I don't understand. I can't hear a thing."

"Well, what I hear is screeching tires and shattered glass. I can hear hundreds of thousands of people talking all at once, shouting to be heard over engines. Crying, screaming, laughing, without pause." He frowned. "And wheels. Razor sharp wheels that turn around and around and around, never stopping. I'm not keeping you here to cause you any harm, Rudy. I want you to stay because I can't let you go on like this. You'll break or you'll burn."

"I'm fine," I said, stiffly. "It's just the sounds of the city."

"You told me yourself," said Ben, "that city magic was sharp and quick and dangerous. You are the walking proof of that. Normally I wouldn't care; I'd let you go back to the city, even if was the loudest noise I had ever heard. But She clearly has plans for you or otherwise you'd have not seen Her. All I'm trying to do is get you to feel some silence. Otherwise you're not going to hear Her."

A thought struck me. "Is that why everyone is so off with me back in the camp?" I asked.

Ben nodded. "Not everyone here is a magic user; there's only five of us, but everyone can hear you to some degree. It took a lot of convincing on my part to let you stay."

"Then just let me leave."

Ben stared at me, then past my eyes and over my shoulder.

"Your city magic is too much for some people, isn't it?" he asked. "I'm guessing you know people who haven't been able to hack it, am I right?"

I couldn't respond; it felt like he'd just slapped me.

"I don't want that to happen to you," he added softly. "I can see your heart, and it's a good heart, but where some people have covered theirs in fat, yours is bound up in smog and oil. If you won't stay, then wait at least another night and witness the ritual. Maybe we can help you out, as well as Leigh-Anne."

Most of me was screaming to leave, to get out as fast as I could, but there was certainly a scrap of me, mainly my heartstrings, that ached in a way I couldn't explain. Sometimes, in my darkest moments when it was all too much, the swirling ink of the Clyde looked mighty tempting. And other times, deep down, I wanted to lose myself to the chaos of the city, to truly lose control and see where it took me. I cast my eyes over the loch, a different animal than the artery of Glasgow that splits her in two like a bronze axe through a log.

"So, we're just going for a dip then?" I asked.

Ben broke into a wide grin and cast his hand out over the loch, coming to point at a large island about a hundred metres from the shore.

"That's where we're going," he said as he kicked off his boots and slid out of his shorts and underwear, standing naked as the day he was born. "Come on, you can't swim in your clothes."

"Can I leave my boxers on?" I asked. Ben shrugged.

"If you like," he said. "But I can promise you it won't be the same."

Without another word, he strode into the water and, once the water was just under his arse-cheeks, launched himself forward into the water and disappeared. I couldn't take my eyes from the spot; how anyone could submerge themselves in the icy water so effortlessly was beyond me. However, I did reluctantly begin to peel my layers off and was down to my pants when Ben broke the surface of the water and brushed the water from his eyes, his usually big hair hanging in defined curls that hung down past his mouth.

"Come on!" he insisted. "The water is amazing."

"I very much doubt that," I muttered, deliberating as to how naked I was going to get. Eventually I thought to myself 'fuck it' and ripped off my boxer shorts before I had time to change my mind and stood fully naked in front of someone for the first time in... Damn. I couldn't remember how many years. I didn't have time to reminisce for long as I dipped my toe into the water and felt my nerve endings scream in a warning to the rest of my body.

"Nope," I said, foot safely on dry land and my hands covering my penis. "No, I can't. I tried but I can't."

"Yes, you can," insisted Ben. "The children can do it. Is the big bad warlock less resilient than the kids?"

"That's an unfair comparison," I complained, but he certainly struck a nerve. I once again put my foot into the water and felt my foot go instantly numb. "Fuck this."

I had never, as I have said, mastered keeping the heat spell on my body rather than the air around me, but I cast it and prayed that reality would bend to necessity. I strode into the water, ignoring as best I could the grasp of the grave that gripped my belly and threatened to pull me under.

"Just jump," suggested Ben. "It's going to be cold but as soon as you cover your head you'll adjust a little."

All I could do was shake my head and try to ignore his empty platitudes. As I belly flopped forwards with all the grace of a beached whale, I let the spell go and hoped that it would do its job. And it did, to a degree; while the water was still colder than any shower I had taken since the gift of a working boiler, and it certainly took my breath away, I felt a gentle warmth roll across my flesh and knew that I wasn't likely to die of hypothermia immediately. My head broke the surface to see Ben clapping gently, arms raised above his head.

"I mean, it's quite clearly cheating," he said, obviously aware of the magic I had just woven. "But it's a start. Come on."

"Would this be a bad time to let you know I can't swim?"

Ben raised an eyebrow so high it was in danger of receding into his hairline.

"I'm joking, lighten up."

My guide turned and began to swim a strong front crawl out into the depths; I followed in a worrying combination of breaststroke and doggy paddle, panicking and swallowing a mouthful of loch-water when I realised I could no longer touch the stony floor below me. I hated this, I realised, and would have liked nothing more than to head back the way I came, but there seemed to be a force, either internal or external, that pushed me forwards through Ben's wake; he was already far ahead of me and nearly at the island's craggy edges.

The islands were a lot less appealing close up than they were as an object in the distance; what from far away looked like a deep green jewel on a sheet of silk was revealed to be nothing but high, almost sheer, sides of rock from which grew trees and bushes so thick that they covered the thin soil and exposed stone. Ben was waiting for me as I arrived, spluttering and struggling for breath, and lifted me out of the water with one arm before depositing me on a mostly flat surface.

"How was that?" he asked.

"That might have been the closest to hell I have ever been," I replied. "And you do this every day?"

"Almost. I've got to stay clean. Can't be reinforcing the cliché of the smelly hippie, can I?"

I had no answer, so I instead glanced up at the small cliff; it looked to be around four metres from bottom to top.

"What now?" I asked, though I was both certain of and dreading the answer.

"We climb."

"We climb. Stark bollock naked?"

"Well, our clothes are on the bank, so yeah."

Shaking my head, I said, "Well, you go first so I have a route to follow. And if I come down awkwardly on a spiky plant, I am going to curse you."

Ben shimmied up the side of the rock as if for him it was the most natural thing in the world, which I suppose it was, and I tried to follow his movements, though I wanted nothing more than to turn away from the view of the naked man climbing the island; it was one thing to just see Ben in the skud, but to see everything laid out in the open as he bent this limb and that limb was a little more than I was comfortable with. Eventually though, he made it to the top and beckoned for me to follow. I was not a natural; I couldn't work my feet into the cracks without the fear that I was about to break my toes off and I didn't seem to have the strength in my fingers needed to support my weight. Jesus, I hoped no one was watching from the shore.

When at last Ben pulled me onto the top of the island, I was freezing, shivering and scratched to all hell from the stone and branches and looked for a place to sit and catch my breath, before remembering my threat about spiked plants and deciding to just lean against a tree. The island was bigger than I had expected, big enough to comfortably house the entire community if they didn't mind squeezing in.

"You'll have to be careful," explained Ben. "There are a few holes and a lot of uneven ground, so I don't want you falling. And the vegetation is thick here so careful you don't trip."

He wasn't lying; the sun's reflection glistening through the leaves was the only evidence of the loch's presence and I suspected that we would be totally invisible from either shore.

"Where are we going?" I asked as I followed Ben's bright white bum further into the island.

"To get the best view," he explained. "Look, here."

The area with the best view turned out to be a large rock that seemed to grow from the island itself, bordered by trees and bushes so that only our heads and shoulders poked through the canopy.

The view was incredible, I had to give Ben that. I could see the perfect panorama of Loch Lomond; in every direction there were islands, mountains and forests. In the distance I saw a large boat, no doubt bearing a few passengers daring a trip during the off-season. There was that peace again, I suddenly realised. That abject silence that filled my head more than any car horn or burglar alarm.

"You feel it, don't you?" said Ben. "Hold onto that."

"I… I don't know if I can," I admitted. "You've been to the city. I don't think anyone could find this in Glasgow."

"Sure they can. The land was there long before the city. Beneath the stone and tarmac Scotland still breathes. You just have to know how to listen."

"And how do I know what to listen for?" I asked. "I've been there my whole life. I've never heard anything different."

"It's different for everyone. I can't tell you how to find Her and hear the earth beneath Glasgow. She is still there, you just have to search a little harder."

I didn't respond; I doubted if this silence truly existed inside the whirring machine I called home, but I didn't want to push the issue. The vista enveloped me even more than the loch had and I drank in what I could. Something caught my eye on a stony beach, a dark pinprick in front of the trees.

"Look," I said, pointing. "Is that what I think it is?"

"Who," corrected Ben. "But aye. That's Her."

With a glint like light through amethyst, the something glinted purple and cast the distant shape in a violet haze.

"You're lucky," said Ben. "She's not always as easy to see."

"I've not got a great view to be honest. Are you going to tell me why there's a massive unicorn stoating around Loch Lomond?"

"Where else should she be?"

Well, he had me there.

"Besides, She's everywhere. Sometimes She's a unicorn. Other times She might be a thistle growing amidst the flowers. You might simply hear the clash of steel in the distance or pipes carried on the breeze. From the furthest reach of the Outer Hebrides to Gretna. Everywhere in this land you can lay your eyes, She is there in some form or another. You're a lucky man."

"What does 'she' want with me?"

Ben shrugged. "It's not up to us to guess. All we can do is listen and hope we glean some meaning."

There was a cry from above and we both glanced up; high above the wisps that floated through an azure sky, a bird described a lazy circle on wings that I could tell easily spanned two metres.

"Is that her too?" I asked.

"I don't know," admitted Ben. "I've never seen Her as a… well, damn."

A speck appeared between us and the bird, as if it had

dropped something from its talons. Whatever it was, it grew as it fell from the heavens, spinning in a lazy circle; it was a feather, I realised. When it was directly above us, my arm moved of its own accord and plucked it from the air as naturally as I might pluck an apple from a branch. It was huge, easily over a foot in length and coloured a marbled brown and cream, though it glowed a soft gold in the sunlight.

"Most people could go their entire lives without seeing an eagle in this country," said Ben, eyes fixed to the feather. "You might see a Sea Eagle on the coast if you're lucky but to see a Golden Eagle is another thing. And for it to drop a feather right into your hands? Someone's teacher's favourite."

It felt oddly heavy for a feather. I held it out to Ben.

"It could have been for you."

"Nope," said Ben, definitively. "If it was for me I'd have caught it, but I didn't even feel the impulse. Could you have ignored it? Could you have let it fall to the ground?"

I thought for a minute before I shook my head; I couldn't have held my arm down if I had wanted to.

"I'm beginning to get a feel for you, Rudy. You're special, aren't you? Unicorns and magic feathers?"

"It's a little on the nose, isn't it?" I asked with a sigh. "At this point just send me a text."

"I think She knows that She needs to work hard to get your attention. Does that sound likely?"

As much as I hated to admit it... yes. The purple glow faded into the treeline, and all that was left was the light on the loch and the wind on my skin.

"What do you think?" asked Ben, spreading out an arm and draping it across the view.

"They're beautiful," I said. "Have you swum to all of the islands?"

"Aye. The bigger ones are a little out of my taste though," he said. "Tourists can reach them easily enough and the amount of midnight raves and parties on them grows each year."

A vague memory of Andy telling me about an illegal party he'd been to on Loch Lomond surfaced, but I buried it deep and decided not to share that with Ben.

"Do you want to head over to another?"

"Not really," I said, a little guilty. "I'm not all that comfortable being naked in front of anyone, and I'm not a fan of seeing others naked either. I'd really like to head back and put some clothes on."

If Ben was disappointed, or even surprised at my admission, he didn't show it. "Okay," he said. "We can swim back to shore. Careful with the feather; I think you might be smote if you lose it."

And with all the agility of one unburdened by the treacherous ground below him, Ben broke into a sprint, reached the edge of the island and curved gracefully into a perfect swan dive. While impressive, I couldn't help feeling that he was showboating for no one's benefit but his own and decided that I would gingerly make my way back the way I came, clamber down the almost sheer face and dally slightly at the water's edge. I knew I had to get back in but felt like if I put it off enough, another option might present itself. Obviously, no such alternative was forthcoming, so I resigned myself once more to the cold, put the feather delicately between my lips and lowered myself into the water.

Which, I was astonished to discover, did not affect me as much as it had on the journey here. I was aware of the dark chill of the water around me and beneath me, but it was as if I had a coating of something that protected me from the cold; the golden feather felt pleasantly warm in my lips. With this new development, I broke into a more confident breaststroke and didn't quite cut through the water like a speedboat, but I certainly couldn't be mistaken for a drowning man this time. When I reached the shore, Ben was nearly fully dressed in clothes that he had most certainly not been wearing earlier in the morning. With dread I looked for my own pile of clothes and found only my boots, next to a pair of thick socks, grey tracksuit bottoms and a bright pink tee-shirt. A woollen jumper was also laid out and everything had the pleasant smell of tilled soil, wet leaves, and tree sap.

"Where are my clothes?" I asked, hurriedly pulling on the trackies and savouring my being dressed once more.

"Being cleaned," said Ben. "What's the point of bathing in the loch if you're just going to put your smelly clothes on again?"

"Did I really smell that bad?" There was no response other than a pitying look. "Noted. Can you please make sure the hoodie is taken care of? It's pretty special to me."

"Don't worry, we won't break any of the magic on it. That's what you meant, right?" he added, off my expression.

"Partly. It's also got a lot of sentimental value. It belonged to someone who… isn't here any more." I said.

Thankfully, Ben didn't pry. "I'll pass that on. Remember though, one good turn deserves another. You've got to do something for us, too."

"Like what?"

I laced my boots and stood, stretching high and tracing delicate patterns in the air with the feather; it didn't feel like other magical objects. I couldn't describe the difference with clarity, but suffice it to say that it felt like I was brandishing hundreds of miles in my hands.

"I don't know," said Ben. "Can you sew? Or weave? Are you any good at carpentry?"

I blinked stupidly. "I might be. I've never tried any of those things."

"Seriously? What can you do?"

"Magic, mainly. Is there any magic needs doing?" I asked. While I might not have had my stones under my feet, I had a feeling that I could tap into the power of feather if I needed to.

"Remember, we don't use magic as a cure-all here. If something is worth doing, it's worth taking a long time to do."

"All right, Treebeard," I said with a sigh. "Those are your rules, not mine. If you want my help, let me help in my own way. Because otherwise you're going to be let down."

"Fine," said Ben. "What are you thinking?"

Well, he had me there. I hadn't planned this far ahead, and I was all too aware of his eyes on me as I wracked my brains.

"Oh!" I exclaimed, taking myself by surprise. "I know. Do you have any candles? Tealights will do, or some longer candles and a knife."

Upon returning to camp, Ben presented me with an impressive folding knife and a box of 12 white candles; I cut one into four pieces and carved the wick free from the stubs, binding it in ancient language, ropes of magic and my own willpower. Using my hands, I dug two holes in front of the shelter that Ben had shared the night before and carefully placed two of the quarter candles in them. With a click of my fingers, both burst into flame and produced more heat than would usually be put out by such a source. I covered them with soil, ended my spell and sat back.

"Test it," I instructed.

Ben climbed in and let out a pleasured sigh.

"Okay, I'll give you that," he said, lying back. "It might be nice to sleep a little less covered than usual."

"I wouldn't get too used to it," I warned. "It should last you the winter, but the candle magic will only last so long. Come spring you might want your blankets again."

Again something stirred, something I couldn't quite put my finger on, but I was already being directed to the rest of the shelters and the ghost of a thought was quickly exorcised as I went through my spell again.

"You know," said Ben, as I finished the last sleeping space. "I think this might endear you to the rest of the community."

"Yeah?"

"I said might."

Very few people had said anything to me during my stay so far, and I realised they said very little to each other. There was no chat or banter, no joking amongst themselves, only necessary speech when situation demanded. If I was truly as loud as Ben seemed to think I was, then I must have been the worst thing they had ever experienced. It was well after midday when I handed back the knife and the remaining stubs of candle; after my morning exercise coupled with the magical exertion, I was ready for either lunch or a nap. Possibly both. I was digging the filth from under my nails when Ben squeezed my shoulder.

"Lunch time," he said.

Lunch, it turned out, was flame-roasted vegetable skewers, seasoned with mystery herbs and spices that I was too hungry to try and identify, washed down with what I think was freshly pressed vegetable juice; I wondered if my dedication to meat was more of an issue with the quality of the fresh produce readily available in the supermarkets. I was among the first to finish, and even took on the burden of Leigh-Anne's unfinished skewers when she offered it to me.

"I don't eat a lot at lunch," she explained. "I can get a bit queasy during the ritual and the last thing I want is to spew on the people fixing me."

"Curing you," corrected Ben. "You're not broken, just unwell. Which is something we should probably make a start on," he added, glancing at the sun's position. It struck me that it was rather high in the sky for mid-October.

Leigh-Anne nodded and rose, making her way around the common area, taking plates and bowls from the others. I watched as some gathered strings of clay beads from their packs, others went to the shore to gather stones while others still collected handfuls of twigs from the surrounding area. It was like watching a single creature, I thought to myself. There were few words spoken, but everyone knew what they had to do and seamlessly they prepared until they all made their way into a clearing I had not been shown. Light filtered differently here, like honey dripping decadently through the leaves and dappling everything in a rich gold. Magic drenched me as I followed the crowd and Ben directed me to a log where I could sit. I'd felt the stirrings the previous night, something older than the city, older even than the beast and I was, despite my previous fears, excited. This excitement was replaced by horror when the heads of every person in attendance snapped around to stare at me.

"It is so good to finally talk to you," said the entire community. The voices rippled out from all directions, overlapping each other until all they all rang out together in a warbled symphony.

16

"I'm just hallucinating," I said, I'm fairly certain out loud. Somewhere in my gut and the back of my skull I recognised the signs of some hallucinogenic or other playing on my senses. Those mystery herbs... Just go with it, I told myself. It might be a hallucination, but that didn't mean it wasn't important.

"I've always been here," I continued, the words slipping from my lips like slurry. "Who are you?"

This time there was no response; instead, the light bent around the impression of a unicorn that galloped around me before bleeding into the shadows as quickly as it had formed. *The* unicorn. Her.

"Thank you for the feather," I said. "It's beautiful. Heavy."

A shower of leaves fell from the surrounding trees and twisted into the shape of an eagle which swooped overhead before dissipating into a breeze.

"You belong to the city," said the assembled, the voice passing from one mouth to another, sometimes one voice and other times ten. "But beyond the city you belong to the land."

"I don't want that. It's too big."

My field of vision stretched and I suddenly realised I was a pinprick in a jungle of dirt and grass, Gulliver in the land of the Brobdignags.

"It isn't about what you want. It's about what you need and who you are. The same wind blows in the streets as blows through my trees. My rain feeds your river."

From my position as a speck in the undergrowth, these words were bellowed from above as if mountains themselves were calling out to me. I opened my mouth to speak but before I could make a sound, a hiss of compressed air and screech of metal buried me in a din, fighting for control of mind and flesh; the vision before me shattered. Something tugged at my shoulders and a soothing cool began to creep down my back. For a sudden second, everything was pleasant.

Beep. Beep. Beep.

I tried to move my head to see where the noise was coming from but it was as if I was bound to the spot. Then my surroundings fell away like a curtain on a stage and I found myself within white walls; the smells of disinfectant and sickness filled my nostrils.

Beep. Beep. Beep.

No, I begged, not this. But it was futile. I was in the hospital again, the place where it all began. In front of me, where Leigh-Anne had been lying on a bed of moss, was my mother, on a bed of metal and cheap linen. God, she had looked awful at the end, a thought I chastised myself for thinking. Her face, once full of cheer, was now canvas pulled taut over her skull, the echoes of forgotten laughter drawn in around her eyes. This was just after the doctors had confirmed that there was nothing else they could do but make her last weeks, or days, as comfortable as possible. But that wasn't good enough for me, the all-powerful wizard (I had been going by wizard at the time) with magic in his hands and arrogance in his heart.

"Rudy," she whispered; is it truly a whisper if it is as loud as you can manage?

"I'm here, Mum," I said, hating the cracks in my voice. "It's okay. It's all going to be okay."

And I believed it. My gods, did I believe it.

The magic came easily; it always does when your emotions run high. One of the greatest challenges any caster can overcome is separating your feelings from your craft; it never ends well, as I was about to find out. I lay my hands over her chest and poured my magic into the cells that had multiplied too fast for us to catch, drawing what negative energy I could reach out of her and casting it away with the wave of a hand. I was doing it, I realised. I was doing what the doctors had been unable to do. Why had I let them 'umm' and 'ahh' for so long, as my mother suffered in unimaginable pain day by day, when I could have saved her from the very beginning? Pride overflowed and a smug smile festered on my lips.

My joy was short lived; I felt the change as it happened, as my mother gasped and began to shake while an alarm sounded. Nurses rushed into the room and pushed me aside. But I was doing it, I said to myself, confused. I had told her she was going to be okay. But then she was gone.

The hospital was gone, too; instead, I was back in the clearing, though now it was cold and dark. Ben sat in front of me; I felt tears on my cheeks. Lurching forwards, my stomach contracted and I purged myself of guilt and vegetables.

"I killed her," I gasped, saying out loud what I usually just internalised. "She's gone and it's because of me."

"Who?" asked Ben, his voice soft. For the briefest second, I thought I registered his eyes dart first behind me to my right, then to my left.

"My mum. She had cancer, and the doctors gave up. They

said it was beyond their power but I wouldn't believe it was beyond mine. I wasn't anywhere near strong enough; I'd only been at it two or three years but still I told myself I could succeed where they failed. All I did was make it worse."

Should tears burn this much? They felt like acid in my eyes.

"It was terminal," said Ben, understanding. "You tried to stop her from dying."

"And it just killed her quicker."

Neither of us said anything for a while; while it wasn't something I had forgotten, because how could I? It was something that I had put in a box and locked up tight, throwing away the key.

"How old were you?" asked Ben.

"Twenty-two," I said. "I was still at uni; she always said she was going to make it to my graduation, since she wasn't able to go to university herself. But she never did."

"I'm sorry."

I shrugged. "Don't be. I did it to myself."

"No, you tried to help."

"And look where it got me," I said with a cruel chuckle. "I killed her."

"No," said Ben. "Cancer killed her, Rudy. Not you. She was already gone." I opened my mouth to snap back at him but he held up a hand. "Life force is an energy that doesn't mix well with magic, and I think you know that. If something is terminal, we can't reverse that. We can't and we shouldn't."

"I should have just let her live her last few days out in peace."

Ben shrugged. "Maybe. But what would those days have brought her? More pain, more suffering? You're under the impression that what you did was an awful thing, but maybe you gave her a gift the doctors never would have. You let her go quickly. Granted, you could possibly have gone about it better," he said, inclining his head. "But don't paint yourself as a murderer."

I didn't respond; what the hell could I say to a man who was trying to paint my killing my mother in a positive light?

"Someone with your heart doesn't deserve this pain," he added.

"My heart, my heart, I'm sick of people going on about my heart," I snapped. "You don't know a thing about me. Do you know how many people I've over-charged? How many people I've ripped off because they thought the unholy stench beneath their floors was a haunting and not just their backed up drains? What about that screams 'good' to you?"

"I'm not here to judge how you survive, we do what we have to. I think you try to do good where you can, to make up for what you believe is your greatest evil," said Ben, his tone even and gentle. "Even if that were true, it doesn't take away from your intent. I'm not here to make you forget, but to let you know that we can't willingly hold onto our curses if we want to walk this path."

"What do you mean?" I asked, a little taken aback. "I'm not cursed."

Ben looked at me, sadly. "They're heavy. Rocks weighing you down, ready to drag you to the bottom of the loch."

I couldn't be cursed, I told myself, as I always did. I'm a *Curse-Breaker*; removing curses is what I do! But I couldn't deny it was getting harder and harder to ignore my ghosts, the curses made manifest that hung about my shoulders, whispering sour nothings into my ears. I could push them back and keep them at bay for as long as I liked, but I held onto them because I deserved it, because I needed that punishment.

"You can see them?" I asked.

Ben shook his head.

"Not quite. I can feel their outlines around you." He glanced behind me again. "They're sad."

"Can you get rid of them?" I asked.

"No," said Ben. "This isn't a curse caused by old superstitions or trauma, or even one like Leigh-Anne's curses. You welcomed these in, fed them and nurtured them, and it's up to you to work this out."

"Other people deserve my help more," I said, bitter.

"Do they?" asked Ben. "When a plane is in trouble, whose mask do you put on first?"

"I've never been on a plane."

"Fair enough." Ben thought for a minute. "When a lioness hunts, who does she feed first?"

"Her cubs?"

"Herself. What good would she be to the pride if she isn't fit to hunt? Rudy, the worst curses are self-inflicted, and sometimes our noblest deed is doing good to ourselves. If you want to keep doing good in your mother's memory then that's great; good done for any reason is still good. But don't try to use it to scrub yourself clean, because that will never work. As for your curse," added Ben with a shrug. "Forgive yourself, is the only advice I can give you."

He stood and held out a hand, which I took.

"Come on," he said, clapping my shoulder. "I bet you're starving after all that."

"How did it go with Leigh-Anne?" I asked as we walked back to camp. "All finished? I missed the ritual."

"It depends how you look at it. I'd say you experienced the whole thing," countered Ben. "And if I had to guess, we have at least another week until Leigh-Anne is free."

"And what then," I asked. "She goes home?"

"If she likes. But she knows that she has an open invitation to stay here for as long as she chooses. The past few weeks have shown that she could do well here."

"You can tell that from a single fortnight? This struck me as a lifelong obligation."

"It can be, some of us have been here for decades, some even longer. Others come and go."

"Longer than decades?"

"Haven't you noticed?" he asked. "The outside world's vision of time moves differently than here; everything is slower, calmer."

I stopped, wide eyed.

"That's it!" I said, too loudly. "Sorry. That's what's irritating me. Your climate is off. You're running on summer while the rest of us are sliding into winter. That's been rubbing me all day."

"No, we just have all the seasons at once."

"Well, that's something you're certainly going to have to expand on," I said, after a brief pause.

Ben rested against a tree and stared out over thirty or so members of his family sitting around the fires, eating together as the night drew in.

"We're magical, but the land here is magic too. When you're so removed from the cities and cars and high streets, does it really matter what year it is? To this loch your city is a newborn. The mountain hasn't even noticed it exists. Out here, it can be any time you imagine it to be." He turned his attention to me. "It takes a bit of harnessing, but with practice some of us can step out into another age."

Time travelling hippies living in a spot where time moves slower than the rest of the world. After the week I'd had I didn't have it in me to be surprised, but it certainly caught my attention.

"Only some of you?"

"The casters. Everyone here exists slightly to the left of the arrow of time, but only those of us who practice can step through the centuries."

"Isn't that dangerous?" I asked; time and magic shouldn't mix.

"Oh, extremely," said Ben, stretching his arms above his head and standing up straight. "That's why we only do it on special occasions. Mostly we just siphon the time magic to grow our garden. Come on, we don't want to miss dinner."

Sombre undertones abandoned, Ben strolled into the community and picked up a wooden bowl while I processed this new information. A coven with access to magic so powerful that they could go anywhere throughout history and Ben acted like it wasn't the most important thing he had said to me all day? All that power at their fingertips and they grew vegetables? I'd never managed to keep so much as a houseplant alive, but if I had their resources I was fairly certain my goals might be a little loftier. Which, I thought to myself as I sat next to Ben, was probably why it was a good thing I didn't. I couldn't be trusted. Not yet.

"One last question for now," I said, quietly. "When I leave, are one hundred years going to have passed in Glasgow?"

"No," said Ben.

"Promise?"

"I promise. That's never been an issue."

Leigh-Anne was seated across from us, clumsily carving something from a piece of wood while someone played a gentle tune on a guitar. There was a smile on her lips and she seemed... softer. When I was finished removing curses my customers tended to look drained, but if anything, Leigh-Anne had been rejuvenated. This was true healing, willow bark to my aspirin.

"How are you feeling?" I asked, after the guitar paused.

"Great," she said, quietly. "I always feel the best directly after. Sort of freer and looser. Until the badness tightens up again, and then I'm right back where I started."

"That's interesting," I said, bluntly.

Leigh-Anne glanced at me, frowning. "Interesting?"

"I mean, it's awful. Sorry. Sometimes I think out loud. I'm working on it."

It was interesting though. Curses that grew strength back over time weren't something I'd come across before. But these synthetic curses were throwing me curveballs every other day.

"You're looking a lot better than you did this morning," I said, trying to move on from my faux pas. "And I think they made some decent progress today."

"You think?"

"Well, there was enough mojo to have me feeling wobbly, I can't imagine why it wouldn't have helped."

She smiled wider.

"Do you think you could stay here?" I added.

Leigh-Anne paused her whittling, looking thoughtful. "I don't know. If you'd asked me a month ago if I wanted to go and live in the forest, I'd have laughed at you. Now, I could see it happening. I'm not saying that I'll stay forever, but I don't really see any need to leave."

"Not even your family?"

"I miss Laura, but she moved out ages ago and I barely see her. Mum and Dad... I think some time apart will do us good."

"Speaking of Laura," I said, pulling my phone from my pocket; it was almost out of battery and my portable charger was running on empty. Still, I expected it would have enough life left to get a call through, if we could find any signal. "Do you think you might give her a call? Just to say hi, touch base."

Despite her obvious apprehension, Leigh-Anne nodded. "Sure. If you can find me all the way out here, I think I can manage a phone call."

I brought up her sister's number and handed her my phone. "Ben said you might get some signal down by the loch. Do you want me to come with you?"

"No thanks," said Leigh-Anne. "I'll be fine."

Ben joined me as I watched her go, a bulging sack over a shoulder. "Will she be okay?" I asked.

"Yeah, no worries. The camp ends there," he said, pointing to where Leigh-Anne had just vanished. "But the boundaries go all the way to the water's edge. It's one of the reasons you're unlikely to get a good signal here. Besides, you saw when you arrived; we've always got people on guard. Here, help me with this, would you?"

He swung the bag off his shoulder and dumped it on the floor. A few bundles spilled out and I snatched one up.

"What," I asked, determined to get a clear answer, "are these called?"

"We don't really call them anything," said Ben, glancing at my hands. "If they had a name it's long since been lost. We just make them."

That was infuriating; the lack of satisfaction felt like talons on my skin.

"I'm going to come up with a name and when I do, you're going to start using it," I said, irrationally irritated. "What do they do? These are the things that led me to you but I haven't been able to work out exactly what they are."

"It depends on what your intent is," said Ben, picking up another. "You can charge it up like a spare battery to store power for later, or you can weave them into a protective talisman. In Leigh-Anne's case we're using them to draw out negativity, like drawing venom from a wound."

With a deft flick of his wrist, he cast it into the flames where it caught almost immediately and blazed in a bright yellow flame.

"How did you find one?" he continued. "They're rarely seen outside of the communities."

"A café manager had one by the till. Picked it up from a tourist stall at Loch Ness."

Ben scowled. "Isn't that always the way? Here, you can help."

Each bundle burst into a brief, glorious inferno as the curses inside were released and destroyed, purified by the fire. As the last one was committed to the flames, Leigh-Anne joined us, her red-rimmed eyes highlighted in flickering glow. She gave me back my phone.

"Did you get through to her?" I asked.

"Yeah."

I sensed that there was going to be little more information forthcoming, so I asked a single question more.

"Does she want you to come home?"

Leigh-Anne shook her head. "No. It took some convincing, but I told her you thought it was a good idea."

"I don't think those were my exact words."

"But you do. You would have carried on trying to take me away if you thought I was in danger. I don't think you'd leave me somewhere I wasn't safe."

She had me there; the worst part of trying to be good was having people make assumptions about you which were all too often accurate. I didn't want to push the issue any further, and I figured since I had put the sisters in contact that I should be able to leave in the morning. And hopefully get my next five hundred quid, said a cackling voice in the back of my skull.

Dinner was delicious, as per, and this time I was sure there were no psychoactive ingredients and went to bed full, sober and eagerly awaiting my exit the next morning.

When I woke, it wasn't to the usual illumination of my tent that I'd come to expect, but rather to a man's voice hissing my name.

"Rudy. *Rudy.*"

It was Ben, I realised.

"What is it?" I asked, sitting up with a start and fumbling for the zip. I fell out onto my hands and knees and scrambled to my feet. I could see Ben's outline, but in the almost total gloom of the forest at night-time his details were lost.

"I need you to come with me," he said. "It's urgent."

Without any further explanation he turned and strode off to the edge of camp, leaving me to fumble with my boots and stuff my feet into them as I hobbled after him.

"What's urgent?" I asked as I caught up. "What's happened?"

"They're here."

My blood ran cold, even if I still didn't entirely know what was going on. "Who's here, Ben?"

I could feel the cold look he gave me, even if I couldn't see it. "You tell me. You're the first outsider to make their own way here in generations and suddenly we have intruders. Doesn't that sound suspicious to you?"

It did, though I still wanted to impress that I had no malicious intent.

"Ben, you have to believe me. The only people that knew I was here are people I trust with my life. Whoever is here has nothing to do with me." He didn't answer and strode on through the trees, leaving me to try and keep up; once more he almost seemed to walk right through every obstacle while I stumbled with each step. "Ben, please slow down. If you want my help you're going to have to wait for me."

Still he wouldn't answer, and the distance between us grew. Was this his plan? To leave me to the mercy of whoever else was out here, and the mercy of the forest itself?

"Ben!" I hissed, desperate to keep my voice down but also make him hear me. "BEN!"

I couldn't even see his outline now and since he made little to no noise as he walked, he might as well have been a ghost. This had been his plan after all. I was alone and, I quickly realised, entirely lost. As far as I could tell, the area I had been led to was mostly flat so I couldn't even follow the decline to the loch. My heart began to beat quicker as I begged myself to remain calm. I had been here in the woods for three days and had been mostly safe. I could keep my cool for a few hours if I needed to. Speaking of cool, I noticed my teeth were chattering and not only through fear. I tried to warm the space between my clothes and my skin and while successful, I couldn't be sure if it would maintain if I moved about too much, so I sat on the damp floor and crossed my legs. I wouldn't let fear of the unknown set in.

Ben had taught me how to find the silence and in my panicked state I now tried to find it once more but all I could hear was the hammering of my heart and the blood rushing in my ears. How am I supposed to find quiet if it's already so bloody quiet that every noise is deafening? This wasn't going to work, not in this state. I drew in a few deep breaths and tasted the wet wood and rotting leaves, inhaling and exhaling, focusing on the orchestra around me; the wind in the trees and the distant lapping of tiny waves on stone. I could hear the roots stretching below and the trees bulging as they grew. I heard the mountains as the plates deep inside the Earth pushed them up ever higher, and I heard the plates rumble as they floated on an ocean of liquid rock and metal. Yet for all the noise, the air around me was as silent as it had ever been. I felt a safety in the silence and revelled in it for as long as I could. That was when I finally heard it.

It was what I imagined a tornado would sound like, if you were stood in the very centre and the tornado was filled with nothing but grinding metal and shattered glass. Phantom voices swirled around me in the maelstrom, laughing and crying and screaming and singing. Gone were the noises of the world around and beneath me, replaced with the violent storm of the distant city. What chaos had I brought to this peaceful community? No wonder they had viewed me with such distaste. And what was worse, I couldn't seem to shut it out. Now I had noticed it I couldn't pull my attention from it, no matter how hard I tried. I had heard the earth breathe and grow moments before and knew that I could still reach it, if I could shut out everything else.

My fingers pressed into the soft earth, begging whatever supplied the magic out here to help me as my eardrums threatened to burst. This would drive me insane in a very short time, I realised; no one would be able to understand why I was writhing around on the floor, deafened by a noise they couldn't hear.

"Come on," I begged. "I know you're there."

But I couldn't focus; if it had been difficult to get past my heartbeat before, then this was impossible.

Then, from just ahead of me, I somehow heard a heavy muffled thud over the sounds that surrounded me, followed by the damp rustling of the undergrowth. Eyes watering and ears feeling as if they would start to bleed at any second, I looked up. There, towering before me with a horn the colour of a thistle's flower, stood the unicorn. A glossy mane of royal blue cascaded down a neck, not of dappled grey as I had previously thought, but a pure white that seemed to ripple like silk under my gaze.

"Please," I said. I did my best to stand but fell into a kneeling position, dmy head heavy and bowed. "Please, help me."

The hooves made soft thuds as the creature moved forwards, walking slowly but not out of caution; the unicorn walked as if this was her space, her time, and I was just a guest. I reached out, hoping that maybe just a single touch of this impossible beast would somehow cure me. To my surprise, the unicorn nuzzled my hand as if it were no more than a common cow. Eyes of glassy indigo studied me and read me, looked into me and through me. Her breath was the warmth of the sun through the trees and her presence on the world around me was heavy, drawing in the world around her like an equine singularity. All I could feel was peace and awe.

You can imagine I was more than a little surprised when my chest erupted into a blinding pain and I looked down to see the purple horn buried deep into where I'm pretty sure my heart was.

The forest around me vanished and instead I was standing on a cliff, watching boats being pulled up onto the beaches of the west coast, their pilots pulling out huge piles of furs, chests and tools. Next, I was standing on a barren landscape, punctuated only by the occasional gorse bush. I must have been far north indeed if no trees grew. There was a roar behind me; after locating the source of the sound I wanted to run. A giant, hundreds of times taller than the tallest building in Glasgow, lumbered forwards, ignoring me completely and stopping only to rip out a strip of rock from the ground. It was easily over a mile long, yet this giant hurled it far into the air as if it weighed nothing at all. I noticed a bird with a wingspan unlike any I had ever seen, turn on its wing and dodge the missile, which fell into the sea with an almighty splash and a wave that rushed to the shore with the speed of a jet. Rock after rock the giant threw, each missing its target and eliciting furious bellows. Yet, when the waters subsided, the great islands of Rum and Muck and Eigg and all the outliers I couldn't name rested in the surf.

The scenery changed again and this time I was in the thick of a battle as warriors in scraps of tattered cloth fought off invaders in furs and leather. Then another battle; swords and axes clashed off each other while spears embedded into shields with violent *thunks*. The dirt beneath me stained my boots a sickly red-brown and the stench of opened guts, stomachs and bowels filled my nose. I watched as mountains burst from rumbling ground and rose like beasts waking from hell, while a vast blanket of trees stretched across almost the whole country. Kings and queens ruled and fell before me; two boy princes were murdered and hurled from the battlements to rot in the meadow below.

The entire history of Scotland played out before my eyes, myth and story and history woven together in an elaborate tartan. I couldn't hear the sounds of the city anymore, nor could I feel the almost certainly fatal wound in my chest; millennia spanned in front of me in the time it was taking me to bleed out. If this was dying, I thought, then it wasn't so bad. It didn't hurt any longer and if I can die experiencing my country's eternity, then I suppose that was okay. I saw Glasgow shipyards burn and Edinburgh ravaged by plague. Dundee pulled whales from the North Sea for fat and corsets while Aberdeen drank the oil from beneath it like a thirsty animal and far into the north, Inverness huddled against the heart of winter.

A sucking sound brought me back to the cold dark of the forest where the unicorn had stood before my weakening body. Which, I realised with no small amount of relief, was not actually weakening. My hand went to my chest which felt bone dry; there wasn't even a hole. There wasn't even a unicorn.

"What was that all about?" I asked myself, breathlessly. I hadn't been expecting an answer and wasn't disappointed, but something rustled in the dark behind me. Still as lost as I had been before, I figured I might as well follow the noise, and pushed forward, peaceful; the noise of the city had vanished, and… no. It hadn't vanished; I could still hear it, but it seemed to follow me at a distance, as if I was listening to it from many miles away. Unsure if this was going to be a permanent change, I was still thankful for the current respite.

I wasn't stumbling any more, I realised, and was sure that I saw a root twist out oy way. Had that weed bent aside to let me past? It was an odd feeling, and though I knew in my core I was still very much a 'city boy', there was a part of me that felt accepted by the wilderness, and that I had accepted it in return. There was still fear of this vast, open land but I didn't dread its company as I had done only a few days previously. I had just experienced the memory of a whole country; a couple of mountains and a loch couldn't hold as much terror any more. Though what I had just witnessed was slipping, like a dream that fades from a photograph into watercolours upon waking, yet I didn't think I would ever truly forget any of it. I felt older, as if those years experienced had stretched me across too much of a timeline; how long had I been lost in the woods? Somewhere between five minutes and a few centuries, I reckoned.

When I found myself at the edge of the camp, Ben was sat by the cinders of a fire, staring into the low red glow. He glanced up at my arrival and grinned at what could only have been clear confusion.

"You found your way back, then?"

"Not intentionally," I said, though not unhappy at finding myself on somewhat familiar ground. "What the hell was that, Ben? Was there even anyone out there?"

"If there was, I certainly wasn't aware."

"So you just dragged me out into the darkness and abandoned me," I said, sitting next to him on the log and joining him in staring into the fire.

"Basically."

"Why?"

"So you could let go," he said. "I wanted you to experience the magic of our world on your own, without anyone guiding you. I could take you by the hand for months but I would only be showing you, and you would not have learned."

"And if I'd stayed lost?"

"Then I would have come to find you in the morning and tried something new." He glanced at me and frowned. "Though I don't think I'll need to try anything else. You're quiet."

"Well, quieter," I said. "I heard the storm of steel you were talking about. It was only getting stabbed through the chest by the unicorn that shut it up."

Apparently Ben had not expected this part of my adventure; his eyes widened.

"She did what?" he whispered.

"She stabbed me," I repeated. "Why? She doesn't do that to everyone?"

"No, She doesn't."

Ben looked at me still in awe, so I told him about the visions I had had before Scotland walked me back to camp.

"Incredible," he said, with what I thought was a hint of jealousy colouring his voice. "I'd wondered if She'd reveal herself to you again, but this is something new."

"Yeah, I've been getting that a lot lately."

"Eagles and unicorns, eh? You have some very powerful beings looking out for you," said Ben.

"What is she?" I asked, determined that I had earned an answer now.

"What do you think she is?"

Very nearly biting back, I stopped and considered this. What had I seen? The history of the country I was made out of. I thought of the white body and blue mane, the deep thistle-purple of her horn.

"The land," I said, immediately knowing it was true.

"*Our* land," Ben corrected. "She is everything you walk on and hear and breath for as long as you stay within Her borders."

"A god?"

"Sort of, though she's older than most other deities."

I thought of my kneeling in front of her and winced.

"I am going to have a lot of explaining to do when I get home," I said.

"To who?"

"The Clockwork Man," I said. "Can't see him being too thrilled about what just went down."

"That's your god of the subway?" asked Ben.

Something far away screeched, the sound echoing along a tunnel that wasn't there.

"That's him," I said warily, wondering if Ben had heard the noise too. "I'm his champion, though I never asked to be, but it is what it is."

"So your mechanical god has made you his knight and now She's bequeathing eternal knowledge to you. You're going to have access to a whole lot more than city magic if you keep this path."

"I don't want more than city magic," I said, feeling a little ungrateful. "All I ever wanted was a boring life reading books and removing curses."

"Well, that's balls," said Ben. "Maybe that's what you used to want but I can't see you living that life. Can you?"

I couldn't. He was right; maybe a tiny office buried in papers and articles had been the dream long ago but that life was gone, as dead as my old name and I couldn't miss what I never had. Besides. . . this *was* more exciting.

"A human cannot live on the city alone," intoned Ben. "I'm not saying give up your worldly possessions and live the life of a monk in constant praise of the natural world, but with that sound out of your ears, maybe you will hear more than you can see."

I didn't want to be a knight, nor did I want to be a monk. But, said that little voice in my head that always showed up uninvited, neither did you ask to lose Jason or your mother. It never matters what you want.

"Shut up," I said suddenly, to a shocked look from Ben. I hurriedly added, "Not you! It's been a stressful day and now I'm talking to myself. I'd like to go to bed, again."

Ben nodded and rose with me. "I should get some sleep too. You and I have a busy day tomorrow."

"Another one?" I groaned. "What are we doing?"

"We're walking back to Balloch," said Ben. "Unless you'd prefer to stay."

"As if the rest would keep me."

"I think they might now that they will be able to hear themselves think. Rudy, I hope you'll remember that you'll always be welcome here. If I thought you'd stay I'd offer you a place, but I know you wouldn't take it."

He was right; for all my revelations over the last few days I still belonged to the city; I wanted my tarmac beneath my feet and bricks surrounding me instead of trees.

"Rest your bones," Ben told me. "It's an early start and it's going to be no mean feat if I want to get there and back in a day. I hope you're ready for a more punishing walk than the one that got you here."

I very much wasn't, but I was prepared for a sofa and a cup of coffee and my own bed, so without further ado I fell into my tent and was asleep before I could even zip up the door.

When I woke for the second time that day, it was to a weak grey light and a fine drizzle that crystallised the camp in countless tiny gems. Someone had brought me my clothes and tucked them inside the tent, luckily out of reach of the rain. Dressing myself in my own clothes again, I saw that someone had stitched the hole in the sleeve and even worked out the bloodstains. The gratitude I felt was immeasurable.

By the spent fire pit, I found Ben stacking up wood for the

morning cook off, his hiking stick once again on the leather holder on his back.

"You ready to leave?" he asked.

"Already?"

"I thought you were eager to get out of here."

"Eager, yes," I confirmed. "Still needing to pack? Also yes."

"Get a shift on then, I want to leave in ten."

Luckily I had lived out of my bag for the past few days so all I had to do was stuff my sleeping bag back to the bottom of my pack before cramming the accursed collapsible tent on top of it. I folded my borrowed clothes neatly and laid them on a log.

"Pass my thanks on to whoever cleaned and fixed my clothes, would you?" I asked.

"Consider it done."

My rucksack resting on my shoulders and feet nestled inside my clean, dry socks, Ben and I set off past the boundaries and into the untamed wilderness. I felt a pang of regret as I realised I hadn't said goodbye to Leigh-Anne.

"Will they be okay without you today?" I asked. "For the ritual?"

"They'll make do. They'll have to."

"Sorry."

"Don't be," said Ben, with a wave. "I'm not the be all and end all of this coven, I'm just the voice. You didn't get to talk to the ones with real power here, the ones that make me look like an amateur."

"How long have you been here?" I asked. "How long have you been the spokesperson?"

"Not long, I'm still only in my thirties."

"And how long have you been in your thirties?"

Ben grinned that cheeky, knowing grin that I had come to expect from him. "Well, a wee while."

The walk back around the loch was a lot more bearable this

time around, not least because now the undergrowth was working with me rather than against me, but also because having a guide like Ben meant that I was able to see what before I would have overlooked. He pointed out which plants could be eaten and which could definitely not be eaten. I was directed to trees and told how long they had been growing, while showing me the tracks that proved which animal had been where.

Morning began in earnest and I know that I was making much better time than before; moving with such ease now, I was embarrassed about how much drama I'd made for myself previously. We stopped for a lunch of fruit while Ben named the birds above us and I marvelled at his ability to recognise them from such a distance; I knew I would never remember any of the names he told me. When we arrived at the limits of the campsite, Ben stopped.

"This is where I leave you, buddy. If I want to get back before dark I should be on my way."

"No worries." I stuck out my hand. "Thanks, for everything. Sincerely."

He took it. "Don't mention it. I won't say it was my pleasure, but I had fun, at least."

"And I appreciate it. Will you be in the city soon?"

"Nothing planned. But you always have a bed here. Figuratively speaking."

Ben took the stick from his back, began twirling it in his fingers and strode off, whistling. I could never imagine being that carefree.

I checked the bus stop and found I hadn't missed the only bus that day. Granted, it wasn't going to come through for two hours. The old Rudy would probably have spent his time effing and blinding, but the Rudy who had just spent three days in a forest was happy just to see doors with locks again. So, I sat in the wooden bus shelter and tried to process everything that had happened over the past couple of days.

It was perhaps lucky that the bus made such a noise that it woke me from the nap I had slipped into, allowing me to groggily stand and flag it down. The rest of my journey was uneventful and peppered with nods into sleep until finally, after the sun had set and the smell of cold stone had set in, I arrived in my city. It was only as I stood in front of the subway station did I think I might be due a talking to.

"If you're thinking of bringing me in, could you please wait until tomorrow?" I begged at the doors. "I really just want to go home and sleep."

The Clockwork Man, mercifully, left me alone and as I turned the key in my lock, the welcoming smells of coffee and tobacco and books embraced me. I found Andy playing on his computer and didn't get a word out of him for five minutes until the match ended. Finally, he pulled off his headphones.

"So, how was the great outdoors?" he asked.

"Tiring. You wouldn't believe the couple of days I've had."

I filled him in on my journey, eliciting a satisfying gasp when I mentioned the unicorn.

"And you found her? The girl?"

"Leigh-Anne. Yeah, I did. She's safe as houses and she spoke to Laura, which I hope will be enough for her." I still wanted to be paid.

"Wow," said Andy with what I think was a proud smile. "Well done, man. I didn't know if you'd be up to this, if I'm honest. But I'm impressed. Well done making it back in time, too."

"In time for what?"

"You're pulling my pisser, aye? Tara and Annie's engagement party the morra?"

Skin of my god damn teeth.

"Oh yeah, of course," I said, fooling exactly no one. "I'd best go get some sleep then, eh? Don't want to be yawning through the celebrations."

If the feeling that surged through me now was job satisfaction, then what the hell had I been doing all these years? I bade Andy a good night and let the comfort of my familiar room wash over me. Though the wonders of the country had, even if I didn't like admitting it, opened me a little to another way of life and magic, I still could not think of anything more comforting than one's own bed after a stretch of rough nights.

I placed the eagle feather on top of my chest, stripped out of my clothes and into a pair of trackies before snuggling down into my duvet. Job done.

All was well.

xcept of course it wasn't, because why would life ever be that simple? The damsel in distress is safe, I've gone on my hero's journey and faced my personal demons, and my flat mate is proud of me; all wrapped up in a neat little package. Though life isn't a story. That should go without saying, but people forget that and go about their days waiting for the next plot device to steer them through their quest, but we don't get the luxury of a plotline; life is a series of events in an incredible domino effect, and sometimes what you thought was the end was really just the end of act two. And act three is always where the shit goes down.

For the second night in a row, I was awoken by my own name, but this time it was a wail that pierced through my windows and woke me with a start. I sat for a moment, wondering if I had dreamed it, before hearing it again, closer to my door. I sprang out of bed and pulled on my hoodie and my docs and made my way out as fast as possible. Andy was already in the hall.

"Who the hell is that?" he asked.

"I have no idea," I replied, pushing past him into the close and then out into the street.

There was a woman at the bottom of my steps, and it took me more than a few moments to place her.

"Linda?" I said, shock most likely registering on my face.

"I'm sorry, I didn't know where to go," she sobbed. "I was coming back from the centre and—"

"GET BACK HERE, YOU BITCH!" bellowed someone to my right, making me jump. I registered the newcomer and immediately placed him as the soon to be ex-husband. I placed myself between him and Linda.

"Andy, please take Linda inside and offer her a cup of tea," I said, my voice calmer than I thought it would be. Andy came down and put his arm around her.

"Get out of my way," snarled the man as he reached me. I stepped in front of him.

"No."

I saw Andy and Linda go through the door and shut it behind them; the click of the snib going into place confirmed that it was now just me and him.

"That's my wife!"

"Not anymore, mate. You fucked it and you fucked it good. I hope you're sad and lonely for the rest of your life."

"What do you know?"

"I know what she told me, and I know what I saw in her cards. And I know that the best thing you can do now is turn around and go back the way you came."

"Aye?" asked the man, eyes bulging. "And who are you to tell me what to do, you wee shit?"

My gods, I wanted to hit him. I wanted to punch him in his ugly red face and knock him straight into the ground. I'm six-foot-four.

"You're angry, so I'm going to let that slide. But I want you to know that Linda is under this wee shit's protection and you are beginning to test this wee shit's patience. Turn away, you miserable little man, and go home, before the city loses its temper."

I saw the lunge coming and probably had time to move, but out of three potential reactions my body chose the least helpful and froze. His fingers grabbed my sleeves and, as I struggled to free myself, the new stitching came undone and the rip burst open, extending all the way up to the seam in my armpit and tearing it almost entirely off. That did it.

Anger coursed through me and this time, despite my best efforts, a crack appeared in my defences and the slightest sliver of rage broke through. With a shove I pushed the man away and as he staggered back, wrapped my hand around his throat.

It would be so easy, said a man's voice in my ear, the voice of one I had known who had given in to the chaos, calling me into the void; I imagined I felt a large, strong hand on my shoulder. A pinch on an artery, a spark in his brain, it said. You could make it look like a dreadful accident.

And I could, I knew it. But what if I couldn't stop? And why did it fall to me to decide who lived and died? I hadn't gone that far yet. I loosened my grip and instead of frying his neurons, gave him a glimpse of the world around him as I had Johnny, but this time I really let him have it.

"You see, what I was trying to say before is that the chaos of this city is in my blood. When you attacked me, you attacked Glasgow. And now you know what creeps and writhes around you, what feeds beneath you. This city is dangerous, old man. It will eat you whole and I promise you that no one will mourn." I dropped him. "Go away. If you ever come near her again, I personally guarantee that next time, I will do more than just scare you."

I didn't give him the satisfaction of waiting; I simply opened my door and left him alone. Andy had indeed made tea and even had the foresight to make me a mug so sweet that I could feel my teeth rotting.

"Rudy, I'm sorry," said Linda, calmer. "I didn't know where to go. He came out of nowhere and yours was the closest place."

"I'm glad it was," I said. "I don't think he'll bother you again, but if he ever does, even if it's just a rumour on the vine, you come to me. I don't care what time it is, you come to me and I'll help. Understand?"

Linda nodded and we shared a few biscuits to calm down before we ordered Linda an Uber and sent her back to the comfort of her home. I glanced at the time; it wasn't even eleven.

"My sleep schedule is so out of whack," I moaned, rubbing my eyes.

"Do you want to sit up for a bit?" asked Andy. "I'm pretty wired after that."

"Thanks, but no. I just want to sleep through the night, and I can't understand why the universe won't let me do that."

I didn't return to my dreaming with the speed I had before, this time struggling to get comfortable as I waited for the adrenalin to subside. I had been so close. So close to crossing the point I couldn't come back from and that dallying on the edge was going to haunt me. Would I have come so close before this new magic had its roots in me?

As my alarm went off and informed me that it was long past dawn, I stretched and revelled in the fact that my curtains did their job so well, before deciding that all I wanted to do for the rest of the day was to lounge about in bed and congratulate myself on a job well done. That lasted all of twenty minutes before I was dragged out of my comfort by a bursting bladder, so I decided to pull out my staff and continue working; while I wanted to jump straight into finally burning arcane symbols across the wood with Tara's wood burner, I still had to sand and smooth the whole thing so I gathered the sandpaper from below the sink and took it out into the garden.

There was one large tree in the centre of the communal yard, ringed by a wooden bench so I played some tunes from my phone and basked in the weak sunlight, bundled in my layers. It was still autumn in Glasgow after all. I worked hard and without pause, meditating on all that had transpired over the past week or so; even now, as I sat beneath the boughs of what I was now fairly certain was a beech, I could only feel the rumbling madness of city magic. How could this tree, many decades older than myself, resonate nothing of the wild magic that I knew lay in wait in the soil and stones? How was I ever going to find the old magic when all I could hear was the bawling of Glasgow?

Sometime after noon, Andy came to join me, carrying two steaming mugs of coffee, and sat beside me.

"So, are you going full wizard now or what?" he asked, taking the staff from my lap and wiping away some of the dust.

"I thought it might be a useful tool," I said, sipping my coffee. "Jason always went on about wanting one, but he never got around to it."

"He never mentioned it to me," said Andy.

"It's not made of binary so I doubt he thought you'd be interested."

Andy swung the staff about a few times before focusing his attention on me.

"Why did you pick up where he left off?" he asked me, bluntly. "The Curse-Breaker for hire was his gig. Did you ever show an interest, before?"

"No," I said. "But I'm good at it. And someone needs to do it. The city needs a body, and a protector. You know what's under the ground, under the tunnels and foundations. The Clockwork

Man keeps it there, I think, but that doesn't stop this city warping in the pressure. Jason left a void that needed to be filled and luckily there was me."

"Did you ever think that was exactly his plan?" Andy asked, sitting and handing me back my staff. "I mean, he loved you, anyone could see that. But maybe he wanted to know that if anything ever happened to him, Glasgow would be in good hands."

I tried gulping down some coffee to shake the lump that was growing in my throat, but all it did was make me cough and splutter.

"Maybe," I said, breathlessly. "I think he'd have wanted someone more powerful than me, if that was the case."

"Hey, he was my best friend for much longer than you knew him. If he thought you'd be strong enough to take up his staff then I'd have a little more faith in him." Andy stood, burped and picked up his mug. "Don't be out here too long. Tara and Annie want you to be at the bar early to help get set up."

I checked the time and sighed; he was right. I finished off the last few inches and resolved to go over the whole thing again the next day with the fine sheet of sandpaper to make sure it was like silk under my palm before following in Andy's footsteps.

As I climbed out of the shower, I saw my phone flashing and after wrapping my towel around my waist, found a message from Moti.

Hey, guessing you've been busy but wondered if you'd like to do something tonight?

Unless I'm being pushy in which case...

Who is this?

I grinned and began to tap out a reply, before pausing and heading out to Andy's door.

"Andy," I said with a couple of taps. "You decent?"

"One sec."

I heard him stumbling over the mess that carpeted his floor before pulling the door open and thrusting two shirts in my direction, one grey and one purple.

"What looks better?" he asked.

"Clearly the purple," I said. "Hey, I have a slightly awkward question. Do you remember Moti?"

"Uh, tall guy? Glasses, dark hair?"

"Yeah, him. Would it be really poor form for me to bring him to the party tonight?"

I'd heard of people's eyes bulging before, but I don't think I'd ever witnessed it happen first-hand. However right now Andy's pupils were in danger of extending past the tip of his nose.

"Like, as your plus one? As a date?"

"Whoa, steady on pal, let's not go crazy, eh?" I said, holding up my palms. "I owe him, big time, and I think I'd like to see him again."

Andy said nothing, but instead continued to stare at me like I'd just explained that humans were in fact descended from cacti.

"Well?"

"Mate, I don't care that you're interested in one of my hookups, that's grand. But are you sure?"

"Not at all. It's been a long time and I'm not sure I'm even interested," I said with a shrug. "But I met him at The Last Drop and he makes me laugh."

There was another moment of staring, until Andy broke out into a wide grin.

"Then do it, you fudd. Just make sure you turn up tonight looking less like shit than you usually do, aye?"

With Andy's eloquent advice in mind, I replied to Moti with the suggestion and set about trying to dress myself like a normal human being might. When my phone buzzed with a reply, it was only with slight anxiety that I opened the message.

The party had been a long time coming and if truth be told, we were closer to the wedding than we were the engagement; both Tara and Annie lived busy lives and an expensive celebration had been quite far down on their list of priorities, but now that the time had finally rolled around, they had pulled out all the stops. A cocktail bar in the west end had been rented out for the entire evening and, depending on how the party progressed, probably the night as well. When I arrived, Annie was balanced precariously on a ladder trying to hang fairy lights and gratefully dumped the thread into my hands as I reached in for a hug.

"It's your own fault for being tall," explained Andy, holding the ladder in position with one hand and nursing a beer with the other.

"Oh, you made it!" said Tara, arriving from a back room with a tray full of candles. She dropped them onto a table and squeezed my calf.

"As if I'd forget," I said, shooting a glare down at Andy. "I'm at your disposal. Point me at tasks."

I owed both Tara and Annie more than I was likely to be able to pay back any time soon, so it was with little griping that I allowed myself to be put to work and by the time the first guests started to arrive, the bar was a twinkling grotto of purples and pinks and I gratefully took a martini glass of something red, sweet and strong from the man behind the counter. No one walking in through the door seemed familiar to me, so I retreated to a table where Andy, already about four beers in, was sitting.

"Half of these people are computer scientists," I said, sitting.

"Shouldn't you be out there schmoozing?"

"They're all professionals. I'm just a hack who learned to code instead of doing homework at school. These guys are Bach to my Good Charlotte, ken?" He pointed his beer bottle towards Tara. "Think any of her pals might be able to help you with your brand-new detective business?"

"For a start, I haven't started a detective business. Secondly, I can't exactly vouch for how legal all my actions have been while detecting," I said, counting down on my fingers. "And lastly, I'd likely be sectioned before I could even get my elevator pitch finished."

"Well, here's to being the spare pricks," said Andy. We clinked and drank, Tara joining us as I rested my glass on the table.

"Having a good time?" she asked.

"A free bar is always a ticket to success," said Andy.

"You know, it wouldn't kill either of you to be a little more social."

"Hey, I need to ease myself back into it," I said, popping the cherry from the bottom of my glass into my mouth. "I've been in the sticks, too much stimulation could finish me off."

Andy snorted.

"I'm getting another beer, want anything?"

"Another of these sweet red things, please."

Tara occupied Andy's chair; tonight her hijab was lavender, embroidered with purple thread and stones, and glittered in the candlelight.

"Is it feeling real yet?" I asked. "Now that you've finally had the party?"

"Honestly, I'm at the point now where I just want to be married," said Tara with a sigh. "Don't tell Annie I said that. But everything is booked and paid for, all that keeps happening now is obstacles keep popping up that we have to deal with. Just give me the certificate and have done with it I say."

I grinned.

"Damn, you're going to be married though. At least one of us had to be."

"Oh, come of it," scoffed Tara. "You were married in every way that mattered before I'd even met Annie. Us having it in writing won't make it any more real."

I don't know if it was a magical disturbance or if I was more anxious than I realised, but at that point I felt my eyes drawn to the door which opened to reveal the tall, dark-haired form of Moti. Tara followed my eyes, which I assumed had widened significantly.

"Did you bring a date?" she asked me.

"Is that okay?"

"Rudy, it's great! Who is he? How did you meet? What are his prospects? Does he seem like a respectable gentleman?"

"Er, can I get back to you on all of those?" I asked, standing and waving Moti over to the table. He joined us.

"Moti, hi. Glad you could make it. This is Tara," I said, gesturing to her. "It's her engagement party."

"Oh, congratulations," he said, holding out a hand. Tara took it and smiled.

"Thanks. Lovely to meet you. What are your intentions with my Rudy?"

"Oh no, I hear Annie calling you," I hissed, gently stepping on Tara's foot; she rolled her eyes and rose, winking at Moti as she left. Moti raised an eyebrow and sat in the empty seat, smirking slightly.

"Your friend seems great. Really subtle, you know?"

"Yeah, she's the 'b'," I said, grinning back. "I'm happy you're here."

"Me too. Wasn't sure if I'd hear from you again."

"I think you would have, eventually. You wouldn't believe

the few days I've had."

"Well, we've got time," said Moti. "Tell me about it."

Andy chose this moment to return with a drink in either hand, freezing as he realised that it was Moti in his seat, not Tara.

"Oh. Hey bud."

"Hey," said Moti, coolly. "How've you been?"

"Dandy. You?"

"Likewise."

There were a few seconds of tense silence before Andy put my glass on the table.

"Well, if you'll excuse me I'm going to find a corner to stand in. It might be a little less awkward."

With a quick turn, he left Moti and I alone; I offered him my cocktail.

"Nah, I don't drink."

"Good to know," I said, taking a sip. "Look at that, we're learning about each other."

I felt my phone vibrating in my pocket but dismissed it; who would be calling me? Everyone I knew was here.

"So, you said you've been busy?" said Moti, flagging down a waiter.

"Mmm. How familiar with Loch Lomond are you?"

"A wee bit. I've taken the nephews boating out there once or twice."

"Quite the family man, aren't you?" I said. "How many nephews do you have?"

"Including nieces, eight," he replied. "Wait, nine. My siblings keep popping children out."

"That must be nice though. I don't—" My phone began to vibrate again and I pulled it out with a sigh. It was a private number. "Sorry, I think this might be a work thing."

I answered the call and held the phone to my ear.

"Rudy, wonderful," said a voice in my ear, before I could even greet the caller. The Clockwork Man? "I have an urgent matter that requires your attention."

"You never call me," I said.

"As I said, urgent. There is a young man on his way to your station; he made it very clear upon his arrival on the platform that seeing you was of the utmost importance. It was quite the scene, really."

"Any idea who he is?" I asked.

"None whatsoever. But he is certainly a magic user and he asked for you directly. I imagine you would want to meet him at the entrance of Ibrox station."

"Could you give me something to work with, maybe?"

"He is a tall man, lots of blonde hair. Dressed in some very unseasonal shorts."

Fear gripped my stomach as the line went silent; what would Ben be doing in the city so soon after I had said goodbye to him at the loch?

"Rudy, Jesus," said Moti, clearly worried. "You're peely-wally, what's happened?"

"Work," I confirmed. "I think something's gone very wrong. I need to jet."

"Do you need a lift?"

"No, no thank you. I think it would be quicker to get to take the subway. I'm so sorry," I added, as I stood and patted down my pockets. "I asked you here and now I'm abandoning you."

"Forget it," said Moti. "We'll catch up later. Let me know how it goes."

I pushed through the crowd, pausing only seek out Andy who I found chatting to a woman by the window.

"Erm. Everything okay?"

"Something's wrong and I have to go check it out. I get the feeling this is bad. If you haven't heard from me in a couple of hours, get word to the Old Man."

"Rudy, I—"

"Don't," I begged. "I'll see you later."

I hoped that was true. Wordlessly I leant forward and, despite our chuckle-worthy height difference, rested my forehead against his before turning on my heel, heading out the door and racing down the road to the closest station. This had to have something to do with Leigh-Anne. The barriers opened for me instantly and I all but leapt onto the waiting train. I found Ben waiting for me on Ibrox platform. He looked at me with dark rimmed eyes.

"She's gone, Rudy."

My flesh froze, and not just because I wasn't wearing enough clothes for October. He could only have been talking about Leigh-Anne.

"This way," I said, leading him to my flat. We sat in the kitchen and he huddled next to the radiator.

"I'm exhausted, man," he said; I could tell. "We went about our night as usual; I arrived back just as Leigh-Anne's ritual was finished. We ate, we did what needed to be done and went to sleep. That's when they came."

"Who?"

"I don't know. It was dark and they were darker. Wrapped in so much hateful energy that even if I'd gotten close I don't think I could have done anything."

"They got past all of you?" I said, incredulous. "You told me the others were even more powerful than you."

"They are. If we'd known what was about to happen I think we might have been okay," Ben said, slowly. "They walked right up to our boundaries and we had no idea. And our spells weren't just repelled. Our protections are gone. They ripped them away and left us bare. That'll teach us to get too comfortable."

He shuddered and I pulled the bottle of cheap blended whisky from the shelf and the tumblers that stood beside it. Ben took it gratefully and knocked it back in one. Impressed, I poured another.

"What can you tell me?" I asked. "What details can you remember?"

"The sounds of the city," he said immediately. "Not as loud as yours were, but I think they were hiding their trail. I could only hear it when it was right on top of us and that was when I woke up. It was chaos. Darkness on darkness and people were falling left and right, curses latching onto them like leeches."

"Dead?" I asked, aghast.

"One," said Ben. "Not directly; she couldn't handle the shock of the incident and her heart gave out. She'd been there longer than any of us."

"I'm sorry."

And I meant it. This was on me; it had to be, though I wasn't yet sure how. It was like Ben had said when he had lured me into the forest; I show up and suddenly they were being attacked. Except this time it wasn't a trick.

"Anything else?"

"I told you, the city. Screeching tires, slamming doors, car horns. The smell of oil and smoke." He paused. "And fruit."

"Fruit?"

"Not fresh fruit though," he said with a frown. "Fruit, but wrong."

"Okay."

Who had known where Leigh-Anne was? Tara, Annie and Andy knew I had been in Loch Lomond but I'd not given anyone any indication of where she could be found. I hadn't, I realised as my blood froze, but Leigh-Anne had. Cursing, I pulled out my phone and for possibly the first time ever, I started a video call; I needed to see Laura's face. She picked up, which was a good start.

"Hey, Rudy. What's up?" she asked.

"Leigh-Anne," I said. "She's gone."

Laura's face fell slightly, before hardening into steel. That seemed genuine.

"She's gone? Gone where?"

"You tell me," I said. "You're the only person outside my team who knows where she was."

"Your team?"

"Who did you tell, Laura?"

"No one," she insisted. "I swear. Rudy, can you find her?"

"I don't know," I said honestly. "Someone has taken her and I don't know if we're strong enough to go up against them. Can you think of no one who might have overheard you talking about it?"

"I've barely seen anyone since the call. It's my days off so I've spent most of the time sleeping. I just saw a couple of friends last night. Oh, and I met my parents for breakfast yesterday morning, but we didn't talk about Leigh-Anne at all."

"I thought you cut them off?"

"I did, but Mum called me waxing poetic about how losing Leigh-Anne made her realise that nothing was more important than family… you know the speech."

I didn't have any blood family left so no, I didn't. I continued.

"Well, what did you talk about?" I asked, fishing for anything I could use.

"Nothing much," said Laura, unhelpfully. "We were only together for about forty minutes."

"Laura, work with me here," I snapped. "What did you talk about?"

"Honestly, we didn't talk about anything in particular," she insisted. "We just spoke about… we… just chatted," Laura finished, looking a little confused.

"You can't remember?"

"No, I can remember meeting them, I know we sat down and had a coffee, but... It's weird, I can't remember a single thing we talked about."

I glanced at Ben, whose face was white. I knew exactly what he was thinking. Something fell into place.

"Ben, I need you to think very hard," I said, my voice clingfilm over the panic that threatened to spill over. "What fruit did you smell when you were attacked?"

He frowned. "I think it was citrus."

My heart stopped.

"Lime?"

"If I had to pick, yeah. But unnatural. Chemical."

I'd been so stupid and so damn *blind*; the stench of bleach had filled my senses and now, as I cast my mind back, I couldn't remember if there had been any curses to sniff out below that stench; there must have been some, only a caster could keep a house free of the wee fuckers. All I had been able to smell was that eye-watering faux-fruit that had now made its way out to Loch Lomond; Douglas and/or Rachel.

"Stay where you are," I said to Laura. "I'm sending someone to you; he'll be able to keep you safe. Go to your nearest subway station and wait there. Say 'Rudy sent me' to one of the cameras."

"What do you—"

I ended the call.

"You're going to go to Laura," I said to Ben. "Keep her safe."

"What about you?"

I relayed my plans as best I could and headed to my bedroom. Ben followed.

"Let me come with you," he said. "You're going to need backup."

"No," I insisted. "You need to go to Laura. You can keep her safe if they come after her and, if I'm wrong and she's just a very good liar, you're the only one I can trust to take her down if you have to."

"Alone?"

"You'll have to be. Who else is there?"

He didn't have an answer. From beside my bed I pulled out my staff; it was still unfinished, lacking the stain, varnish and sigils I had planned, but it had been by my side long enough now to pick up something. At least I hoped it had. I opened my chest and pulled out the few IMPs I had remaining and went to conceal them in my hoodie, before realising that I wasn't wearing it because it had been torn almost to shreds. I needed pockets that I could dip my hands into easily and my jeans weren't going to do the job. I wasn't going to like this, but right now it seemed I had very little choice.

The jacket was on the hanger it had been on for years and the green leather was cold under my fingers. The hoodie had been his too, but this was different. This had been what he had worn to set himself apart, to cultivate the aura of mystique that I had never possessed, nor had I wanted to. Jason had been the real Curse-Breaker, and I a pale imitation walking in footsteps that I had no right to follow. But the night was cold and there was no way I could cram my shoulders into anything Andy owned.

I slipped it on and felt, for the briefest of seconds, something familiar warm me, like the smile of a loved one. It came down to just past my knees and the thick inner lining would work wonders against the night air. With an elastic band I attached the eagle feather to my staff and joined Ben in the hallway.

When we arrived at the station, we were thankfully in time for the final train, albeit the one that only travelled in one direction so that if you wanted to go to a station two stops one way, you'd have to go thirteen stops the other. I glanced at a camera.

"Take him to Laura Baxter. Please." I didn't feel any sense of recognition of my request. "We're supposed to be doing good, right? Then help me now. I have to try and help."

I wasn't going to beg. If I got down on one knee now, like I had the Unicorn, then it would be to convince him to do something for me. That didn't feel right. You shouldn't have to beg someone to help you save a life. There was no response, and I was ready to say fuck it and send Ben off on a wild goose chase when the display monitor faded and in place of the waiting times read the name of St Enoch station. An empty train pulled up.

"Come on," I said, bundling Ben into the carriage.

Taking the subway to what you have already accepted might be your death feels a little lacking in gravitas, but I had no other choice. An Uber would have taken me all the way around the city before I got where I needed to go and walking would have taken me upwards of an hour, so Ben and I sat in a heavy silence, heads bowed and shoulders tight. We didn't pull into any stations that we passed through, so thankfully we were making good time and in less than five minutes the train slowed at the station Ben was due to get off at.

"Listen," he said as he stood half-on half-off the train. "If there's anyone who can help Leigh-Anne now, it's you. You're on your own patch and though you might not have the upper hand, I can feel your power here and it's unlike anything I felt at the loch."

"It's not going to be enough," I said, weakly.

"Maybe not. But remember; the silence doesn't just go away because of the city. It's always there. You just have to find it."

Without saying goodbye, Ben exited the carriage and raced up the stairs, leaving me alone with my thoughts. My stop arrived all too soon; I could happily have ridden the train around the circuit a few times to try and psych myself up, but deep down I knew that if I didn't step out now then I never would. I disembarked, climbed the stairs and stepped out into the cold night air, heavy with the moist promise of rain. I turned up my collar and stared at the tarmac as I strode forwards.

You know, said a voice, this time a woman's. You don't have to do this. You did your part. You found her and told Laura where she is. This isn't your responsibility anymore.

"Shut up," I hissed.

The air evacuated my lungs with a 'WHOOSH' as I felt a soft, warm hand on my cheek. I stumbled back and readied an attack, but the energy left me as I registered who was standing in front of me.

"My beautiful, brave boy," said my mother, a weak smile on her lips. Of all the faces of hers the ghost could have taken, why did it have to be her skeletal, wasted face, inches from death? I knew the answer though; what other avatar could the embodiment of my guilt and responsibility have taken?

"I'm so proud of you," she continued. "You have done exactly what you said you would do. This isn't your fight any more. It's going to be dangerous."

"She's just a lassie, Mum. If she's in trouble, I can't leave her."

I couldn't fault her reasoning though. I had done my job, and I'd done it damn well. But I'd also been the reason that a peaceful, untouched community had been invaded and attacked. The same community that I credited with helping me begin the long process of letting go. I may not have been obliged to carry the guilt of my mother around with me but if anything happened to Leigh-Anne, then that would be another ghost I could never shake.

"I'm going to help her," I confirmed, half to myself and half to my mother. "Could you please do me a favour and just... fade, for a while? I don't need you distracting me."

My mother, or the aspect of my mother who lived on in my mind, looked at me sadly and, despite my being at least a foot taller than her, somehow leaned in and kissed my forehead.

"I'll be here if you need me," she said, before she bled into the night and left me alone.

I appreciated the sentiment, but I couldn't see a scenario in my immediate future in which I'd need my guilt to come and hover around me.

The house wasn't far, less than a five-minute walk, but it was at the top of one of Glasgow's many hills and my boots felt like they had been filled with cement; each footstep was a trial and each thereafter grew more difficult. I could just turn. I could just run.

I could. But I wouldn't.

I didn't bother trying the door handle this time. Instead, I gripped my staff tight in one hand and held the palm of the other hand out to the door, which wrenched itself off its lock and slammed against the entrance hall wall. As I strode inside, assaulted by the odours of ammonia and chemical citrus, Douglas raced out of the living room and fixed me with a stare so foul I could smell it.

"What the hell do you think you're doing in my house?" he roared, reaching out to grab me but retracting his hand as if he had just tried to grab a saucepan from the hob. A terrified looking Rachel stood behind him.

"Enough," I said, more calmly than I felt. "Where is she?"

"Where is who?" spat Douglas as he nursed his hand.

"Don't play stupid, you're too educated a man. Where is Leigh-Anne?"

He stepped forwards again but I held the end of my staff in front of his eyes; I'm not entirely sure he knew what a staff was, but the top was thick enough that it could have made an effective club in a pinch, so he settled down. I stepped in and pushed forwards.

"Isn't that what you're supposed to be doing?" he asked. "It's why my wife convinced me to let you off the hook, so shouldn't you be out there doing your job?"

"Where. Is. She?"

"I don't—"

"Go to sleep, darling."

Douglas crumpled at my feet in a heap, and as I turned I saw Rachel, clad in sensible jeans and comfortable shoes, step out of the living room and face me.

"Men. Useful as they are, they do tend to get in the way sometimes, wouldn't you agree?"

"Your aunt," I said. "Laura wasn't the only one she shared her life with, was she?"

Rachel's voice had changed, I noticed. Gone was the weak, watery woman who had fed me cake and lamented the loss of her daughter. Instead, this voice was low and confident; the voice of one who had won before the fight had even started.

"Oh, that old cow wouldn't have recognised power if it had spat in her face." Rachel joined me in the hall so she could face me properly. "She had herbs, she had potions, she had nothing. She never realised that you could replace blood for basil. Fear for fennel."

"You're cursing your own daughter," I said, sickened.

Rachel shrugged. "I made her. I can do what I like."

Too late I realised that Rachel was now the only thing between me and the front door. I began to back away.

"Where is Leigh-Anne?" I asked again.

"Where she should be," said Rachel. "Tucked away in bed, in her family home."

"Dosed up to the eyeballs on your magic," I added.

Rachel sighed, looking genuinely weary. "Have you ever raised girls? No, of course you haven't, you said so. They're unruly, Mr. Renfrew. After Laura walked out, who had to deal with the repercussions? Me. Suddenly every eye of every family member was on me. 'Oh, Rachel can't control her children.' Our social standing plummeted. Clients wouldn't take Douglas on. I couldn't let that happen again."

"You're sick," I said with a grimace. "You're poisoning your kid for your image? Laura was right. She's just jewellery to you, isn't she?"

"It's how I was raised. I told you; I was the obedient little Catholic girl who never went to university, never learned any useful skills, save one. It is not for us women to stand in the spotlight and bathe in the glory," said Rachel, walking forwards and pushing me into the kitchen. "I have spent my entire adult life behind the scenes, doing what I need to do to manipulate us into good standing; influence, the ears of ministers, *money*. I gave this family everything. Then of course, Laura decides that I'm a monster and runs away to live her bohemian life, squandering her grandmother's inheritance. I gave them everything I never had, and still it wasn't enough? Fine. As soon as Leigh-Anne reached the age where she could become wild, I made sure that she wouldn't. She only has her sister to thank."

"You repulse me," I said, backing into a chair as I allowed myself to be led to the conservatory door. "All the bleach in the world can't cover up your stench."

And I could smell it now. What had before been a house scrubbed clean was now the odour of a thousand curses writhing over one another like snakes in a pit, the bleach not doing a thing to cover up the current corruption. Rachel let out a surprisingly beautiful laugh.

"To be honest, I can't believe that worked. I'd expected someone to come have a poke around and thought ridding the house of any trace would be a good idea. Though I would never have expected it to be you. My money was on that little blonde rat who gave my daughter that peasant magic; I needed that out of my house as soon as possible. You were disappointing," she said. "I'd pictured a wonderful battle which would have seen me feeding you to the plants. Instead all it took was a little bleach to throw you off the scent and a cup of tea to get you out of my hair."

"And breaking me out of the jail?" I asked, desperately trying to make enough time for me to find the door handle.

"I needed Leigh-Anne found and I couldn't risk the police finding her, could I? That way lies questions and paperwork and the child protective system." She sighed. "I'm sorry Douglas is such an old snob. It really doesn't do to have such clouds hanging over an otherwise upstanding household. But old money is as old money does, and his first reaction was to let you know who was in charge. But of course, he never really was in charge, was he?"

I could feel the energy crackling between us, like the air before a lightning strike.

"What's your endgame here?" I asked. "Leigh-Anne stays at home, doesn't make any waves, can't embarrass you like Laura. And then what? You care for her for the rest of your days?"

"Goodness, no!" said Rachel, eyes wide. "You see, that's the glorious thing about being bedridden; no one is going to notice if you fade away until there's nothing really left. Eventually, my darling daughter will pass and we will mourn and sympathy will replace judgment, my power will grow and I shall be free to take more and more. The city is bending under my will, Rudy, and eventually it will break to me. Glasgow is mine, and neither you or my daughters will change that."

I was up against the glass door now. The handle was under my elbow but it if I tried to open it, Rachel would take the opportunity to come for me. I still had to keep her back.

"I don't understand one thing though," I said, pulling the

first thought that floated into my mind. "Cursing Leigh-Anne is one thing. But what about the others? What about Hannah? That poor woman at Kinning Park?"

A flicker of confusion appeared on Rachel's face, before she set her features once more.

"I have no idea what you are taking about."

Cold steel spikes wrapped around my throat and pulled tighter than a vice; the intangible thorns dug into my flesh as my eyes bulged and my breath caught; I had been prepared for an attack, however, and before the curse could truly incapacitate me, it faded from my skin into a cloud of noxious exhaust fumes. Rachel hurled multiple curses at me which might have ended me then and there had I not brought the staff up in front of me; the dark magic was absorbed into the wood, which began to vibrate in my hands and as she recovered the energy she had just siphoned away, I took a steady stance and thrust my staff in her direction.

Where, of course, nothing happened. The magic didn't even fizzle out; it just wasn't there. Not even the eagle feather offered up anything. Slightly cross-eyed as she focused on the tip, Rachel began to chuckle.

The chuckle ended as I channelled my inner Ben and cracked the hard wood directly between her eyes. I felt bone and cartilage crack and Rachel howled in pain. I, however, did not wait to see what damage had been done; I took this opportunity to wrench open the glass door to the garden and stumble out onto the patio. A curse whizzed past so close I felt the razorblades brush my skin. I didn't know what benefits the garden might hold for me, but it had to be better than the kitchen where the gas and sharp, sharp knives lived.

A phantom hand closed around my ankle and sent me crashing to the patio; I dropped my staff and tried to roll onto my back, only for Rachel to press a foot into my chest, nose streaming blood.

"Are you a mage or a Neanderthal?" she asked, stamping on my ribs.

I didn't answer because my mouth was already forming the syllables to twist her foot away. Sensing this, Rachel kicked me in the chin, almost making me bite my tongue clean off. This strength was unnatural, I realised; she had done this to herself. Luckily, my fingers were still free so with a complicated pattern her leg was twisted round and she was sent spinning into the floor. I formed as many spells as I could muster, not really caring what the effect was, and hurled them at her as best I could. The first couple hit with the sound of screeching tires and crunching glass, leaving her with extensive road-rash on one arm, a deep cut across her nose and two black eyes. The rest she resisted.

"Impressive," she said, standing. "But am I right in thinking you're beginning to wear yourself out?"

"Not at all," I said. "Just getting started."

Which was a damn lie; I had just unloaded most of my power and Rachel had batted it away like a wasp at a picnic. If this went on much longer, I wasn't going to have anything left to throw at her.

"You know, I'm beginning to understand you a little more; I see your story written all over you. You dance in both worlds yet embrace neither. You play pretend in the mundane, but it's not your home. You feel your power begging to be set free, but you turn it down." I felt for the first concrete step with my heel and tried to climb them backwards. "I wonder, if you don't live in either world, are you truly alive?"

"Oh, I'm feeling pretty alive right now, trust me," I said, painfully aware that these could be my last moments of feeling any degree of alive at all.

"I don't doubt. Imagine how much more alive you could feel

if you just took what was yours?"

"Is this the part where you offer me a place at your side if I give in to my darkness?"

"God no!" said Rachel with disgust. "No, I prefer to work alone. But it's a shame to see such skill wasted."

Breathing hurt; some of my ribs were cracked and with her current strength I knew she could do much worse. I dodged as I felt something come towards me and threw a spell back at her which bounced harmlessly into nothing. I wasn't so lucky the second time; her curse caught me right in the sternum, my broken ribs buckling and digging into my flesh as I was lifted bodily from the steps and landed haphazardly in a pile of limbs and leather, face down in the damp grass. For the second time in a week I was winded, and my breath came in shallow gasps. Damn. I had been right. I couldn't win.

My right arm was jarred from shoulder to fingertip and would not move, while the fall had knocked the air from my lungs; I could neither sign nor speak. Rachel walked towards me; she was favouring one leg, true, and one side of her face was mottled and shiny, but her victory was assured, we both knew it. I didn't have much time left. I was too far from the subway for the Old Man to help me and I couldn't hear anything over her roaring noise; my own sounds of the city bubbled away in the back of my brain.

Give in, Jason's voice urged. Surely, *surely* she deserves it. Let it out and you can destroy her.

"No," I whispered. How dare it, how dare *I*, use his voice for my temptation?

"No?" asked Rachel. "No, don't kill me? No, how will you get away with this? Dear Rudy, yours won't be the first body I have had to hide. My hydrangeas will bloom all year."

Flower food: there are worse endings I suppose. I tried to stand but my knees buckled and my arms wouldn't support me as I fell. I couldn't win this, I thought as I lay on my side. Not without losing myself to that part of me, kept buried all these years. I was going to die.

The city held its breath, a hush of anticipation fell upon us all and for a second, there was no sound, yet I heard everything.

The silence in the clamour.

A single raindrop fell onto the palm of my cupped, outstretched hand. Even as the wails of the cars and the screams and roaring of planes above me returned, far beneath the tarmac I heard the ground shift under the weight of the city. The river wound through the earth, through silt and stone, a cacophony that drowned out everything else; the wild magic that had lived and breathed since before the first settlers arrived on the riverbank bloomed within me, embraced my city magic and two voices rang out in a clear, tight harmony. Two faces of a coin, both separate and one, imbued me with a wealth I had never had before.

A new plan fell into place with ease. As the rain fell in heavy drops that exploded like grenades around me, my injuries became less important than they had been a few seconds ago and I rose in one fluid movement. Rachel stopped as she felt the atmosphere change around her. A new thought occurred to me, one that blazed like a sun in the front of my mind.

I was going to win.

From my pocket I pulled the final piece of the jigsaw and bent the flimsy carboard between my fingers.

The world around me changed from crystal clear HD into bleeding colours, an oil painting by the greatest artist in centuries. The figure that had once been Rachel lurched forwards in a futile effort to grab me, but I had already dissolved into the inky blues and murky greens that made up the garden. This was beyond illusion; I felt myself melt and I could take in the scene from every direction at once. Revelling in the energy that passed through me and became me, I reformed behind Rachel and picked up the long smudge that was my staff. I turned, tapped into the eagle feather and whatever awful magic Rachel had poured into the wood, and pale brushstrokes burst from the ground. The roots of her well-fed flowers wrapped around Rachel's legs and arms, tying her into place. But not too tight, I realised, loosening the magic a little. Otherwise this wasn't going to work.

I raced through the kitchen and into the hall, where the oil painting faded; everything went back to normal which made me a little dizzy and I ran into the doorframe. Righting myself I stepped over Douglas and made it to the busted front door. I heard a scream of frustration from the other side of the house and guessed I only had a few seconds before Rachel was on me once again, so I didn't hang about. The rain fell in sheets and soaked me to the bone as I hurried down the hill, pausing only to glance behind me.

Rachel stood at the steps to her house, wreathed in an angry aura of pitch black and gnashing teeth. Please, I begged silently. Please, don't be sensible. Don't make the right choice…

My prayers were answered as Rachel leapt down the steps in one move and landed gracefully into something that looked like a well-executed plie. As she made for me, a single step seemed to cover at least four of mine; that was something I hadn't counted on. I sprinted back towards Byres Road, weaving through the few cars and pedestrians passing through. Hillhead station was closed, iron shutters having been pulled down over the entrance and barring my passage. I rattled the barricade a few times, as if I was suddenly going to be able to rip it off its rails but, obviously, it didn't budge.

I turned to face my opponent. This was it. This was where it had to end. I felt the wild magic, around and below the bubble that was the city. I could reach out to the power. I just needed a little help to channel it.

Come on, I prayed. Come on.

From below I felt a ghost train rumble and as the energy surged upwards through my boots, my eyes flicked open and everything around us froze, locked in a moment as we stared each other down.

"You can still walk away," I said to her. "You and Douglas can leave the city and go ply your fuckery elsewhere. Just not in my city."

She considered it. Fuck's sake, I know she considered it; I saw it in her eyes. But then those eyes set and she raised her hands, pain and hatred slicking from her fingers like gore.

"I will not be sent away by you," she hissed, before launching everything she had left.

I slammed my staff into the ground; Rachel was knocked off her feet and into a car, her spells were blown away and a crack opened in the pavement. I had never been in an earthquake before, and as such had always imagined them to be jerky up-and-down movements. What I felt instead was a rolling wave beneath me, as if the soil and rock under the ground had suddenly become a stormy sea. I was knocked off my balance and, as the crack widened at my feet, I felt the sputter and spurt as time took control again.

Chaos reigned. Cars came grinding to a halt and people stumbled and fell as the earth, the one constant solid, betrayed them. There were screams of terror and the whine of stressed steel, car alarms and shattered glass. Despite the destruction, I only had eyes for Rachel, who screamed as she scrambled away from the growing fissure. She pushed herself up and locked her eyes on me.

With the screech of a steam train, the likes of which had not operated here for decades, a thick white cloud burst upwards and enveloped Rachel, obscuring her entirely from view, her scream one amongst many. Then, sucked away back into the earth, the plume was gone and Rachel with it. The ground stopped shaking and the split before me closed, like a wound being stitched. That was it. She was gone.

While the earthquake might have ended, the resulting panic was still in full effect and already there were sirens beyond the alarms and sobs. Adrenaline flushed from my system and with it the magic from land, city and god. I leant against the shutters and allowed myself a couple of soothing breaths. They didn't do a good job, and I didn't feel good in my victory; while I wasn't sure how I had wanted this to end, it certainly wasn't like that. But I couldn't stay here. I needed to be very, very absent when the police arrived, and my job still wasn't complete. My staff little more than a walking stick at this point, I slowly picked my way back up the hill to the Baxter house, where the door still lay wide open; I slipped through the growing rabble easily and shut it.

"Can you walk?" I asked Douglas, crouching down beside him as he sat against the wall.

"What happened?"

"Your wife happened. She's gone now."

"Gone?"

"I'd like you to go too," I added. "I don't know how involved you were with what she was doing but I don't really care. I just don't like you."

"Who the hell are you to—"

"Rachel is gone," I repeated. "Lost to the thing below the city. Take a look."

And with that, I punched him in the face and as I did so, I gave him a quick glimpse of exactly what that was. Only for as long as our skin was touching, but it was long enough. Douglas scrambled to his feet, pulled a set of car keys from a hook by the front door and hurried down the rain-slicked steps. Another problem down. Now for the big one.

Leigh-Anne wasn't hard to find; I could follow the tendrils all the way to the attic where she lay, eyes half open; if I thought she had been bad before, then this was tortuous to witness. Curses like cheese wire ate into her flesh while heavy chains bound her in place. Her skin was milk-white and her breathing laboured. Without immediate attention, the long-term damage would be disastrous.

"Oh, you poor woman," I muttered to myself.

She is alive though, I said to myself, and that's all that matters for now. I pulled out my phone and called Laura.

"Did you find her?" she asked immediately. "Is she okay?"

"Yes, I found her. No, she isn't okay. You need to come to your parents' house." I hung up; I didn't have the energy to continue. "This is going to be shit."

Falling against the wall beside Leigh-Anne, I allowed myself to feel all the pain that had been building up as I held it at arm's length and as the tide of magic-tinged agony washed over me, I let out a barrage of swear words that literally coloured the air around me blue. Gods, I hoped I wasn't bleeding internally. My ribs were going to need as much attention as I could give them after I had them looked at by a professional, and there were more than a few cuts that were going to need stitches.

A car pulled up shortly after the call and when two heads popped through the hatch, one with blonde dreads and the other with a shock of blonde curls, I unclenched my jaw and relaxed.

"Oh, god, Leigh-Anne," cried Laura, rushing past me and to her sister's side.

Ben crouched in front of me. "How do you feel?" he asked.

"Like I've just had the living shit kicked out of me by a middle-aged woman," I said with a wan smile. "Can you fix my ribs?"

"I could, but not quickly and not here," said Ben. "It would be quicker to go to A&E."

"Gods, I doubt that," I groaned, thinking of a Glasgow A&E on a Saturday night; for many, the weekend was just an excuse for a fight that didn't get in the way of work. "Have a look at Leigh-Anne."

Ben joined Laura and put his hands above Leigh-Anne, moving them in and out, up and down, as if he was kneading an enormous lump of invisible dough. He winced and drew back.

"I need to get her back to the community, tonight."

"No," said Laura, vehemently. "No, she stays with me."

"Laura, listen to him," I said, struggling to move to her. "Ben and his people were helping her before. They were making great headway into removing the curses that your mum had put on her. They can do it again, with time."

"My mum," growled Laura. "Where is she?"

"I don't know exactly," I admitted. "But I'd bet my remaining ribs that she isn't ever coming back. Nor your dad."

"Good," she said with more venom than I would have liked. I wouldn't wish the world below on anyone, regardless of their deeds. Still, I kept on track.

"I trust Ben, with all my being," I assured her.

"Can't you do it?"

I shook my head. "Not yet. These curses are something new and I haven't perfected the technique. It turns out I have a lot to learn."

"You can come with us," said Ben. "You'll be more than welcome and you can stay by your sister's side. You'd have to pitch in around the camp, but you'll eat well and Rudy has made sure we'll stay warm all winter."

Laura stared hard into Ben's eyes with a severe frown. He, however, returned her gaze with cool, gentle composure.

"How quickly can we be there?" she asked, eventually.

"You got a car?" asked Ben.

"I saw my mum's outside and I don't think she's going to report it missing," she said with a glance at me.

"Good. I don't want to wait for tomorrow and besides, dragging her through all sorts of public transport isn't going to do her any favours. I can organise a boat to get us along the water when we arrive."

"Hey," I said. "You couldn't have organised a boat to take me back to Balloch?"

"It was still a part of your lessons," said Ben, cheeky grin flashing once more.

Between the two of them, they managed to manoeuvre Leigh-Anne through the house and out to the car.

"I'll be along soon," I said to Ben as Laura carefully secured her sister in the back seat. "I'll come check on Leigh-Anne. Do what I can for the camp."

"I wouldn't," warned Ben. "Not for a while at least. I think everyone's going to be a wee bit wary of outsiders for a while."

"That makes sense," I said, a little deflated. I would have liked to return, I realised with a start, even if it were only to drop in on Leigh-Anne. But I understood. Even if Ben didn't blame me, I sure did.

I watched them leave and sat down on the curb, allowing the events of the night to wash away in the light drizzle the torrents had become. Although it felt like it was all I had been doing lately, my body cried out for sleep but I knew it wouldn't be happening any time soon. As my Uber pulled up and the promise of a night in a hospital waiting room loomed, I began to wonder if Rachel had gotten off lightly.

18

"ou kneeled in reverence before another god," said the Clockwork Man, disapprovingly. His most devout tutted as he poured two cups of tea.

"Shut up, Campbell," I said. "Yeah, I did. She's a massive unicorn who could have skewered me right through. Which she did, incidentally."

"You can understand why I might be a little upset that my Champion is bowing before other gods, surely."

"I would like to make one thing clear," I said. "Last time I was here you made out that we were partners. I respect you, I appreciate your blessings and I'm even a little in awe of you, but you are the god I work with. You are not my god. I am not your follower."

Campbell dropped a sugar lump in shock and caused my tea to spill; I tutted, loudly.

"You prayed to me."

"It's the only thing I knew would get your attention," I said, with the smallest ember of satisfaction. "I don't follow anyone. Just another atheist."

The Clockwork Man frowned. "How can you not believe in gods when you have witnessed them first-hand?" he asked. "You know they exist."

"Yeah, well, I know the Prime Minister exists, but I don't believe in him." I tried to change the subject. "Where is she?"

"Oh, I think you know where she is," the Clockwork Man said, casually. "She remains at the leisure of the beast. I must say, the earthquake was impressive. Wherever did you learn that?"

"From the earth itself, I think. It's difficult to explain." What had seemed so clear and simple as unfamiliar currents fuelled me was now murky and far away. "Thanks, by the way. For helping me with the time."

"Yes, I shall be making that up in travel delays for the foreseeable future. Be wary, Rudy," the god warned. "Wild magic is just that; wild."

"I've seen enough of the city to know it's not exactly safe either," I said. "I think I need to learn what else I can do. I'm not going anywhere, but it can't hurt to broaden my horizons a little."

The Clockwork Man focused his attention on his tablet.

"It's still all over the news," he said, disapprovingly. "You rather put paid to subtlety when you gave Glasgow its strongest earthquake in recorded history, wouldn't you say? I'd advise you to keep a low profile, for a while at least."

"Duly noted. Well, if that's everything?"

"I'm afraid not. There is someone here who would very much like to meet you."

"Meet me? Who?" I asked, dreading the worst.

"Please, be polite," warned my host. "Campbell, if you would?"

Campbell disappeared into the kitchen and returned with a woman who radiated power like heat from a flame. Before I could even register her appearance, I found myself standing with my hand outstretched, as if puppeted by invisible strings.

"Rudy Renfrew," said the Clockwork Man. "May I introduce you to Amelia Bracken, of the Three."

"A pleasure to meet you," I lied.

"Likewise," said Amelia, smiling sweetly. "Please, sit."

I did so, of my own accord this time.

"Well, I shall leave you to get acquainted," said our host. Was the Clockwork Man *uneasy*?

Once I was alone with someone I had hoped never to meet, I was able to take her in with greater attention. If not for the evident potency, I wouldn't have pegged her as a mage; she wore a fuzzy purple jumper and glasses on a crystal chain. Her mousey hair was cut into a sensible bob.

"We've been looking forward to meeting you, Rudy," said Amelia, kindly. "You have certainly been making a name for yourself lately."

She spoke with a drooping lilt and I wanted to place her from somewhere around Birmingham.

"Sorry," I said. "I'll do my best to keep my name-making to a minimum from now on."

"Oh, not at all! It's been fascinating to watch you grow these past years. Lately, though, we have had a little more to watch, haven't we?"

"Thank you, I think?"

"You are most welcome." Her smile was beginning to unnerve me. It felt like a wild animal baring its teeth. "We were, however, disappointed to not receive a reply to our gracious invitation."

"Oh right, that," I said, hurriedly. "Sorry. I've been pretty busy lately. The Clockwork Man has been sending me off on missions and I was a little preoccupied with a missing young woman."

"Ah, yes, Miss Baxter. How is she?"

"Pretty bad, but I guess you already knew that."

"We are aware, yes," said Amelia, with a little less concern than I would have liked. "Perhaps you would care to fill me in on your side of events? Obviously we have a rough idea of how events played out, but t hear it in your words could prove helpful.

Wanting this to be over as quickly as possible, I gave Amelia bullet-point list of my escapades, leaving out the unicorn and the community as best as I could, focussing more on Rachel and her dealings.

"Feeding from the life force of her own daughter. Ingenious," said Amelia, with a hint of what sounded like admiration. That stoked my ire and before I could stop myself, I snapped back.

"You know, you could have stepped in at any time. I thought you were supposed to keep the peace but there Rachel was, taking over my city, one curse at a time. Where were you?"

Amelia removed her glasses, folded the arms and let them bounce gently against her chest.

"Young man, unlike yourself, we are not limited to Glasgow. We have a much wider net to cast." She beamed at me. "I'm sure you understand, Steven."

She might as well have slashed my throat.

"That man is dead," I said quickly. "I made sure that name would never be used again."

"Come now," Amelia chastised. "You more than anyone should know that the dead leave ghosts. It is our business to know the ins and outs of practitioners across Britain. And yes, we knew about Rachel Baxter and her actions; our eyes were fixed on her and we had plans to neutralise the situation had she pushed much further. But of course, now the issue has been resolved. In quite a spectacular fashion, I might add."

I couldn't even take the compliment. I had discarded that

name nearly a decade ago and had wrapped it in so much magic that none should have been able to find it. Her use of it was a threat, plain and simple.

"Who else knows that name?" I asked.

"Only us," assured Amelia. "And we fully intend to keep it that way. Call it our collateral, if you will. We are not here to be your enemies, Rudy. We wish you no ill will, and we look forward to a wonderful partnership. But please remember that we will always be watching, and should you prove… problematic, we will be forced to step in."

Again, I began to snap back but caught myself; if they had found that name, I didn't want to think what else they could do.

"So, without wanting to be rude," I ventured. "Why are you here? To invite me to breakfast in person?"

"Partially," said Amelia, with a nod. "But also to issue a warning. Rachel Baxter was not exaggerating about how far her reach extended. Her influence will be missed and thanks to your removal of her, there is now a power vacuum in the mundane world that will need to be filled."

"I don't follow."

"Dogs pull at their leads and if those leads are cut then the dogs wander into traffic. We don't only deal with mages, Rudy. When the need arises, we step in to deal with some of the issues of the mortal world."

Don't think that her use of 'mortal' escaped me, though I said nothing.

"Isn't one of your rules to not get too involved?" I asked.

Amelia pulled a glass tumbler from the air, its contents fizzing around a slice of lemon. "One rule for thee, another for the Three. It is not a regular practice, you understand, but please be aware that Glasgow may need us to step in at times." She threw back the drink and let the empty glass go back to wherever it had come from. "And other times, we may rely on you to step in for us."

I shook my head. "That's not my area."

"No? Perhaps Linda MacDonald and her husband would care to differ. I told you," she said, clearly pleased at my shock. "We watch. Now, if you don't mind, I must be going. When should I tell my colleagues that you will be joining us for breakfast?"

We set a date, reluctantly on my part, and once we had shaken hands she made her way back into the Clockwork Man's house. The god returned a few seconds later.

"Well, how was that?" he asked. I didn't respond, choosing instead to raise my eyebrows and exhale through my teeth. The god nodded sympathetically. "I know, she does tend to have that effect. Anyway, if that will be all, please don't let me keep you."

I took my leave and walked down the garden path to the ever-clean station. I had no fixed destination in mind and mainly I just wanted to ruminate, so I rode the inner circle for a few spins before making my way into the centre of town.

The job was done, the case was closed, my bank account had another half ton resting in it until rent was due. So where had that job satisfaction gone? Leigh-Anne was safe, albeit worse off than when I had set out to look for her. Rachel was gone, lost to places unknown, though her damage had apparently left holes to be filled. There was still the subject of the phantom dark mage who enjoyed putting curses on people. I didn't think that Rachel had been the one responsible for Hannah's affliction; she had seemed genuinely confused when I mentioned it.

And on top of the news that I was to be the Clockwork Man's champion, and the Unicorn's… something, I now had the Three to worry about, no longer just a word in my ear but flesh and blood and arrogance. And they knew my gods damn name. My birth name, I quickly corrected myself. And that put me entirely under their power. There were too many unsatisfying endings and loose threads. But that's life; it's not a story.

I found myself in the wynd that led to Moti's bar and popped my head in; he was bent over the bar, lost in something on a clipboard. He looked up as I sat down on a stool.

"Hey stranger," he said. "You never called. Again."

"Yeah, sorry about that. You wouldn't believe the night I had after I left you. I've been recovering. Any chance of a pint?" I asked.

"How about I take my lunch break and we go eat?"

"Well, now that you've twisted my arm…"

Not wanting to waste any of Moti's precious free time, we went to the café we had visited previously; the bundle still sat by the till, as clear as the day it had blown my investigation wide open. Moti ordered our food and sat down.

"So, to what do I owe this visit?" he asked. "You're making a habit of just dropping in on me when I'm not expecting it."

"I needed to talk to you," I said. It was true, though I hadn't realised it until now.

"About?"

"Dating. Going on spontaneous lunch dates."

Moti looked suddenly nervous. "Are you about to tell me that you don't like boys, or something?"

"No, it's not that, it's…" I took in a deep breath. "I had a partner. We'd been together since my last year of uni. His name was Jason. He was like me."

"A warlock?"

"Well, yeah, though he preferred magician. But that's not what I meant. Anyway, he found me and took me in, pulled me off the streets when he found out that's where I was. What I do now, it was his gig first and he was twice the mage I could ever hope to be. But he could never tune out the chaos like I can. This city is alive, Moti. It lives and it breathes, and it feeds. And beneath it all, the beating heart of the beast below. I can't stress how easy it is to lose yourself in the rage and mayhem around you. We did well, for a few years. We worked together and I learned more from him than I ever would have from the scraps I'd found on my own. Till one night, I wake up and he's nowhere to be found. I assumed he'd been called out on a job, till the morning and I couldn't reach him. Then things fell apart pretty quickly.

"It didn't take long to find him, but by the time they did, he was gone."

"Shit, Rudy, I'm so sorry," said Moti, looking as if he was going to put a hand over mine but deciding against it. I was grateful.

"Thanks. I never truly got an answer as to why he did it, but I have my suspicions. I'd noticed him getting smaller and further away, and I think I know now what was wrong, what he was hearing. Since then, I've been interested in a few guys and girls, but I've never pursued any of them. Yeah, girls too," I added, off Moti's look. "I've never had an issue between guys or girls or anyone who falls anywhere on the spectrum. It's never bothered me what bodies people were born in, Moti, because..."

I drew in a deep breath, my mouth suddenly dry.

"Because I don't like sex. I've never found the thought of it appealing in any way. Jason was the same. I think that's one of the reasons we stayed so strong; neither of us wanted any more than we were getting."

Moti didn't reply right away, and I wondered if he was going to react badly; despite being in the same trench, I've known queer people just as unaccepting of asexuality as straight people.

"Thanks for telling me," he said eventually. "I really appreciate it."

"So, I wanted to tell you that now," I said, quickly. "Because I enjoy your company and you're pretty cool, but I didn't want to lead you on only to disappoint you later."

A soft smile played on Moti's lips. "You understand how exciting you are, aye? Your stories. Look, let's eat and you can fill me in on your adventures. We can talk about everything else later."

Once again, I entertained my audience with my journey, enjoying his animation as I detailed my battles and once again getting the best reaction when I mentioned the Unicorn.

"Wait, so is that why the Unicorn is our national animal?" asked Moti.

"Actually, I think it's the other way round. But that's just one aspect of her, she could be anything she wanted."

"You live a weird life, you know that?"

"I do," I said, nodding. "I've been wondering how different it could have turned out if I'd never picked up magic and focused on academia instead."

"That's not you," said Moti. "I think you'd die of boredom."

He was right, I knew. For all my moaning and being thrown great distances by things more powerful than me, I did have more fun than I would have had sitting in a cramped office, marking essays and snapping at students.

Moti paid this time, and we walked back through the windy street. I turned my collar up against the chill.

"I like the coat," said Moti. "I think if you'd been wearing that when told me you were a Curse-Breaker I might have taken you more seriously."

"Please never let Tara hear you say that." I turned to him. "I'd like to hang out again, maybe for longer than it takes to eat a sandwich. But I'd understand if you feel like it would be a waste of your time."

"Stop that," said Moti, sternly. "Yeah, I enjoy sex, but that doesn't mean it's all I think about. This is new for me, sure, but I'm willing to give it a go if it means getting to see more of you."

"Aye?"

"Aye."

I grinned what felt like my first proper grin in days. "Well then. I have your number and you have my card. I'm sure one of us will call the other soon enough. For now, I'll let you get back to work."

"I guess a quick kiss on the cheek wouldn't be appropriate?"

"I'd prefer it if you didn't."

There was a short pause before Moti reached out and squeezed my shoulder. "How about that?"

"Acceptable," I said with a smile.

I still didn't want to go home, I realised as I walked back into the busy street. Normally I would go to the river to think, but today I wanted to avoid it. So, I walked without destination, shoulder to shoulder with the single-minded entity that shuffled past on a thousand feet, my ghosts hanging back enough to give me the illusion of independence. My thoughts wandered to what Rachel had said to me, about how I walked in both worlds but belonged to neither. It had shaken me for a few days, I couldn't deny, but I had decided it didn't matter. So what if I didn't belong in the world of bills and taxes and rent; I still paid them, mostly. And what did it matter if I didn't truly belong to the peripheries; I made my presence known there too and clearly my actions weren't going unnoticed. What really counted was that I belonged to the city.

And the city belonged to me.

Raised on the coast of Fife in Scotland, Ieuan Ledger-McQuade moved to Glasgow at eighteen to study, and to enjoy life in the 'big city'; now living in Mexico City, they have since reconsidered this title. Working as a freelance writer/teacher, Ieuan lives with their partner and three dogs, two of which are mostly housetrained.

One of their proudest achievements to date is being a member of the inaugural year of Glasgow University's Fantasy Literature postgraduate masters course, now one of the institution's most popular degrees. When not writing, Ieuan can usually be found in front of some sort of console or waging war against an unforgiving garden.

CPSIA information can be obtained
at www.ICGtesting.com
Printed in the USA
LVHW102058100622
721011LV00005B/47

9 781928 011750